ALWAYS JULIA

Always Julia

THE ART OF A LIFE

Ava Zacardi

This novel is a work of fiction. Names, characters, places, and incidents are the product of the author's imagination or are used fictitiously. Any resemblance to actual persons, living or dead, events, and locales is entirely coincidental.

ISBN 979-8-9865810-0-2

First Printing, 2022

For my grandparents,

Carolina and Sabatino

Contents

1

The Swing

Sam has not been able to stop thinking about the girl he loved wholeheartedly in first grade. He remembers her tiny body on the swings sweeping through the air like a pendulum. She would reach the highest point of the arc and then suddenly fly off into the sky like a bird, land gracefully and then pivot towards him with a shy smile. He sighs at the memory of her sitting next to him, feeling the tenderness in the little curled serifs she added to each letter as she meticulously printed her name at the top of her papers. She was so delicate, like a cherished Wedgwood tea-cup in his wife's buffet cabinet. Angie, his wife, died a year ago, and instead of thinking of her, he has become obsessed with the girl with long black ringlets from almost sixty years ago. He falls asleep with her in his mind, feels her long thin fingers holding his hand on the playground, longing for her smile. At night Sam hears her calling to him in a whispering song as he dreams, and the melody lingers all through his waking hours.

2

Last Fall

The long shadows of fall swept across the driveway as Angie pulled her car into the garage. In her trunk were the makings of the night's supper. Sam had said he'd felt a chill in the air that morning as he stretched himself awake. She thought it would be a good idea to make the family's favorite winter recipe, the one her mother-in-law taught her years ago. Angie woke up that morning to the same dull headache she'd had for the last several weeks, but it seemed to disappear every day after her second cup of coffee and not return until the following day.

Angie brought the grocery bags into the house and started cooking as she put boxes and cans away. Beef cubes were tossed in flour, and she browned them to a crusty amber in the red Dutch oven. Then she caramelized the onions, and the smell brought back distant memories of her husband's parents. They had been gone for so long, but this aroma reminded her of when time passed in slow, savored moments. Memories of her young children all piled into the car on Saturday nights for get-togethers at her in-law's house weaved through her mind as she added the fresh parsley. Angie knew this aroma would greet Sam at the door and make him smile. He'd been anxious ever since he decided to retire at the end of the year. She'd wondered what it would be like to be together again all day. They had plans to cross the country to see the Grand Canyon and California in January, then visit their children and grandchildren who had settled all along the east coast. Angie daydreamed as she poured the stock over the rest of the vegetables and smiled, thinking about their early days when they were inseparable. She lowered the heat to simmer when the morning headache returned unexpectedly with an urgent throb. She took two steps sideways to reach for the Tylenol in the cabinet but crumpled to the floor. Her last thought was, "I never wrote down the recipe."

3

Julia

"My life prepared me for heartbreak."

"What do you mean when you say that?" Martina, the therapist, pushes Julia to explain since her new patient had a penchant for bold statements without a flicker of emotion showing on her face.

Julia shrugs her shoulders. "I don't know. It's just how it is."

"There has to be a better explanation than it just is. We can't progress if you don't at least try to explain why you feel this way."

"You're asking me to explain emotions. There just isn't an intellectual answer. You figure it out. You're the therapist." Julia cannot sit still in the swiveling leather chair and keeps swaying back and forth frenetically.

Martina remains calm in the wake of her client's growing hostility. "Let's take a step back, Julia. Tell me one thing from your childhood that caused you anxiety."

Julia spins around. "Anxiety? Everything caused me anxiety. That's like picking out one scene from Pieter Bruegel's painting of hell." She stands up and starts to play with the lock on the window, clicking it open and shut as she stares down to the ground thirty-two floors below.

"Okay, come on, Julia, sit down. Let's rephrase the question. Why don't you address what you said when we started today? Think back to one incident that broke your heart as a child, or as you said, prepared you for heartbreak."

Julia oozes frustration. She shuffles through her memories, trying to pick one incident from her mental list of traumas, and finally decides on the one that recently resurfaced in her memory. The one that she can't explain. "When I was five years old, we moved from the city to the suburbs, you know, near here, to the North Shore."

"I imagine it wasn't just the act of moving. What about the move made you sad?" Martina has to prod Julia for every nugget of information.

Julia shakes back her head and clasps her hands tightly together. "I don't know. It sounds ridiculous."

Martina leans in. "Nothing is off the table if it's caused you pain."

"It's not pain in the typical sense. More of a longing, you know, a what-if kind of thing. Oh, forget it, it really is childish."

"Well, Julia, you're the compilation of all the events in your life. Things that sound silly as an adult could've had profound meaning to you as a child."

Julia stops her continuous motion. "You really know how to lay it on with your psychobabble, don't you?"

Martina maintains her even, soft-spoken tone. "Julia, let me say it in another way then. Pain is pain no matter when it happened. If you were a child or not, it still lives in you somewhere."

Julia crosses her long legs and tosses back her head of gray curls. "Okay, okay. There was a little boy in my class that I loved. I had to leave him without even saying goodbye."

"That's a very natural reaction to miss someone from so long ago when times are hard. We sometimes make long-lost acquaintances better in our memories than they were in reality."

Julia turns and faces the window. "Yes but, I hear him singing to me in my dreams."

4

The Beachcomber

It's a beautiful fall day as Sam gazes out of his bay window. His eyes draw a line up and down the block. Each house on the street is the same Cape Cod in its seemingly infinite variations framed by the red, yellow, and orange oak leaves getting ready to fade. Few of the original neighbors remain, and they are replaced by strangers. He laughs to himself that he recognizes the new occupants only by their shoes that he observes as their garage doors close when he walks the dog.

* * *

No one except the few old-timers stopped by when Angie died. He was not really surprised but only surprised that he was hurt by it. The reality was that most of the new people did not even know his name. Sam liked to say, "I think the world passed by but forgot to stop and say hello to us, Angie."

After the funeral, his oldest daughter, Caroline, tried to persuade him to leave Long Island and move in with her family in North Carolina. "Dad, you would love Raleigh. You could golf all year."

"No, I'm fine here. It's too hot there to golf in the summer."

"But the snow, how long can you keep shoveling for?"

"I can pay anyone to take care of that, and I'm not that old anyway. It's not a problem."

His son from Tampa battered him even more. "Why don't you go to Raleigh, Dad? Caroline and Vi are both there. You can spend more time with the grandkids."

"Maybe when I'm older."

"Dad, think about it. You'd still be close to your friends on the east coast. I mean, half of them are in the south now anyway."

"It's not about my friends. It's about where I'm comfortable living. This is my home."

The one question that none of his children asked was how he was going to live without Angie. This wasn't the plan. But somehow, he did. There were days when he felt like he was showing disrespect to her by not spending all his waking hours being sad. And then there was the time when he opened the jar of cinnamon to sprinkle on his oatmeal that he was overwhelmed with grief by a simple scent. On those days when being home alone was too much to bear, Sam would get in his car and drive to the last parking lot at Jones Beach and walk along the shore, letting the ocean air and the sound of the waves fill him. Now on this warm fall morning, Sam senses the chill of winter closing in on him. All last night he'd heard the lilting voice of his childhood playmate crooning a wordless song in his dreams. Sam feels guilty for enjoying it and decides to head to the ocean. The beach will be deserted except for the walkers like him, the runners, maybe the occasional holdout still fishing from the shore. He has begun to recognize the faces that share this quiet space with him day after day. Sam parks in the almost empty lot and heads down to the beach. The rubber paths that lead to where the wet sand is solid are still in place. He likes not having to bend down and take off his sneakers. It is so simple to just leave the empty house behind, drive for twenty minutes and then enter this cocoon of wind, smell, and sound. Sam used to tell Angie when he went for his early morning walks on week-ends, "I feel like one of those monks in a monastery when I am at the beach. It's so peaceful."

This morning Sam can see how the sun tilts towards winter above the horizon. Unlike his usual routine, he stops and speaks to one of the men fishing. "Catching anything?"

"No, not yet. I caught a striped bass late yesterday. I was hoping for a fluke, but it's kind of late in the morning for anything."

"You just like trying, huh?"

"Yeah, it's my escape."

"I know what you mean. Good luck." Then Sam smiles to himself and keeps walking. He can see a group of women in the distance heading towards him. They have matching Yankees baseball caps, dark sunglasses, and one has her long gray hair in a ponytail. He puts his head down and lifts it for a second just to wave a hello. Then he quickens his pace, so he won't overhear their conversation. He can hear a voice calling to her friends, "I'll catch up to you later," and heading back toward him. Sam starts walking faster until he hears her speak, "Sammy, Sammy, is that you?"

Sam knows the face but can't remember the name. It's one of Angie's friends from church. He forces a smile as she bubbles. "Oh, Sammy, it's so good to see you out. How are you?"

"Good, good, you know, keeping busy."

"We were just talking about Angie. It's almost time for the holiday bake sale at church. We'll miss her cookie trays this year. They were always the biggest seller."

Sam smiles some more. He knows there are some cookies still in the freezer from last year. He's saving them for when the children come for the holidays. "Yes, she was a wonderful baker."

"We miss you at church. You should come to the nine o'clock mass. There's a nice coffee hour afterward."

"Well, maybe, maybe next week."

She touches his hand to his shoulder. "Oh, Sammy, don't isolate yourself. It's been almost a year now since Angie left us. We all miss her so, but you have to take care of yourself. She would want that."

Finally, Sam remembers her name. "Linda, it was nice to see you. Go ahead catch up with your friends. I'll stop by for mass soon. I promise."

Linda gives Sam a warm hug and takes off towards the rest of her group. He keeps walking alone towards the lighthouse.

5

With Friends Like These

Linda runs back up to her group, her ponytail swaying with the effort. Bending over to catch her breath, her hands resting on her knees, she laughs. "I better stick to walking; this panting must be a sign of turning into an old lady."

"Stop with the old lady business. You're in great shape." Dina pauses and puts her hand on her hip. "For someone your age. Does your husband know that you like to chase after other men?"

"Stop, Dina, that was Sammy, Angie's Sammy."

"Isn't that weird? We were just talking about her. That's some kind of odd coincidence," Dina looks up to the sky. "Maybe Angie heard us?"

"Jesus, Dina! Seriously, he seems a little lost. But you know it's hard to tell with men. I invited him to come back to church on Sunday."

Carol chimes in. "I didn't recognize him, Linda. You have eagle eyes; he barely looked up at us."

"I don't think he knew who I was at first either until I mentioned Angie."

Carol shakes her head. "She never complained about him, not like my Cosmo, the buffoon. Do you know he asked me how do you turn up the heat yesterday? I'm surprised he figured out how to lift his legs in the lazy boy chair."

Dina runs ahead and turns, walking backward against the wind. "Good thing it's warm today then... since you left Cosmo alone this morning."

"The only thing Angie ever said was that he plays a lot of golf, but she didn't seem to mind. He was always home by supper time and washed the dishes afterward." Linda picks up the pace, and they all try to keep up with her.

"And he is so handsome...with that salt and pepper hair," Dina shouts up to Linda, who is five strides ahead. "If my Cosmo drops dead, Sammy is my next stop!"

Carol huffs. "Dina, stop! She was lucky to have him, that's all. Slow down, Linda. What's the rush?"

"Oh, my friend Julia called last night. I haven't heard from her since she moved back into the city. We're having an early lunch near her house."

"Linda, don't start coddling Julia again. You're always worrying about everyone else. Chasing Sammy down just now, your kids, and her...my God, you don't owe her anything."

"Carol's right. She's stressed you out all year. You can't solve her problems. Saint Linda, punching bag for the world's troubled souls."

"Oh, I know I should try to *disengage*, as my daughter likes to say. Julia's like a little wounded bird that I have to help. Besides, anyone who lived through what she has would be a bit crazed."

Dina stops walking and reaches for Linda's hand, then pats it. "Dear, it's one thing to be crazed. It's another to treat you so badly. I mean, she's just so rude. Why does she even bother calling you?"

"Because… I'm her only friend." Linda sighs and takes off in a run towards the parking lot.

6

Two of a Kind

Julia is running late, still frazzled from her therapy session. There is a pack of cigarettes hidden under a pile of old maps in the glove compartment. She takes one out of the almost empty pack, lights it, and tries to blow the smoke out the window, but it drifts back in, giving her a second dose of calm. Julia clutches the rose quartz prayer beads she has around her neck and takes one last deep breath, then flicks the cigarette out the window. Bella would probably be waiting for her on the sidewalk outside of Immaculata High School. When Julia pulls up, her granddaughter sits on the curb talking to two boys with their ties undone and jackets rolled up next to them.

Julia puts on a smile and pushes the button to lower the window. "Bella, Bella! I'm sorry I'm late, honey, got stuck on the expressway."

Bella waves to the two boys who call to her as she sashays to the car. "Oh, don't go…Come to the party tomorrow night!"

"Yuck, why does it smell like smoke in the car?"

"Oh, the garage attendant was probably smoking. I'll turn up the fan."

"Maybe I can just stick my nose out the window like a dog." They both laugh. Bella is feisty like Julia. She is in ninth grade, old enough to stay home alone, but still insists on staying with Julia when her parents are on call.

"Do you have all your things for the weekend?"

"Yes, I stuffed my backpack, and I left extra clothes at your house last time."

Julia double-checks her mirrors and pulls away from the curb. "What's new?"

Bella doesn't hesitate. "Well, I overheard my parents talking, and my mother said you were going to a shrink, and then my father said you're a batty bitch and that it's a good idea." Unfazed, Bella starts changing the stations on the car radio.

Julia wishes she could have one more puff of that cigarette. "What do you think about that?"

"I love batty bitches."

Julia sighs. "Thank God your father still lets you stay with me. You're the only real thing I have in my life."

"Oh, Grams, he likes you deep down. You know he's English. He doesn't get it all the time."

"Get what?"

"Emotion...stiff upper lip and all that...Why are you going to a shrink anyway?"

"It amuses me."

"C'mon Grams, really, why?"

"Maybe I hear little voices in my head singing to me."

"Okay, I get it. It's private."

"Yes, let's talk about something else, don't worry about this batty bitch. Who were those two boys?"

"Just two guys, you know, from the Chess Club. They're in love with me…I guess you could say they are my pawns."

"Don't break their hearts, Bella. One could be your knight in shining armor."

"Oh, Grams, please! I thought only fathers made up corny jokes." Bella gives an embarrassed laugh.

The drive from Glen Cove to Astoria is slow and plodding in the early rush hour. But along the way, Julia's mood brightens. Bella always brings out the person who still lives under the surface in her. They laugh and sing along with the radio for the whole ride and scream in unison when a plane landing at LaGuardia roars over their heads. Without fail, Julia feels a surge of nostalgia every time she exits the highway and heads down Ditmars Boulevard towards the East River. Time has done very little to change the contours of Astoria. The slender streets are still lined with two and three-story buildings, some with new signs but many the same from her childhood. After a string of unfortunate financial turns, she sold her house in Great Neck, in the tony neighborhood on the north shore of Long Island and moved back into the house she grew up in across from the park on the East River. The renters did not renew their lease, and Julia finally decided a change would be good for her. It would be easier to live without the financial pressure of the big house with high taxes. Everyone thought she was crazy to leave Long Island, except Bella, who loves the idea of city life.

Julia squeezes the car into the narrow driveway, and Bella has to scooch over to the driver's side to get out of the car. They both stand at the end of the driveway, pause for a moment, turn, and face the sun setting over Manhattan.

Bella speaks first. "Isn't it beautiful?"

"Yes, you know I used to stand here with my grandmother after school and watch the sunset with her."

"Do you ever feel her presence, you know, in the house, Grams?"

"Yes, Bella, I do, actually. Why do you ask?"

"In religion class, the teacher was talking about the afterlife and stuff. I think it's all bullshit." Bella smiles and walks into the house like she owns it.

7

—

November 1971

"Mom, I don't want to go back to live with Dad. Why can't we stay here with Nonni?" Julia pleaded.

"We have to give him another chance. He promised me he'll be better this time," Julia's mother, Gracie, was caught between a world of guilt and one of hope. Her slender fingers shook as she lit another cigarette. Looking down, she dusted ashes off her skirt. "I made a vow for better or worse."

"I don't know why you ever married him." Julia tried to focus on her mother's reaction to find the truth in her face.

"He wasn't like this when I met him." She blew a long stream of smoke into the air.

"You mean he never hit you before you were married, or he wasn't an asshole?"

"Please, Julia, don't make it harder for me than it is. Your brother needs a father. Besides, you'll get to go to that nice high school on Long Island."

"But Mom, I love my new School for the Arts." Julia was insistent. "I'm not leaving! Look at how good I can draw now!" She held up her sketch pad under her mother's nose. "Take Jeffrey home. Please, please let me stay here with Nonni. I'll come home on weekends." Julia was starting to hyperventilate when her grandmother stepped out of the kitchen and into the living room.

"Gracie, let her stay. You go…leave the kids, see if he change, the *cornuta.*"

"Oh, Mom, please don't interfere. I'll have to ask Dennis what he thinks about Julia staying. He really misses Jeffrey."

Julia's grandmother moved close to Julia, wrapped her arms around her, and whispered in her ear, "I fix. Don't you worry. I fix." Then to lighten the mood, she said, "Come on, play me a song on the piano."

Julia wiggled out of her grandmother's arms and sat down at the old blue piano. It was a small upright Steinway piano called the G.I. Vertical that her grandfather helped make during World War II for entertaining the troops. Unfortunately, it had been accidentally dropped while on the loading dock, then smashed again when a forklift backed into it. Antonio, Julia's grandfather, asked the boss to let him have the damaged piano to bring home. His two brothers and a cousin with a truck helped him move it into their tiny house. It was a perfect fit. The soundboard was not damaged, and Antonio meticulously put it back together. The Steinway factory was only a few miles away, and Antonio worked there as a carpenter. When he first arrived from Italy, he worked as a laborer for Con Edison but learned English quickly from reading the newspapers, an ability that got him a job at the piano factory. They needed men who could follow directions in a schematic, and even though he only hammered nails into the soundboards all day, everyone in the family was so proud of him. He never complained about the monotony of his occupation, got up every morning content, and walked the few miles to work with his lunch pail tucked under his arm.

The family's biggest achievement was when they stopped renting and bought the one-family house with three tiny bedrooms that sat in the shadow of the Hell Gate Bridge on the East River. It was made of brick and had a tiny patch of yard where Antonio grew plum tomatoes, basil, long cubanelle peppers, and a narrow driveway that never had a car parked in it. Whenever relatives visited, Antonio would greet them at the sidewalk and point, "You see, I got a view of the *oceano*." Then the roar of the trains above their heads would drown out their laughter.

"Play that Christmas song that Perry Como sang on the television last night."

"Nonni, it's barely even December!"

"Play it, *per favore* …no "Wichita Lineman" you always playing, I no like. What you call that, country music?"

Julia laughed; her grandmother always cheered her up with the silly things she said. She started playing the first refrain from the "country song" just to get her grandmother riled up but then quickly switched to "Have Yourself a Merry Little Christmas." Without a trace of an accent, her grandmother sang along. When she was done singing, she said, "That's my kind of country." Gracie sat quietly in the armchair with a worried look on her face.

It was Friday night, and Gracie's older sister, Rosie, was coming over for dinner with her family. "Come on, Julia, help me in the kitchen."

Julia followed her grandmother, took an apron, tied the string tightly around her waist two times, and knotted it in the front so it wouldn't fall off. "You know, I know there's something wrong with your father when I met him. But no, no, your mama, she no listen to me. She wanted a college man. Now look what she got, *bastia*."

"Nonni, please… maybe Mom's right… maybe he has changed."

"A wolf no change his coat."

"I get nervous when he is home. It's like walking on eggs all the time. You know, trying to not upset him. Jeffrey is too little to understand what's happening. He'll probably be fine if he goes back."

"You stay with me."

The front door opened, and in blew a burst of cold air and a frenzy of noise. Julia's Aunt Rosie, her husband Freddie, and their three teenage boys squeezed into the living room. Tony, the oldest, his curly brown hair piled on his head like a bird's nest, came into the kitchen and kissed his grandmother. "How's that new high school, Julia?"

"I love it. I'm actually learning how to paint in oils now. And the teacher lets us listen to the radio during class. I really really love it."

"That's cool. What about you Nonni, are you cool too?"

"I give you cool. Why you no do your homework?"

"Did my mother tell you that?" Tony started inching away from his grandmother, pretending to be scared.

Maria started shaking the wooden spoon in her hand at Tony. "Never mind who told me. You see this house your grandfather buy for the family? He work! Work, make something of yourself. He roll in his grave if he know you no study."

"Oh, Nonni, it was because I was playing soccer on the team after school. That's over now. I'll catch up on my homework, don't worry about me."

Tony walked over and, towering over his grandmother, bent and gave her a bear hug to make her stop swinging the spoon at him.

"Okay, Tony, don't make me cry when I see your report card."

Julia went to the rescue of her cousin. "Nonni, why do you always just blurt out what's on your mind?"

"Because I love you, that's why."

Tony took the giant pot of homemade minestrone soup and placed it on the table set up in the living room.

The family tore chunks of the crusty bread fresh from the bakery that sat in the middle of the table, thanked God for their blessings, and ate, not knowing what the future would hold.

* * *

Along the same East River, near the Whitestone Bridge, Sam was sitting down to dinner in the dining room. His new girlfriend, Angela, was in the kitchen helping his mother. He could hear them talking in cheerful banter. They had been dating since the start of the school year. Sam had two older sisters who were away at college, and his mother welcomed the female companionship. Angela never met a boy who was so polite and considerate. Her own brothers, although good men, were rough around the edges. They had both come home from the Vietnam War transformed. Angela's mother was often shocked by how they guzzled six-packs and the language she overheard them using when they thought she was out of earshot. To Angela, Sam seemed untouched by the vulgarity of life, a boy destined to be a gentleman. When Angela walked into the dining room, Sam stood up and pulled out her chair. His father, still dressed in his suit, did the same for his mother. They placed their napkins on their laps, said grace, passed the plate of bread to the right, and saw their future together.

8

Tuning In

Julia found the blue piano beat up in the corner of the basement when she moved back into the old house in Astoria. The paint was peeled and chipped, but all the keys still worked. She spent one long afternoon sanding and repainting it so that it looked like a MacKenzie-Childs masterpiece, then called movers and a piano tuner to finish its resurrection. It is now the centerpiece of her new living room, and Julia is determined to relearn how to play it.

"Grams, I brought you my old Suzuki books so you can practice." Bella hands Julia a stack of books.

"Most of these are probably too hard for me still … but thank you." Julia has no intention of ever opening them. She only wants to play the songs of her childhood from when she entertained her own grandmother.

"Were you the only one who played piano in the house?"

"No, my mother played. She was very talented, a natural, really. She taught herself then had some lessons."

"How did they afford music lessons?"

"My grandmother was a seamstress. People brought clothes to the house for her to fix. She made a lot of money on the side, cash only. That's how she paid for the little extras."

Bella's cell phone starts to buzz. "Grams, I'm going to my room to study for a while."

"Okay, I have a painting I'm working on. We'll get pizza in about an hour."

Julia and Bella spend the night eating pizza, texting, and watching a tearjerker movie. Tomorrow Bella is going to help Julia decorate for Christmas. That is one task she always has trouble doing alone. Bella always looks forward to driving upstate, trekking through the forest, and picking out a tree. Julia likes to go right before Thanksgiving, so she has time to get used to the idea of Christmas.

They watch the weather report before going to bed. "Grams, it's going to be so warm tomorrow. It'll be weird sweating, picking out a Christmas tree."

"Don't complain that it's not cold, but I do agree it's strange," Julia laughs. "But then, life is strange."

Bella, even at fourteen, still loves the trip and the company of her grandmother. She seems immune to being a typical teenager. They always stop for the giant apple fritters sold at the farm stand and then eat another one in the car, making a sticky mess. In Julia's return to her old home, her whole life in reduction, she hopes to keep some semblance of normalcy with Bella.

Julia is glad that she has something to look forward to in the morning. She is still bristling inside from her performance at the therapist's office and needs the distraction of her granddaughter. Julia knows she is pushing away again but can't seem to stop the momentum. Bella is her only tether.

At three in the morning Bella shakes Julia, who had fallen asleep on the couch, trying to wake her. "I thought I heard the piano playing." Bella has a tired, confused look on her face.

"You must've heard one of those fancy car horns or a train. Go back to sleep. I'll check the door." Julia tiptoes in the dark. Everything is locked. She tosses and turns for a while in her bed but finally falls to sleep. In the morning, she is up before Bella and again tiptoes into the kitchen to make coffee. The cabinets are ajar, and the table is perfectly set for three. Julia shakily puts the extra place setting back in the cupboard and shuts the doors. Then she goes to her car and finds the last cigarette in her pack.

9

Christmas Eve 1971

"Your grandfather would have loved this tree." Maria strate-gically placed strings of tinsel on the fresh pine tree.

"I can barely remember Papa, except that he always hugged me and let me taste his wine."

"He was a good man. He work too hard, that's what killed him. He loved you, the only granddaughter. He would say, Julia, she's a *bellisima principessa.*"

"What does that mean?"

"A beautiful princess," Maria translated, and Julia blushed.

"Nonni, why do you always wait until Christmas Eve to put up the tree?" Julia was under the tree trying to get water into the small stand.

"Because that's when they go on sale."

Julia had grown used to not worrying about money. Her father earned a good income at the newspaper as one of the editors, and her mother worked part-time as an accountant. Money was never the problem. Julia had managed to negotiate her way into spending the school week with her grandmother and taking the subway into Manhattan to go to school. On Fridays, she would leave school and take the Long Island Railroad home to Manhasset, where her mother picked her up at the station. Julia would secretly scrutinize her for bruises when her mother looked ahead at the road as she drove. It was hard to tell, but as the month wore on, her mother was smoking more. Tonight, Christmas Eve, her parents and brother were coming for dinner with all her aunts, uncles, and cousins. She would go home with them and stay for the rest of the school vacation. Julia tried to keep out of her father's way when he was around, but it was nearly impossible. At night she would lay in her bed trying to rationalize her father's behavior and her mother's acceptance of it. The only thing that made her feel better was imagining she was adopted. She would tell herself, "These people who acted so strange could not possibly be my parents." Julia even contrived an adoption story that she told some of her new acquaintances at her high school.

Julia squeezed the angel onto the top of the tree. There was only an inch left before it hit the ceiling and the living room became even smaller with its presence. There would barely be enough room to set up the extra tables. Maria switched all the tree lights on, and they sat on the couch to admire their work.

"Okay, enough fun, we have to finish cooking. Come on Julia, you make the pizzelle."

Julia followed her grandmother into the kitchen. "Nonni, I don't want to go home this week. Can't I stay here?"

"Why, why you ask that, Julia? Is he starting up again? When your grandfather was alive, he no tried his funny business."

"No, not as bad as before. But he's always grouchy." Julia decided not to tell her grandmother everything that was happening.

"You keep your mama safe. It'll be okay."

Julia thrived in the shadow of her grandmother. There were no condescending remarks, reminders of how lucky she was to live in such a nice house, angry retribution for trivial infractions. The first weekend Julia was back with her parents, she walked to an afternoon matinee with her friend from elementary school. When she got home, her room had been torn apart, closet door open, dresser drawers pulled out, bras and undergarments along with all her clothes smashed under a heavy foot in a pile in the middle of the room.

"I told you to clean your room this morning, dammit," her father shouted. "Now you have to clean it, you lazy bitch!" He stood at her doorway, lurking with a glass of Scotch in his hand, breathing heavily until her mother coaxed him away. That night she could hear her father still ranting at her mother. She could only imagine the rage as he was throwing her clothes into a heap while she was innocently spending a Saturday afternoon like all her normal friends. After that, she rarely left the house but stayed in her room with the door closed and worked on her paintings, waiting for Sunday night when Uncle Freddie came to rescue her. He worked a second job on weekends at a lawn and garden center near her parents' house and had agreed to drive her back to her grandmother's on Sundays. Julia especially liked when he got off work early, so she did not have to stay home for dinner on Sunday nights. Yet somehow her father left her brother alone and even coddled him. Julia could not understand why.

* * *

Everyone was coming for dinner at five o'clock. The plan was to eat and open presents then go to midnight mass together at Immaculate Conception Church on the boulevard. Julia went outside to wait for her family and cousins to arrive. Inhaling the crisp cold air felt like renewal, so fresh with the promise of snow. The trees in the park across the street were frosted with ice crystals from the sleet earlier in the day. The lights of Manhattan sparkled in the misty air.

The relatives piled into the house, throwing their coats on the bedroom beds. Julia watched as her parents and brother arrived, squeezing the Cadillac into the narrow driveway. Her six-year-old brother dashed from the car to the house yelling, "Dad ran over a squirrel! On purpose!"

Then her father pushed his door open with so much force it bounced back on him and hit his knee. "Goddammit!" His face burned red as he stood facing the open door.

Her mother sat stiffly in the front seat, and he shouted, "Get the hell out already, Grace."

She put out her cigarette in the car's ashtray and meekly replied, "I can't open the door on my side. There's not enough room."

Dennis got back into the car, put the car in reverse, and gunned the gas. The tires squealed as he turned the steering wheel to bring it to an abrupt stop in front of the house. Her mother jumped out and ran inside with her head down. Julia noticed her mother had a scarf tied unusually high up on her neck. Her father then repeated the same maneuver in reverse, slammed the car door, and cursed as he got out. "If there was any goddam parking around here, we wouldn't have this problem."

Julia was too afraid to say anything. She walked back into the house, headed straight to the kitchen, and helped her grandmother and Aunt Rosie prepare the food for the table. Julia gently lifted the fried fish out of the pan and let the oil absorb on paper towels, grated cheese onto the pasta, and went along as if everything was right in the world even though the ground beneath her was shaking.

10

Christmas Day 1971

After nine o'clock mass at Holy Trinity Church, Sam and his family stopped at the bakery for bread for the afternoon's feast of homemade ravioli. They also picked up a copy of the *Daily News*. The Cross Island Parkway had one lane closed, and the traffic was backed up all the way onto the ramps, so they had to take side streets home.

Sam's mother looked down as they crossed a bridge over the traffic jam. "I hope they clear the parkway soon. Everyone is going to have a hard time getting to our house by two o'clock if it stays like this."

His two sisters chatted away in the back seat next to him, talking about all the exciting things they were doing at college. Sam just gazed out the window daydreaming, bored. He picked up the paper he had on his lap under the bread and saw why the parkway was backed up.

Everyone stopped talking when he read the headline out loud. *Tragic Car Accident on Parkway Christmas Eve: Parents and Young Son Killed, Daughter Survives.*

"*Marone mia!* Does it say who?" Sam's mother shouted into the back seat.

"No, just says the driver appeared to be intoxicated according to witnesses...driving erratically before hitting a tree."

"I hope it's no one we know, what a Christmas, oh my God," Sam's mother made a sign of the cross, and he could see her lips moving in prayer. Sam turned the paper over, stared out the window, and silently sent a plea out into the universe.

They drove the rest of the way home in silence. Then, turning onto their tree-lined street, Sam's father parked the car in the driveway, opened the car door for his wife, gave her a hug, and said to his children, "Come on, everyone, let's go have a merry Christmas."

11

The Other Christmas
1971

Julia opened her eyes at half-mast. A flimsy white curtain hung on both sides of her bed. The space directly in front was a hazy gray. Voices filtered through a dense fog. She closed her eyes again and tried to listen.

A muffled voice came from the other side of the curtain. "Can I keep the bullet?"

Someone's booming voice answered, "No, it's evidence."

Heavy footsteps and the sound of clanging metal punctuated the air. Julia thought she must be dreaming and fell back into a deep sleep. She was awakened by someone shaking her shoulder gently. Her eyes opened to a nurse smiling into her face. The nurse pulled a cart with a tray over her body, plopping down a paper plate of toast and a little container of orange juice. The sight and smell of congealed butter on burnt white bread made Julia nauseous, and the room began to sway.

"Honey, try to wake up. You had surgery. Your ankle was broken. They had to put a pin in it."

Julia strained to focus. "Where am I?"

That same booming voice came from out of nowhere. "Is she up yet?"

Suddenly the filter of sleep dissipated. Julia heard loud, agitated voices coming from around a corner.

The nurse's now-irritated face turned towards the noise. "Your relatives are here. There's quite a crowd out there." Her smile returned as she checked Julia's blood pressure. "There's a policeman who wants to talk to you. But you tell me when you're ready. C'mon, try to eat a little something, honey."

Julia sat up in the bed. The white plaster cast came up right below her knee, and she began to shake. The memory of last night was upon her.

The nurse came back into her little space. "We are moving you to a private room now."

An attendant quickly entered and wheeled her bed into the hall. Her grandmother and a crowd of family members surrounded the rolling bed, crying and grabbing onto Julia's hands, caressing her hair.

Julia reached for her grandmother's hand. "Nonni, where's my mother? Jeffrey?"

The question set off more wailing. Aunt Rosie was being held up and guided by Uncle Freddie, and no one could look Julia straight in the eye.

Julia's cousin Tony, still in his suit from Christmas Eve, rushed up to her bed. "Let's get you to your room."

The police officer ran down the hall to catch up with the crowd. He waved his hand as if hailing a cab. "Wait up, I just have to ask the girl a few questions."

Tony spun around and confronted the cop.

Julia heard her cousin whisper aggressively, "Give us a few minutes, will ya?"

The conversation faded as they moved her bed into the private room. Now Julia only caught tidbits of bitter voices echoing down the hall. The sun streamed through the blinds, and the air smelled like rotten lemons.

A new nurse walked in. "You must be special to be set up without a roommate." She shook the thermometer in her hand. "Say ahh, I have to take your temperature."

A policeman blocked the doorway. He was an intimidating six feet tall with a broad chest and close-cropped jet-black hair.

Julia heard hushed voices ping-ponging out in the hallway, but the family had apparently yielded to authority and let the policeman in first.

They all knew it was inevitable.

He addressed the nurse. "I'm terribly sorry, but I have to see if she remembers anything about the accident."

She nodded, and he approached the bed.

"Hello, young lady, Julia, right? I'm Officer Calloway."

In that split second, Julia decided to lie. "Yes. But where's my mother...why are you here?"

"I'm sorry to bother you at a time like this, but do you remember the accident last night?" His loud, deep voice rattled Julia's eardrums.

She answered in a barely audible voice, "Kind of. I was sleeping in the back seat."

"I have several eyewitness reports that your father was driving erratically. Was he drinking before you got in the car?"

"No, no, he wasn't. We were going home after midnight mass."

"Are you sure young lady?"

"Yes, I'm sure."

Looking down at his notepad and tapping his pen, Officer Calloway continued. "Why was he on the Cross Island Parkway? That's kind of out of your way to go home, isn't it?"

Julia turned her head away from the officer. "I don't know where we were. It was sleeting. The wipers were freezing up. He said he couldn't see very well before I fell asleep."

"Is there anything that happened right before the accident that you can recall?"

Julia bit down on her lip. "No, I woke up when he slammed on the brakes. Someone was leaning on their horn. Then the car started to spin. I don't remember what happened after that."

Officer Calloway studied Julia's expression and finally spoke. "Okay, you might remember some details later. I left my name with your grandmother, in case you think of something. Good thing you were wearing a seat belt."

Julia needed proof that all of this was not just a bad dream. "Officer Calloway, did I hear someone ask you if they could keep the bullet earlier?"

"Yeah, that guy was a jerk. He got shot in the ass by a friend he double-crossed." Officer Calloway shook his finger at her. "Kiddo, remember to treat your friends right."

The policeman left, and Julia's family came barreling through the door.

"Nonni, where is my mother? Jeffrey? Are they okay?" Julia tried again to get an answer. She realized everyone, not just Tony, still wore their dress clothes from last night.

Her grandmother's eyes were puffy. Tears streaked her cheeks. She stooped over to kiss Julia. *"Oh, bella mia, bella mia."*

Aunts, uncles, and cousins formed a fortress around Julia's bed. There wasn't an empty space to look past them.

The sun pushed through the Venetian blinds, illuminating the crowns of their lowered heads. Julia, still woozy, felt as if she were surrounded by angels.

Tony stood next to her. He bent down and whispered in her ear what she already sensed. "They're gone, Julia. Thank God you survived. It's a miracle."

* * *

Uncle Freddie and Tony came to the hospital to bring Julia home the next day. "Have Yourself a Merry Little Christmas" was blaring on the elevator as she sat in a wheelchair on the ride down to the lobby. It had started to snow, and they lifted her gently into the car.

Uncle Freddie, who rarely spoke, turned to Julia as he left her at her grandmother's house. "Tony is going to stay here with you and your Nonni for a few days. Let him help you, don't be stubborn."

The living room was still piled with half-opened presents. The needles on the tree had started to dry out and drop to the floor.

Maria sat on the couch with a crocheted handkerchief in her hand. "Oh, Julia, I'm so glad you're home. We take care of each other now."

Tony carried a pair of crutches into the house and stood them against the wall, then sat on the arm of the couch.

When she saw her grandmother sitting in her usual spot, Julia was filled with relief and emptiness at the same time. She felt like she should protect her grandmother from the truth, but the truth overwhelmed her. Still, she couldn't keep it in. "Nonni, I have to tell you something." In a torrent of words and tears, Julia let the truth tumble out.

The midnight mass had stretched into the early hours of the morning. The three-block walk back to the car was miserable in the cold rain. Jeffrey was crying that he was tired and wanted to sit on his mother's lap. Julia offered to have Jeffrey next to her in the backseat. Her father had calmed down from earlier in the evening. He had finished the bottle of Chianti before they left for church, and that sometimes mellowed him out. Julia thought it was safe to make the suggestion.

"Dad told me to shut my trap and put Jeffrey in the middle upfront. The wheels squealed when he pulled out of the parking space, and Mom yelled at him to slow down."

Julia took a deep breath. "He shouted at her, 'Do you want to drive, dammit?' She just sat there and didn't answer him. By the time we got down to the highway, he was driving normal. Like some switch turned off."

Maria wiped tears from her eyes, and Tony anxiously ran his fingers through his hair.

"Everything was fine for a while. Jeffrey was sound asleep leaning on Mom…but when we were near our exit, a guy in a red car cut us off …we missed the ramp. Dad just flipped out and started cursing, 'That sonofabitch, fucking idiot.' He started chasing that car like he was trying to drive it off the road. Mom was shouting at him, 'Slow down,' and 'Dennis, you're going home the wrong way!'"

Julia's grandmother handed her the embroidered handkerchief, and Julia stopped talking. She stared straight ahead with silent tears rolling down her cheeks.

Tony kneeled down next to her and peered up into her eyes. "It's okay, Julia, don't hold it in. It's not a secret. Just tell us."

She took a deep, shuddering breath. "He kept driving like a maniac, and it was starting to sleet again. I pulled my seat belt tight because I was so scared. We must have been going like eighty miles per hour. Dad kept swerving in and out of lanes. Mom lit a cigarette and kind of sucked all the smoke in. Then as nicely as she could, she said, 'Please…please, Dennis, slow down.' Dad turned to Mom and slapped her on the back of the head so hard that her cigarette went flying out of her mouth into the windshield."

Julia stopped talking and started to gasp for breath. Her grandmother moved next to her and held her tight. Julia knew she had to finish the story but could only whisper the ending. "We were going so fast. He turned to slap Mom again and didn't see we were about to hit the car in front of us until it was too late. He swerved, and we went flying off the road. I don't remember anything after that except Mom screaming."

Tony got up and punched the wall. "That asshole."

Julia whimpered, "I lied to the policeman. I didn't want him to think we were bad people."

The truth filtered through the family like a shock wave.

12

Girls Do Lunch

Julia is late for lunch as always. She pulls the used silver Mini Cooper into the parking lot and eases it into a spot.

Linda waits at a table near the window and sees her friend stepping out of the distinctive car, but no one could miss the driver either with her long curly gray hair, perfect posture, high-heeled boots, and long trendy embroidered jacket. Even gray, she looks young. Linda stares down at her walking sneakers, tugs at the waist of her stretchy pants as she gets up to greet Julia, and immediately feels inadequate.

The two women hug, and Julia slides into her chair. "Sorry I canceled last minute on Friday. I don't know what I was thinking. I completely forgot I had to pick up Bella early for the weekend."

"That's okay, Julia. I didn't mind." Linda turns away, assuming that excuse is a lie. "How do you like your new car?"

"Oh, my clown car?" Julia laughs. "It fits in my narrow driveway, and I can fold down the seats for my canvasses."

"Well, I think it is very cool." Linda takes another look at it, sitting in the space next to her Ford Escape. They meet at the chain restaurant across from the Roosevelt Field Mall because Julia likes being able to sit for hours, refill her coffee for free, and not be bothered by waitstaff. Linda is not as enthusiastic; she'd prefer not to stand in line to order at a counter like a college cafeteria, eat food on a tray, or spend money on a salad obviously "fresh" from a bag. Still, she also needs the coffee and the free cookie to get through another afternoon with Julia. So they find a booth in the corner of the restaurant and put their trays down.

Linda stares at the giant mound of green in front of her. "Look at all this organic lettuce piled up on a plastic plate with plastic forks. We are helping and hurting the environment at the same time."

"Well, the world is full of hypocrisy, isn't it?"

Linda can tell Julia's mood right away with that retort. She decides to start with an easy question. "So, how's Bella?"

"She's great, but I can't believe that my daughter let it slip that I was seeing a therapist again." Julia steams.

This is news to Linda also. "How did Bella react?"

"She was nonjudgmental. But I don't want her worrying about me. My daughter can worry, but not Bella."

"How did your daughter know?"

"My daughter decided I was crazy." Julia makes an effort to laugh as she speaks. "She gave me the referral. Someone she knows from the hospital,"

"So, who is this new therapist? Do you like her...him?"

"I don't know. It's a her. She sits there like some damn Marcel Marceau most of the time. Making weird faces and not saying anything."

"Oh, Julia!"

"Well, I went for help, not eyeball rolls...."

"Please, you must be imagining that. I'm sure she isn't mocking you!"

"It feels like she is. She just seems shocked sometimes by what I say....and I don't even know where she got her degree ...Podunk Community College, for all I know. Really, why should I trust her?"

"I don't know. I never went to therapy."

Julia smirks. "No, Miss Perfect, of course not."

Linda settles in for one of Julia's tirades. Somehow the warm and funny person from freshman year in college has morphed into someone who wallows in pain, maybe even enjoys living in a state of constant anxiety. Julia, with her quick wit and observations, can wear a person out with her intensity. Linda often goes home and takes a nap after spending an afternoon with her. She's tried at times to pull back from the friendship like her daughter suggested, but something prevents her from abandoning her old college roommate. Loyalty is her curse. But Julia is a poison she can only handle in small doses.

Linda decides to try 'shop' talk. "Remember in our first drawing class in college, the professor was always making us start by sketching the negative space?"

"You mean that guy with the lit cigarette hanging out of the corner of his mouth? The one who always mumbled?"

"Yeah, that one. We learned a lot despite that."

"Did you forget he smelled like burnt toast? Ugh, disgusting."

Linda leans in. "Okay, forget the toast, just seriously, listen for a minute. Maybe that is what you are doing with your life. Seeing the negative space first instead of all the positive."

"My God, do I have to pay you for that advice?"

"Julia, please, I'm only trying to help. I mean, what do you want from me?"

"Oh, geez, there I go again, you're right, I'm sorry. You're not the enemy." Julia looks down and comes up again, trying to be pleasant. "Really, too much caffeine. I'm wired today."

"Maybe you should try decaf." Linda jokes because she can't bear the discomfort.

They sit silently for a few moments, Julia pushing the leftover cranberries in her salad around the plate.

In the awkward pause, Linda remembers that woman in her church group, Angie, who passed suddenly last year during the holidays. "Look, as a friend...I'm only saying we are not getting any younger. It's time for you to resolve those old hurts. I know the divorce was hard, but get on with life. You can only change your future, not your past."

"Positive about my future? Me? I had to trade in my Lexus SUV for a banged-up clown car! Sell my beautiful home in Great Neck and move into a tiny house under the Hell Gate Bridge!" Julia puts her boots up on the bench and launches into a list of humiliations. "I could be the star in my own stupid cable TV reality show, Divorcee's Half-assed House."

Linda stops her with one sentence. "I thought you loved that house."

"I don't know if it loves me."

"What do you mean?"

"Nothing, nothing, forget I said anything. No, forget I said everything."

13

Home Again

Under the canopy of a dreary near-winter sky, Sam and Julia wake up in their separate worlds, each achingly alone. Sam has started sleeping on his wife's side of the bed because he can't face the emptiness. He hoped it would tamp down the singing he hears in his dreams. Though there are nights when he feels the warmth of Angie's body encompass him, the songs persist. Sam's daughter Caroline noticed the bed unmade on only her mother's side on her last visit. She asked him about it, and Sam responded, "I can see the alarm clock better on that side." Later that day, she again brought up the topic of coming to live with her in North Carolina.

Julia sleeps in a twin bed in the same room where she spent her teenage years. After the divorce, her daughter had tried to convince Julia to move in with her husband and Bella. But, in her inimitable style, Julia responded, "No, I'm not about to have you lock me down in a basement."

Both Julia and Sam know life would be easier if they surrender to the arms of their families. Neither Sam nor Julia would be dropping plastic capsules into a machine for a lukewarm cup of coffee in the morning if they gave in to their children's wishes. Bella would be greeting Julia in the mornings with a pot of steaming coffee, and Sam could teach his grandsons how to golf, making them forever companions. Yet both bristle at the thought of giving up their independence and would rather suffer loneliness.

Under the low gray clouds, Julia takes her morning walk on the path up and down the East River. The sounds of the city obscure the voices in her head, and she only hears the sweet song from her dreams calling to her. Not wanting to run into Linda and Angie's church friends again, Sam heads to the golf course in Bethpage. He finds it almost as soothing as the ocean, playing each hole in his imagination as he walks the course along the cart path. "Next time, I'll use my nine iron if I'm this close to the green," Sam speaks to no one. It has become his custom. Both relax and are lost in thought on their walks. The real problem is when they open the doors to their houses and step inside again.

On this same day, when the pallor of a gray sky makes time feel like it is standing still, they both decide to walk their lives into another direction.

14

Resolutions

"Mom, why don't you come and spend the week with us for Christmas?" Julia's daughter Andrea is barely audible. She has the habit of calling from her car on the way to work at Mercy Hospital. Her ride is exactly twenty minutes, the time she allots to her mother each weekday. If Julia doesn't answer her cell phone, the house phone starts ringing, sometimes waking Julia up from a sound sleep.

"I don't know, Andi."

"C'mon, Mom, Bella would love it, and I'm off most of the week."

"Is Phil going to be home?"

"Well, yes, part of the week anyway."

"I don't think he wants me around for a whole week."

"Oh, Mom. He loves you…really… but…." The cell phone starts breaking up, and Julia can't hear what Andrea is saying.

"But, what?"

"His British accent makes him sound cold...too formal. You know you, of all people, should understand him."

"What does that mean?"

"He just says what's on his mind at the moment. No filter."

Julia processes that reply for a few seconds. "Maybe for a few days. I'll bring *my* filter," emphasizing the my. "I have to discuss something with you when you're not in the car."

"What? What's this about?"

"Nothing earth-shattering. Just some decisions I've made, that's all."

"Should I worry? How are things going with Dr. Blanding?"

"Dr. Blanding, oh, she's so boring. Blanding! Mary Shelley couldn't have come up with a better character name." Julia's pitch goes up an octave.

Andrea knows that signals her mother is upset about something or someone. "Oh, Mom, really! Don't be so dramatic. She's highly regarded."

"Well, she's not exactly interactive."

"Please, give her a fair chance."

"Oh, I will." Julia quickly changes the subject. "Any ideas for a Christmas present for Bella?"

"Maybe you should buy tickets to a Broadway matinee. You two could go, or maybe a museum."

"A musical would be fun, but I'm not up to going into a museum yet."

"Okay, then take her out to dinner or something instead."

"Yes, dinner after a matinee, we both would enjoy that."

"Why don't you go to that Italian restaurant, the one owned by that chef from your old, I mean new, neighborhood? It just opened in the theatre district."

"No, I'm not going there. That woman is rude. Nothing like on TV. People aren't really who they seem to be."

"Oh, Mom, how do you know that?"

"I know, believe me, I know…and we never went to her restaurant when it was in Astoria."

"Why not?"

"As your great Uncle Freddie used to say, 'Why go out when the food is better at home?'"

"Please, stop with your ridiculous stories."

"It's true! Besides, we couldn't afford it."

Andrea knows her mother is itching to tell her side of the story. "So, what's wrong with the chef?"

"I went to a book signing a few years ago. The weather was terrible, freezing rain and all, but I wanted to get her new cookbook as a gift for one of my colleagues."

"That was nice of you."

"It was…so I told her I was there to get the book for a friend who watches her all the time. Then I made the mistake of saying that I love Food TV. You would have thought I mistook her for that happy one with the talk show with the look she gave me. I didn't know she was on a different station."

"That doesn't sound so bad. Did you tell her you were from the same neighborhood?"

"Yes, and it turned ugly. She kind of glared at me and said, 'Oh, there's a lot of Italians like you there' …she was so derogatory!"

"Oh, Mom." Andrea becomes impatient with her mother, partly because she has started to focus on work. She has the bad habit of doing the same thing to Bella, half-listening, anticipating her thoughts, and always in a time crunch. The chronic pressure to get too much done in a day can make her short-tempered. "Don't take everything so personally. Maybe she was just having a bad day. You're so defensive all the time."

"You're always giving everyone the benefit of the doubt, Andi."

"Good thing for you, huh?"

"Well, I'm taking Bella to that Thai restaurant she likes."

Andrea pulls into her space at the hospital. "Later, Mom."

"Have a good day, honey." Julia goes back to sleep. It is only six a.m.

15

Resolutions 2

In the early light of summer, Sam started a daily practice of writing out a schedule as he sat drinking his morning coffee. He thought if he gave himself some structure, the hours would pass easily, and he would feel each new day as a small victory. But now, as the last bits of Indian summer succumb to the bitterness of winter, Sam realizes he is only filling up time with meaningless tasks. Angie had died in this space of time last year, and he aches with melancholy. He knows he has to accept his new reality but isn't quite sure what to do.

One thing Sam doesn't want to erase from his schedule is Saturday evening dinner at his sister's house. They are home from Florida for the holidays, and he can see his extended family that still lives on Long Island. They had all been so kind to him after Angie passed away, but as the months wore on, fewer and fewer phone calls and casseroles arrived to bolster him. Sam understands. People have busy lives, he seems in control, and they move on. But, he also wants to move on. Sam longs to listen to the voice in his dreams. Something or someone is calling him out of his deep well of sadness.

Sam drives down Southern State Parkway a few exits to Westbury. His sister and brother-in-law live in a modest split-level house like the thousands of others that line the streets of their town. The aroma of his sister's traditional Saturday night meal, baked chicken and oregano, envelopes him as he walks in the back door. He realizes he never had lunch and is famished.

"That smells terrific, Franny," Sam steals a piece of bread from the table and starts devouring it.

"Look at my handsome brother, you lost weight," Fran kisses him and then hugs him for a long minute.

"Are Lucy and Bob coming up for Christmas?"

"She didn't want to drive in from Jersey, but I convinced her. Catie, Dan, and the crew too."

"How'd you convince her to do that?"

"Oh, big sisters have their ways," Fran laughs. "My kids and the grandkids will be here too!"

Sam mockingly looks around and spreads his arms. They practically touch the walls of both sides of the dining room. "Where are you going to put everyone? We should have never sold Mom and Pop's big old house."

Franny laughs at him. "Don't worry. Nick's setting up tables in the basement. We'll fit, so what if we have to sit on top of each other."

"My three are coming up too, you know."

"I know, don't worry. The more, the merrier," Fran tightens the knot on her apron. "God bless us if only Angie was still here."

Sam turns away from his sister and looks out the window. "Fran, I've been thinking. Maybe I should try to get out more, you know, with old friends."

"Of course, you should, Sammy. Angie wouldn't want you to be so alone. Look at you. You're like a stick."

"I ran into one of her friends from church. Maybe I'll go tomorrow morning."

"Yes, yes, you should."

Sam would never say it out loud to his sister, but the thought of sitting alone in the pew without Angie next to him has kept him away. He can still hear her singing earnestly off-key and feel her holding his hand like a teenager during the *Our Father*. Yet, he misses the times of peaceful contemplation he feels in church and finally decides to force himself to go. The last time he was there was for the funeral.

The following day, Sam wakes up early, has his one cup of coffee, dresses in his best Friday casual clothes, and drives to Maria Regina Church. He parks by a side door in case he feels the need to make an early exit and finds a seat on the opposite side of the church from where he and Angie used to sit. He always struggled with his belief, but somehow the experience is so ingrained in him that the familiarity of it all comforts him. Life always seems better when light filtering through stained glass streams down on you.

The same priest who presided over Angie's funeral gives one of his familiar stale sermons. Sam thinks he feels his hand warm during the sign of peace as if Angie were holding it. It frightens him and comforts him at the same time.

Familiar faces line up for communion, and as each of Angie's friends pass by him on their way back to the pews, they smile. Some touch the sleeve of his coat and whisper, "Sammy, so good to see you...come have coffee." His instinct is to sprint out the side door, but he resolves to at least try one time to get back into the stream of life. As the final hymn plays, Sam joins the line of people heading for a cup of coffee and a donut in the community room.

"Sammy, Sammy, it's so nice to see you. I was afraid I scared you away forever when I ran up to you at the beach." Linda is glad she chose her newest stylish scarf and best-fitting jeans to wear to church today. She can hear her mother's voice, "Dress nice when you go out. You never know who you are going to run into."

Her husband Hank looks at Linda confused and then reaches out to shake Sam's hand. "Nice to see you, Sam."

Before Sam can even get to the coffee, a circle of women surrounds him. Each one compliments how good he looks and then says how much they miss Angie. "God bless her" filters through the air like a chant.

"Oh, it must be hard for you this time of year, Sammy." A woman he doesn't recognize hands him a donut. She stands so close he can feel the heat of her body through his jacket.

Linda comes running over again. "Sammy, this is Gloria... you remember her from the teacher's union?"

"I'm sorry, I don't. But it's nice to meet you now."

"You were the principal at one of the schools where my committee was negotiating a contract...we had a bit of a heated discussion over study hall assignments," Gloria tries to spark his memory.

Sam shakes his head and laughs. "So, we were enemies?"

Using all the charm a nearly sixty-year-old woman can muster without looking ridiculous, Gloria smiles back into his eyes. "Well, I was hoping we could make up and be friends now."

16

Evergreen

After her daughter's morning call, Julia has trouble falling back to sleep. She is anxious about her ten o'clock session with Dr. Blanding.

On her walk the previous day, Julia resolved to stop with her sideshow and confront her problems. She knows all too well that she speaks harshly and carelessly to people she cares about. Only Bella is spared what her daughter refers to as her acerbic charm. Why lashing out is her chosen method of coping is a mystery to her. It is a pattern that she knows is self-defeating. Sometimes when she makes an off-handed comment, she can hear the sarcasm and bitterness of her father channeling through her veins.

Last week when Julia left the psychologist's office, she blurted out, "I'm genetically programmed to be an asshole." She didn't turn to see Martina's reaction but walked straight to her car and put her head down on the steering wheel.

So today, on this crisp morning with snow in the air, Julia braces herself, puts on her favorite teal silk blouse and walks outside to face herself.

"Why don't we start with a good memory today?" Dr. Martina Blanding is adamant about shifting the dialogue today. She has to admit that Julia causes her not only concern but personal anguish. Yet, despite all of her client's shortcomings, she understands how people are drawn into an uneasy alliance with her.

"I don't remember too much about my grandfather...but there's one memory that is so vivid."

Martina leans in. Julia seems to be trying to readjust her thought process in today's session, as if thought balloons are swirling around her head, informing her speech. "Tell me about it."

"I must have been five years old, maybe six. We were walking in the park near my new house on Long Island...you know, Manhasset. I was sad about moving, and my grandfather knew it. It was freezing out. He held my hand... his skin was so rough but warm."

"Did he say anything to you?"

"Yes... I hear him like it happened yesterday...that accent." Julia looks down at her hands, replaying the story in her mind, and stares out the window. Her grandfather's voice still echoes in her mind.

"Julia, see those trees, the ones all fallen down in the forest?"

"Yes, Papa."

"Now, you see that little pine tree standing alone, just starting to grow?"

"I see it. It's as tall as me!"

"You're that tree, principessa. The forest she change... to make room for new trees."

"I don't understand."

"It's time for you to start a new life. It's your turn to grow."

Julia turns her face up towards Martina, who has been patiently waiting for her to speak.

"He tried to console me about moving away from him and my grandmother. He pointed to a little tree in the woods and told me it was my turn to grow without them. But it was like a fairy tale."

"What do you mean by fairy tale?"

"I guess because I never really walked in the woods before, being a city kid. I was enraptured… the leaves crunching under my feet. It was like we were alone in some mystical world."

"Maybe there is a moral to this story."

"I'm waiting for the light bulb to go on." Julia sits there and looks at Martina and then keeps the promise she made to herself. "Help me."

"You're not that little girl anymore."

"Obviously. That innocent part of me seems to be lost forever. I was still too young to really understand family dynamics, as you say."

Martina decides to go out on a limb. She usually does not prompt her clients with her own ideas and prefers a process of self-reflection, but Julia seemed to be teetering on a breakdown in their last session. Martina wants to force her to focus on her strengths. "But the part of you that can deal with change, maybe reinvent yourself, what about that?"

"That's been the story of my life." Julia watches Martina's body language for a clue.

Martina continues in a flat tone, "You've always been able to survive whatever misfortune has come your way."

"Barely."

"But you've been that new little tree over and over again."

"I suppose you have a point. It's this divorce and losing my job all at once. I mean, how much is a person," Julia pauses and tries to maintain her control. "This time is different."

"Is it?"

"I'm old and tired, worn out from all the pretense…trying to act…I don't know…I probably seem like…." Julia stops herself. She isn't really ready to reveal herself fully to this stranger, and today's session is about over. She quickly shifts gears. "Are there any side effects from those sleeping pills you told me to ask my doctor for?"

"Oh, did he prescribe them for you?"

"Yes, over the phone."

"Not really anything serious short term. Rarely, maybe a little dizziness."

"Well, I am sleeping better."

"Good, good, see you after the holidays then."

Julia makes a pleasant exit for once. Martina feels like she has crossed some threshold with Julia. She didn't want to push her too hard. The risk she took interjecting her own opinion seems to have worked. Martina doesn't fully realize that Julia has decided on her own to participate more fully in her recovery. Both are blinded by their own tunnel vision of each other, but that doesn't matter. Something is clicking between them.

As Julia walks out of the office, she sees a framed embroidered sign she never noticed before. It says, "Survival is a beautiful thing."

17

Gifts

It is the Saturday morning before Christmas. Bella is watching Dude Perfect on YouTube at the kitchen table with her friend, Artie, from the chess club. Andrea walks in to get another cup of coffee and stands still for a moment to look at Bella's iPad.

"I hope that's not what you two aspire to."

"Oh, Mom, it's just like a joke," Bella stands up and follows her mother to the espresso maker. "Mom, what did you get Grandma for Christmas?"

Andrea pushes the button for a cappuccino. "The usual, a nice scarf, jewelry...some pottery thing for her new house."

Bella starts to talk again, but Andrea can't hear over the whirring milk frother. "What did you say?"

"God, Mom, listen to me, will ya?"

"Okay, sorry."

"I said we should get Grandma one of those ancestry kits."

"What is she going to do with that?"

"You know how she doesn't really know where her father was from."

Andrea starts sipping her coffee, leaning against the counter. "I don't think she really wants to know."

Bella moves to stand in front of her mother, touching her arm. "I think she does. Whenever I ask her about him, she says, 'He came from white bread.'"

"I know. That's her way of saying he wasn't Italian. But I do know from talking to Aunt Rosie, a long time ago, that he was from the Midwest, maybe Chicago, but he was estranged from his family."

"Really, how bad was it?"

"They didn't talk to each other at all. Bad blood. No one from his family even came to his funeral." Andrea heads towards her laptop in her office.

"I don't know …I still think it's a good idea. She needs to figure out things, and I just think it would help for her to know. Besides, he's part of us…I mean, Dad could be your cousin for all we know."

Andrea spins around. "Bella, please, you are starting to sound like your grandmother. That's ridiculous!"

"C'mon, please, Mom. It's all part of my plan." Bella blocks Andrea's path to her office.

Andrea looks at her daughter's determined face and decides to really listen. "What plan?"

"Artie said he would help me, right Artie?"

Artie stops the video for a moment, smiles at Bella, and shakes his head in agreement.

"You know how Grams has been sad lately. I think she is really lonely."

"That's true, but I don't think it's something you can fix."

"Mom, listen…we talked about this in health class…about people needing a community."

Taking Bella's words seriously, Andrea puts her coffee cup down on the counter.

Noting her reaction, Bella is animated and waves her arms in the air while looking back and forth at Artie. "We are going to set up a Facebook account for her! Show her how to join groups. Start an Instagram page for her artwork."

"So, what does this ancestry thing have to do with all of that?"

"Well, it's part of the big picture. She can find some of her long-lost relatives. You know, make new friends… connect with people. I bet we have a ton of relatives in Italy. C'mon, Mom, she needs this."

"Okay, okay…maybe you're right. All the cousins she was still close to moved to the west coast after her grandmother died. She kind of lost touch with them over the years. Plus, I wouldn't want to get in the way of your grand plan."

"Order it two-day express mail, so it gets here in time," Bella orders. "And a new iPad…hers is like five years old."

Andrea picks up her coffee cup and feels the warmth between her palms. Then as she looks up at Bella, she has a sudden twinge of regret. She realizes her daughter is growing into the person she wishes she could be. "You know, honey. You're a lot like my father was…Gram's cheerleader."

Bella's face turns pink as she sits back down next to Artie. "Oh, Mom, I just love Grams, that's all."

"I know. We all do." Andrea leaves the room and sits down at her computer. She orders two kits...one for her mother and one for her husband, Phil.

18

The Advent

Sam sleeps soundly for the first time in months. He wakes up on Tuesday morning and realizes that last night was not filled with songs or dreams but deep uninterrupted sleep. He doesn't know what to make of it but welcomes the peace of mind. Sam has a busy day planned, and on this morning, he writes his to-do list with purpose. His mood is buoyed by the anticipation of his children's arrival this afternoon for Christmas week. He decides to go out to the new bagel shop near his house instead of inserting a pod into a machine, pushing a button, and sitting alone in his kitchen drinking a cup of glorified instant coffee. Sam gets into his car, says, "Gentleman, start your engines" as he turns the ignition, and heads out.

He orders the largest cup of coffee they offer and a breakfast sandwich. He is surprised to see so many people crammed into the small space, sharing tables, talking loudly over the pumped-in music. There is one empty table, and he sits down. The first sip of coffee is a magic elixir; his whole world has suddenly awakened. He picks up the paper left on the table when he hears a voice. "Can I join you?"

Sam looks up and registers a bit of a shock wave. "Oh, sure, um, here, let me move my tray out of the way." He struggles to remember the name.

"Sammy, it's me, Gloria, in case you forgot." Gloria smiles and sits down, inching the chair a little closer to Sam.

"Yes, yes, I remember. I was just caught off guard for a second." Sam really looks at Gloria, and on this second meeting, he notices how her blond hair is cut to frame her face and her striking blue eyes. Her smile is irresistible. The second shock wave is that she arouses his interest.

Never in his whole married life has Sam glanced at another woman. Angie always answered her friends' questions about her handsome husband, "Sam's a gentleman. He's not that kind of guy." And Sam knew that was true when he overheard Angie with her friends. Over the years, the passion did fade but never the love. The love only grew. There would never be any tremendously dramatic movie or book written about Sam and Angela, but they had shared a quiet life that seemed charmed until last year.

"I hear you're a golfer," Gloria says as she takes one half of her whole-grain bagel and slides it into a to-go bag.

"Yes, not exactly Tiger Woods. But I enjoy the walk." Sam tries to be witty.

"Oh, I never use a cart either."

"You play?"

"Oh, I've played for years on the teachers' after-school league. My team won the year-end tournament last year." Gloria nibbles on her bagel.

"I thought you were retired?"

"I am, but they let me stay on the league. Half the league is retired. Young women don't seem to be interested in golf anymore."

"Yoga maybe."

"Are you going to the school gala next week?"

"Maybe. I know I should. But I do have my ticket."

"They are handing out all the plaques. You know the golden handshake, for us retirees, is part of the event this year. I've heard it's really a lovely dinner."

"I know, I missed it last year because...well..." Sam looks down at his untouched bagel.

"It's next Friday, right before school starts up again in the new year."

"Oh gee, I have to get going, Gloria. My kids are flying in this afternoon." Sam packs up his bagel and puts the plastic top on his coffee.

"Sam, we should go together. It would be fun." Gloria looks into his eyes and touches his arm. "Here's my business card. I use it for tutoring. Call me."

"Okay, well, maybe...I really have to get moving. It was nice running into you again."

Gloria shouts out as he turns away, "I come here every morning!"

Sam reaches his car, takes a long sip of his coffee, and breaks into a sweat. Through the glass window, he can see Gloria reading the paper he left behind. A voice in his ear whispers *she is nice and harmless*, but Sam can't get past the guilt he feels. Luckily, he has his list of chores to distract him, and he heads off seeking refuge at the supermarket.

* * *

Sam's daughters, Caroline, Vi, and families will be arriving from North Carolina at LaGuardia early this afternoon. His son Matt is flying into JFK from Florida later that night. He wants to go to all their favorite places for the food they can't get outside New York. Antonio's for ravioli, the deli on Broad Street for cold cuts, and the wax-coated provolone hanging on a braided piece of twine. Sam is looking forward to cutting big wedges for his grandsons and watching them wrinkle up their mouths at the sharp taste. The bakery in Massapequa Park near the train station for bread will be his last stop. Sam loves the blast of heat that hits him when he swings the glass door open; he breathes in the smell from the brick ovens that permeate the bakery.

Most importantly, he has to remember when he gets home to defrost the cookies in the freezer that Angie baked over a year ago. It will be a special surprise for his children. Angie always baked in double and triple batches so that there would always be a dessert she could defrost in case company stopped by.

Last year, Sam's first Christmas without Angie was spent in Carolina. He only found the cookies this past spring when the temperature finally climbed to sixty degrees, and he went look-ing for a hamburger to barbecue in the basement freezer. That day he discovered buried treasures. Frozen chicken parmesan, meatballs in sauce, soups, the cranberry beans cooked in garlic that he loved, all neatly stacked and labeled in the freezer. Over the next few weeks, he savored each bite of these remnants of his life with Angie. He felt stupid and embarrassed that he never really paid attention to what she was doing in the kitchen most of the time or why she was always walking up and down those basement steps. The food always appeared magically...he never thought about it until he had to.

The cookies... he saved. Sam knew how much they would mean to his children and stopped himself from eating them even though he craved the taste of almond and chocolate. They looked better than the ones in the cases in the bakery. Delicate flowers, frozen in time, decorated the tops of the bonbon cookies and stared at him, reminding him of what he had lost.

Sam knows it isn't the cooking or the baking that he really misses. It is how Angie cared for him. Her love was unconditional, unfettered by the outside world, and now he realizes how easily he took all of that for granted. So today, he plans to put them on a silver tray with a paper doily like Angie used to do and set them out on the kitchen table for his family. He knows that the last tangible traces of Angie will soon be gone. Despite all of this and his morning encounter with Gloria, he feels optimistic and intent on making the best of Christmas week.

By noon Sam is home with all his bundles of goodies. His phone buzzes with a text from Caroline. "Landed. Picking up rental. Home in an hour."

He has a spectacular Italian feast ready for them when they arrive. He opens a bottle of Barolo wine and sets the table in the best imitation of Angie's handiwork he is capable of. He fumbles through the preparations, folding napkins into contorted triangles, and finally decides that paper plates will be okay to use. He finds the spot high up in the cabinet where Angie kept the glasses with the Twelve Days of Christmas painted on them and places them strategically on the table as the rental car pulls into the driveway.

His three young grandsons burst into the house first. "Papa, is it going to snow?"

"I think so tonight. Come give me a hug!"

All three of them start jumping up and down, chanting, "White Christmas! White Christmas!"

"Dad, oh, look at what you did. Everything looks terrific." Vi has tears in her eyes as she looks at the kitchen table.

"What's Christmas without a little soppressata and provolone?" Sam smiles warmly.

Caroline and her husband walk in carrying the suitcases. Caroline looks at the table and then just drops hers by the kitchen door. "Dad, where did you get these cookies? They look just like Mom's."

"They are hers. I found them in the freezer."

Caroline takes in a deep breath and looks at Vi. They both start to cry. Their sons and husbands look at them confused.

Sam walks over to his daughters and hugs them. "I didn't mean to upset you. I thought this would be a nice surprise."

"Oh, Dad, it is, it is…we just miss her so much," Caroline wipes her tears and smiles at her father.

Vi's husband spies the wine on the table. "C'mon everyone, let's pour a toast to Angie."

Sam takes three glasses for the boys and fills them with a half-inch of wine and the rest of the glass with soda. They swing their legs with excitement under the table.

Everyone squeezes around the table. "Here's to Mom, *salud!*" and they clink the glasses, eat the food they always eat at Christmas time, finish all the cookies, and let life go on.

19

Christmas in Glen Cove

Bella and Julia are both up early and tiptoe down the steps. The Christmas tree towers over them in the two-story entryway. Julia always feels like she is stepping into a grand hotel lobby when she enters her daughter's house. It is a gray morning, and Bella switches on the tree lights filling the room with a hazy glow as they both get comfortable on the nearby couch.

"That's really some tree," Julia whispers to Bella.

"It is, but I like yours better. At least we got to decorate it together. My parents paid some decorator to put up ours this year."

"They're just so busy. At least they think it's important to do for you."

"I guess so...here, Grams, open this present!" Bella's eyes widen as she hands Julia a gift wrapped in iridescent silver paper and a deep blue velvet bow.

"I don't know why you are getting so excited about a scarf. That's what your mother always buys me. I could rappel down from the staircase balcony if I knotted all of them together," Julia mutters under her breath, "or hang myself."

"Stop joking, Grams! Just open it!"

"Shouldn't we wait for your parents to get up?"

"No, they know what it is already. I can't wait!"

"Is it for you or me then?"

"Oh! Just c'mon already!"

Julia continues to tease Bella, shaking the box, flipping it several times until she finally unwraps it. She can't suppress her shock. "Whoa, what am I going to do with this?"

Bella swipes the box from Julia and points to the advertising written all along the sides. "Grams, don't you see? You can finally figure out who you are."

Julia quickly realizes that this gift was Bella's idea and reverses course. "What a nice present, Bella."

"You see what it says? Find relatives, your nationality. You know how you don't really know where your father was from? Maybe we are royalty or something."

"Oh… I always assumed he was Irish being Catholic…well, maybe Scottish…with all those freckles. We're more likely descendants of poor potato farmers."

"Yes, but you don't know for sure."

"You're right. I don't…for sure…but for probably."

Bella is half listening to Julia and keeps talking. "Plus, think of all those cousins you must have in Italy…you can make a family tree. This is going to be really awesome!"

"What's in this other box?"

Bella starts laughing hard. "A scarf!"

"Let's make some breakfast for everyone. Then we can open the rest of the presents." They both get up from the couch and walk into the kitchen. Julia feels small standing by the open door of the SubZero refrigerator. "My God, look at all this stuff…eggs?"

"No, let's make pancakes, those ones you make with ricotta and blueberries," Bella shouts across the kitchen.

"What am I? A short-order cook?"

"No…a celebrity chef!" Bella turns serious as she helps Julia find the flour in the pantry, "You don't seem very excited about your gift."

"Oh, Bella, honey…it's just…some things I just want to forget."

"But why? Aren't you curious? You see, I have this plan."

Julia hands Bella two eggs to crack while she assembles the dry ingredients. "Here, mix the ricotta in with the eggs…use the whisk…. what's your plan?"

Bella hesitates but then blurts it out. "Grams, we have to get you back on track. I can tell you've been sad."

Julia doesn't look up but takes the small bowl of eggs and ricotta and mixes them into the flour. "Bella, don't worry about me so much. I'll be fine. I always seem to find my way out of the tunnel."

"Not this time. I think it'll be good for you to try something new. Maybe meet new relatives. You must have more cousins than the ones who moved to California. Artie and I set up a Facebook and Instagram page for you…." Before Bella can finish, Julia interrupts.

"Facebook? What am I going to do with that?"

"Talk to people!" Bella shouts into Julia's ear. "There are all these art groups and things. You can post your paintings."

Julia distractedly mixes the batter. "I don't know…although it'd be nice to get in touch again with my cousins Gabe and Joey. We were so close growing up."

"Grams, whatever happened to that cousin Tony?"

"How do you know about Tony?" Julia can feel her face burning with anxiety.

"You showed me his picture when I was little, like five. You said that he was like a big brother to you."

"How on earth do you remember that?"

"Because I was in my wanting-a-brother phase then, and you showed me his picture on your dresser."

"Oh my, Tony. I guess you're old enough to know now…he was a fireman. He died on 9/11."

"Oh, Grams…I'm sorry. I didn't mean to make you sad on Christmas!"

"No, no, it was terrible at the time. But now…well…he's a happy memory now. But that's why everyone left New York. They had to get away from their sadness. His wife and brothers just couldn't take all the constant reminders…funerals going up and down the boulevard every day, well…they just had to look out their apartment window to be reminded. So, they left."

"How come no one told me any of this? I thought they moved because your grandmother died?"

"I don't know…why burden you with all that? It was all before you were born."

"God, I'm not a baby anymore. I'm in ninth grade!"

"Just protecting you, I guess," Julia starts fumbling with all the knobs on the stove. "C'mon, show me how to turn on the griddle on this stove."

"Just promise not to lie to me anymore, please."

"It's not lying, really…I won't anymore, okay?"

"Then what happened to grandpa? My real one, not that last jerk you were married to."

"Oh, Bella, hasn't your mother told you?"

"No, she never really explained."

Julia reaches for the plates. "Bella, it's Christmas. Let's talk about all this some other time. How long do I have to wait after I eat to spit in that damn tube?"

Bella senses Julia's anxiety, and she too is ready to switch back to the happy version of Christmas. "About an hour, I think…maybe you should skip the blueberries."

"Let's make some cappuccino. I hear footsteps upstairs."

Within a minute, Andrea and Phil come plodding down the stairs. Phil surveys the kitchen. "You two are up bloody early. What smells so good?"

Bella smiles at her parents. "A merry Christmas breakfast."

Phil heads to the kitchen island and piles a plate full of pancakes, then squirts some whipped cream on top. "Julia, who thought I'd say this, but I'm so glad you're here."

"Phil, please. You promised…Mom, this all looks wonderful." Andrea sits at the table and then yawns.

"It was Bella's idea." Julia looks up from reading the instructions in the box of her ancestry kit.

Andrea watches for her mother's reaction. "She's got a lot of ideas, doesn't she?"

Julia doesn't reveal anything. "Oh, she sure does…she sure does."

20

A Great Week

Sunshine sparkles on the icy crust of snow. The boys are outside sledding down the little hill in the backyard. The husbands are in the basement watching a bowl game. Sam and his three children sit around the kitchen table. "Dad, this has been a great week," Caroline says as she sips the remnants of her coffee. "I can't believe we are leaving tomorrow morning."

Vi stands up and peeks through the slats of the Venetian blinds. "Look at the boys. I can't remember them getting along so well. They're having a blast!"

"It's been wonderful having you all here, a little noisy...." Sam's eyes smile.

Matt puts down his cell phone. "Dad, did you call that Gloria person?"

"No, I don't think I'm going to that banquet. It's really just a fundraiser."

"That's not what I asked," Matt shoots back.

"Dad, don't lock yourself up in the house once we're gone. You said yourself that you need to get out more." Vi comes back to the table and pours everyone more coffee.

"I don't want to drag you back to North Carolina, so I don't have to worry about you being all alone." Caroline starts dinging her cup with her spoon.

"Hey, stop ganging up on me. What is this...an intervention?"

Matt leaves the room to answer a work call, and Caroline continues to prod Sam. "Dad, you know it's not a sin to ask someone out for coffee."

"I know. It just doesn't feel right."

Caroline stares down into her cup. "It's alright, Dad. We just want you to know we wouldn't be hurt if you...well, if you wanted to see someone."

Vi, always the one to cut to the point, says, "Mom, wouldn't want you to be alone, really. Didn't you two ever talk about this?"

"My God, who talks about that seriously? We joked about it, but neither one of us ever expected that Angie would be well...you know."

Matt, who is just as handsome as his father, walks back into the room. "You've got to get out there, back in the game, Dad. You're young still. Want me to set you up on one of those dating sites?"

Even though the kitchen is chilly, Sam begins to sweat from the cold draft seeping through the kitchen door. "Stop, every-one! I'll think about it, okay? Happy now?"

The grandsons come running into the house looking like three tiny snow cones. Their faces are bright red, and frost coats them from head to toe. They start to melt all over the kitchen floor. Caroline and Vi jump up and grab the paper towels to dry the floor. Sam thanks the boys silently for arriving just in time to save him from his own children.

21

Thought Horizon

"I can't believe Grams is taking me to see *Hamilton*." Bella carries her small suitcase for the overnight stay at Julia's house to the kitchen door and drops it. "I love that song…you know, the one they keep playing on the radio."

"What song? Who sings it?" Phil asks.

"Oh, Dad, c'mon! Like the most famous singer in America!"

Julia walks into the room, ready to head back to Queens. "Your dad only knows the Beatles, Bella."

"Okay, that's enough, you two. Have a great time. Remember, Mom, we are going to the fundraiser for Bella's school. Bring back a fancy dress." Andrea is getting ready to head into work for a few hours, even though she is technically on vacation.

"Do I really have to go?"

"We bought you the ticket. It's part of Bella's grand plan." Andrea tries guilt to manipulate her mother.

"All right, all right, but I'm driving there in my own car in case I want to leave early."

Phil puts his iPad down. "Fine with me."

Bella opens the door, and Phil calls out, "No kiss goodbye? Trying to be cheeky?"

Bella hugs him. "Oh Dad, you really are so weird!"

Julia and Bella throw their overnight bags into the tiny trunk of her Mini Cooper. "I was listening to the news. Looks like we might be stuck in traffic this morning."

"That's okay…let's put on the soundtrack from the play…you know to get ready."

"I don't have it."

"Oh, Grams, it's on Spotify…see that button on your car…stream it."

"You do it for me, honey…I guess I need an upgrade…as my phone is always telling me."

Julia is embarrassed that she never learned how to link her phone to the car or master any of those techie things. She is beginning to see Bella's point about being connected with the outside world.

By the time they reach the expressway, traffic is at a virtual standstill. Bella lowers the volume on the radio and turns to Julia. "Grams, really…what happened to my mother's father?"

"That's a long story."

"Well, we aren't going anywhere. Please, Grams, just tell me."

Julia rarely speaks about Mike. She keeps all memories of him hidden in a secret place. But somehow, she feels safe sharing some of it with Bella. "You deserve to know, you're right…your mother and I have to stop treating you 'like a baby,' as you keep saying."

Bella leans her back against the door and turns towards Julia.

"He was the love of my life. After I met him and we got married, I felt like everything from then on was going to be okay."

"Mom said he was your biggest cheerleader."

"He was…it was what they used to call a match made in heaven."

"So, what happened to him?"

"It was a terrible accident…on the parkway." Julia wishes she still had those cigarettes in the glove compartment.

"Oh, no, Grams… but why can't Mom tell me that?"

Julia wipes the hair away from her face. "Every family has its secrets. You'll see that as you get older."

"I *am* older now, so tell me, please," Bella's voice cracks.

Julia pauses and then speaks words she hasn't spoken in twenty years. "He was drunk."

"Driving drunk?" Bella slumps down in the seat.

"Yes, he was at a business event, and everyone was having a few drinks…social drinking. That's what they called it then…. I mean, he wasn't an alcoholic…well, he made a bad decision."

"Did he hurt anyone else?"

"No, not in the accident, but your mother had a hard time forgiving him…even now." Julia's hands are sweating on the steering wheel.

"Forgiving him?"

"For not thinking of her, well of us, before he got in the car."

Bella hesitates. "Is that why she volunteers at that rehab place?"

"Yes, she's trying to save the world from itself."

"Wow, Grams, maybe you were right about not telling me." Bella stares out the windshield at the lines of cars in front of them and feels protected with the car crawling along so slowly. "What about you, Grams?"

"You know Bella, that happening to me, losing my husband… was never on my thought horizon."

"Thought horizon? What's a thought horizon?"

"Oh, a little phrase I made up at the time to cope, I guess…Things that you never expect to happen that happen…it's the story of my life."

"So what did happen… I mean after the accident and all?"

"I kind of went into shock for a while…just staying in my studio for hours, not really doing anything good. Your mom was only about your age, so I had to pull myself out of it. I needed to protect her."

Bella is silent for a long time. Her heart is saturated with emotion.

"Grams…have you forgiven him?"

"Yes, but it took me a long time to forgive myself."

"For what?"

"I should have gone with him…maybe I could have driven…oh, well, it's complicated, but I miss him every day still."

She grips the steering wheel tightly and stares ahead. Julia knows she is about to be overwhelmed by the memory and switches topics. "I hope we make it to my house soon. We still have to catch the subway into the city."

"Let's just Uber in Grams. That'll save time."

"Oh, Bella, you and your good ideas. You were never on my thought horizon either."

"That's a good thing, though, right?"

22

The Banquet

"Mom, you look lovely. That blue is really your color," Andrea says. "Aren't you glad you decided to come along now?"

Julia balances on one heel and spins around in her dress. Her hair is tied in a knot on the top of her head, and curly gray strands drape themselves around her face. Her deep brown eyes are even more expressive in their rim of mascara and eyeliner.

"Bella didn't give me a choice. All she talked about at dinner at the restaurant last night was Artie. She's insisting I meet him tonight," Julia grins. "I think she's in love."

"Do you? I thought they were just friends." Andrea has a twinge of jealousy, fearing her mother is more attuned to Bella than she is.

"No, it's definitely more than that. She made me buy an Amazon gift card at the drug store yesterday. I'm supposed to thank him for setting up my media empire."

"Really? Maybe Artie was part of this big plan of hers."

"I don't know, but I'm not sure I really want to thank this little Mr. Zippy Drive for complicating my life."

Phil walks into the room dressed in his new black suit with narrow lapels and a vest. He has a red handkerchief stylishly folded in his pocket. "Why do we have to have these fundraisers? Don't we pay enough tuition for this damn school?"

"Phil, please…Mom, are you sure you want to drive alone?"

"Well, I think Bella is riding in my car now."

Bella comes down the stairs before Phil or Andrea can protest, looking five years older than yesterday. "Ready, Grams?"

In the car, Phil turns to Andrea. "Your mother really is a beautiful woman, despite that smart-ass mouth of hers, isn't she?"

Andrea has to reluctantly agree.

* * *

The day after Sam's children leave, he decides to go to the bagel place for breakfast. He reasons that if he runs into Gloria, it wouldn't be something he actually planned.

She is in fact there, and smiles when he approaches her table, tapping the chair next to her. "I've been waiting for you."

Surprisingly, he finds her easy to talk to, and before he leaves, he asks Gloria if she wants to drive with him to the banquet. Sam feels he has nothing to lose. She is a pleasant reprieve from talking to himself or his dog.

Later that night he picks up Gloria at her condo, and they head to the country club on the north shore for the Catholic Schools Annual Banquet. Gloria had searched the racks at Macy's and finally found what she thought was the perfect black dress for the occasion. Sam notices how she glitters in his headlights as he walks Gloria to the passenger side of the car. He can't remember Angie ever glittering.

"I think this place looks like a castle. Have you ever been there?" Gloria is especially bubbly.

"Yes, a few times for conferences. Never at night, though."

"I hear it's beautifully decorated for the holidays. Thank you again for driving, Sammy."

"It's nice to have company."

"I wonder if they're going to call our names out at the dinner?"

"Oh, probably not. I imagine we'll only be listed in the program."

* * *

The country club is shining with big bulbs of colored lights and boughs of pine decorating every available surface. The wait-staff roams the growing crowd with trays of scallops wrapped with bacon, tiny kabobs of olives and cheese, and flutes of champagne. Everyone is in a festive mood. A high school student hammers out Christmas carols on the grand piano above the chatter of the guests.

A waitress approaches Gloria and Sam. "Mini spanakopita?"

Gloria takes everything in, enjoying the opulence. "This is some party. No wonder teachers only get invited when we retire. If they knew about this, they'd go crazy,"

Sam holds his table seating card and is surprised to see that he is on the dais. While he frets about being asked to speak, he tries to listen to Gloria and absentmindedly replies, "That's certainly true."

But he is distracted, not only by his surprising place on the dais but by vibrations passing through his body. It feels like a truck is rumbling past him. Below the murmur of the crowd and the piano playing, he hears a low hum in his ear. Instead of occurring in his dreams, this time is real and palpable. His whole body is pulsing with its own tempo.

Gloria looks at him. "Sam, are you alright? You look a little pale."

He stops a waiter and takes a glass of champagne. "Yes, sorry…I'm fine."

He downs the champagne and realizes that it is the non-alcoholic kind by the sweet taste. Gloria turns away to talk to another retiree, and Sam quickly excuses himself. He heads to the bar for a real drink.

Julia stands alone in the country club lobby; Bella having left her to look for Artie. She surveys the room and notices everything seems overdone and garish. Julia bristles at the bright sound of the piano. She quickly judges it inferior to the elegant tone of a Steinway. Andrea and Phil are nowhere to be found, and she tries not to feel anxious. Julia starts to drink one of the glasses of champagne she is offered and, after a few sips, begins to relax even though it tastes like apple juice. She hums along with the song that is playing in her head and suddenly realizes that it is not the one being played on the piano. Julia panics for a second and then is soothed by the warm undertones vibrating through her body. As she moves about the room, the sound ebbs and flows. Whatever it is, she doesn't feel alone anymore.

23

Chatter

The lights in the lobby start blinking, signaling the attendees to move into the ballroom for dinner. Gloria circles the room looking for Sam and finds him standing by the entrance to the bar with a drink in his hand. "It's time to go in, Sam."

"Uhm, my card says that I'm seated on the dais…not with the other retirees."

"Let me see that." Gloria grabs the card and then smiles broadly. "Sam, look, it says *and guest.*"

Sam takes the card back and just stares at the words. He remains quiet for a minute. "Maybe I should just go sit with you and the other retirees."

"Don't be ridiculous, Sam. I'll sit with you on the dais. Won't this be exciting?"

Sam can't form the words to say *no*, slumps forward and makes his way up front. Gloria follows closely behind, turning her head and smiling at everyone she passes. They sit on the end of the dais with Gloria positioning herself between Sam and the Superintendent of Schools.

Gloria looks out at the crowd and then speaks to her plate. "Doesn't this look lovely? Look, there are craisins in the salad!"

* * *

"Oh, bollocks. Salad from a bag, God help me." Phil glances down at the salad plate already waiting at their table.

"Phil, don't start complaining. Look at this crowd they are feeding. I mean, what did you expect?" Andrea speaks in a hushed voice, trying to signal her husband to tone it down.

"But with what we paid for this? We're going to have to stop at that diner on Northern Boulevard on the way home. I can't eat this rubbish," Phil mumbles.

Julia comes up to the table just in time to hear Phil's last comment. "You really are complaining a lot for someone who has such an affinity for pancakes."

"Oh, Mom...I was looking for you. Did you meet Artie yet?"

"No, and I kind of lost Bella too."

"Hey, Mom, since Bella's not here yet," Andrea leans in and whispers to Julia, "What have you been telling her anyway?"

"What do you mean?"

"All of a sudden, this afternoon, she was asking me all these questions about Dad. Then asking me if I had photos."

"She's just been curious about her family tree."

"Mom, don't tell me you told her everything...without consulting me first." Andrea tries to control her temper and takes a deep breath.

"I didn't tell her everything. God knows no one needs to know all that."

"But you told her about Dad's accident, didn't you?"

"You can't hide that forever, Andrea...I mean, she's going to find out no matter how you try to protect her."

Even though Andrea knows her mother has a valid point, she bristles. "Oh, Mom...do we really need to have Bella haul around all our family baggage? Can't you just let her be a kid?"

"She's not a kid anymore."

Andrea's voice trembles. "For once, admit you're wrong...I'm the one that has to deal with all of this now."

Julia's first reaction is to get up and leave the table in a dramatic display. Instead, she stops, reminding herself of what she had resolved to do on her walk last week. "I'm sorry, really I am."

Andrea is shocked by her mother's admission of guilt. She was preparing for their usual back and forth and losing the argument. Andrea suddenly feels guilty for harassing her mother and concedes, "Mom, it's okay...just let's talk about it later. Here comes Bella."

Bella walks up to the table, holding onto Artie's hand with his parents following behind. "Grams, this is Artie."

Artie's mother sits down next to Andrea. "Hi Andi, looks like we have a little romance going on."

"He's been a good friend to Bella lately."

"Is that your mother? She could be your sister."

"Well, yeah, she doesn't act her age." Andrea shakes out her napkin and sighs. She picks the Bermuda onions out of her salad, and everyone else sits down and starts to eat and chat.

Artie breaks out in a big grin when Julia hands him the Amazon gift card, then Bella grabs his arm and pulls him close to her. Even Phil settles down and talks congenially to Artie's father.

Up on the dais, Gloria chatters away while Sam realizes he has made a big mistake.

Phil notices the new principal of the high school walk up to the microphone. "Look, they are going to do the program before dessert."

"They don't want anyone to leave before the boring part," Julia jokes. As soon as the words stream out of her mouth, that pulsing in her head and ringing in her ears returns.

The new principal taps on the microphone. "Welcome, everyone. We are going to acknowledge a few special people who recently retired. First, Mr. Samuel Testa, a man I will never replace but will forever model myself after."

The audience erupts in applause. Sam reluctantly stands up, and Gloria kisses his cheek. Stunned, he walks up to the podium, takes his handkerchief out of his pocket, and wipes the wetness of lipstick off his cheek.

Sam can't tell if it is the roar of the applause or something else that is modulating in his ears. He can hardly speak standing in front of everyone and simply crosses his arms on his chest, then opens them like the pope on the balcony in St. Peter's Square. He mouths the words, "Thank you!" The applause follows him all the way back to his seat.

Julia is so preoccupied with the sound in her head she misses his introduction and leans into Andrea. "Who was that man, again?"

"Mr. Testa, such a lovely man. He was the principal at the high school for twenty years."

"He looks so familiar."

"Maybe you saw him at one of Bella's concerts or something. He retired, I think, in March. Poor guy, his wife died suddenly last year right before the holidays."

"Then, who is that blonde sitting next to him?"

Bella pipes up, "That's Ms. Johnson. She was my sixth-grade math teacher... I hated her."

"Bella, hate is a bit of a strong word." Andrea can hear her mother's voice coming from Bella.

"She was just so happy, like fake-happy all the time. She wore me out."

"Worn out by happiness? Now that's a first." Andrea eats her dessert and skips the coffee.

24

New Year's Eve

The first one up, Julia takes her coffee into the sunroom. In the icy morning light, she looks north through the barren trees to catch a glimpse of Long Island Sound sparkling in the distance. She is thinking about last night but also remembering when she first moved to a street not far from here with her parents. Her father had some *Great Gatsby* dream of being a famous writer living in a mansion on the sound but ended up working for the local newspaper. She wonders if perhaps his diminished dreams were the reason for his bitterness. Julia's solitude is soon interrupted by her daughter, who enters the room and sits down next to her, a cup of mint tea warming her palms.

"Mom, remember last week…when I was driving to work? You said you had something to tell me? I want to talk to you too."

"Oh, yeah…never mind. I don't want to bother you."

"It's no bother, really. When was the last time we spent so much time together? Now's your chance to get it out."

"It's nothing bad…well, I guess it isn't."

"Is it about Bella?"

"No, no." Julia dislikes the pungent aroma of her daughter's tea and turns away.

"Bella told me that last time she stayed with you, she heard the piano playing in the middle of the night. She found you standing kind of dazed in the hall."

"She told you that?" Julia suddenly wants to go back to bed.

"You're not the only one she talks to, you know."

Julia tries to get up to leave the room, but Andrea puts her hand on Julia's arm and speaks in a softened voice. "Mom, sit down. What's going on?"

Julia feels her daughter's hand on her arm and shifts her weight on the couch. She sits for a moment, staring down at the fringe of the rug while assembling her thoughts. Finally, she lifts her head, rubs her hands up and down on her knees, and answers. "I've been having these strange dreams. And when I wake up in the morning, things look out of place…but I don't remember moving them. I'm not becoming that forgetful, am I?"

"No, Mom." Julia sees Andrea's eyes darting back and forth, analyzing what she just said. "What medicines did your doctor prescribe?"

"I don't know…they have some long generic name. Dr. Blanding told me to ask my family doctor for a sleeping pill, and I was already on an anti-depressant."

"Go get the bottles. Let me look them up. I have a hunch."

Julia climbs the stairs back up to the guest room and brings down the bottles she had on the dresser. Andrea starts scrolling through lists of drugs on her phone.

"Mom, it's not a common side effect, but these sleeping pills can cause sleepwalking, and sometimes the combination can cause that fuzzy thinking."

"Sleepwalking? You mean it was me playing the piano?"

"Probably."

"But I heard it too."

"You were most likely semi-awake, coming out of a REM cycle when it happened. Maybe you should stop the sleeping pills at least."

Julia shakes her head. "I don't know if I'd ever be able to sleep again."

"There are other things that work besides pills."

Andrea starts listing all the natural remedies, but Julia's attention drifts to a cardinal nestled between the leaves and berries on the ivy bush that brushes against the windowpane. She wishes she had her phone with her to take a picture. She is always so easily distracted by beauty, but distraction is also her best coping mechanism.

"Mom, are you listening?"

"Yes, yes...maybe I'll try yoga before bed." Julia doesn't want to believe all the songs and apparitions are just a drug reaction. They seem too real. And she doesn't want to talk about it anymore with Andrea, who always has a scientific explanation for everything. "Okay, why are you up so early?"

"I wanted to tell you something when we were alone."

"Good, I'm glad it's your turn to talk."

"I appreciated how you apologized last night," Andrea starts.

Julia is proud of herself. She has been working hard at her newly acquired skill, as Dr. Blanding had suggested, of reflecting before speaking when she is anxious.

"Well, that's the other thing I was going to tell you. It's my New Year's resolution...to think before I speak. I just started a little early."

"That's wonderful, really. If only I could get Phil to do the same...although he's doing better lately, don't you think?" Andrea pauses and looks straight at Julia. "Mom, you didn't answer."

"I try not to notice...Oops, sorry, I forgot the new me. I meant yes, Phil is doing better!"

"We, all three of us, are really going to need to get along, especially this summer."

"What's so special about the summer...and we do get along, don't we?"

"Let's say we co-exist, Mom. But I'm really going to need your help."

Julia turns around abruptly. She feels a wave of anxiety sweep over her, and all the blood drains out of her face. "What's wrong? Are you getting divorced?"

Andrea holds her hand over her mouth to cover a laugh. "Oh, Mom! No! I'm pregnant!"

"Pregnant? How is that possible?" Julia is stunned.

"The usual way," Andrea is still laughing and continues, "I know, I know...it's beyond explanation."

"After all those treatments... I thought you stopped trying?"

"We did when I turned thirty-five. Now here I am, closing in on forty, and well, who knows what happened?"

"My God, I've read about things like this, but not…." Julia is overwhelmed with joy, but before she lets Andrea know, she stops and asks, "Are you happy? Is Phil okay with it?"

"Yes, Mom, he's ecstatic…I can't wait to tell Bella."

"What a beautiful Christmas gift…for everyone."

Julia decides later that day to pack up and let her daughter rest and go to bed early and not feel obligated to stay up to watch the ball drop on New Year's Eve. Julia drives home at dusk. Feeling sentimental, she stops at the market and buys the ingredients to make lentil soup so she can celebrate good fortune in the new year like she had so long ago with her grandmother. She doesn't need a recipe book or a card to assemble the soup. Julia cooks instinctively as if her grandmother is standing beside her, watching. At midnight she toasts the new year with a glass of Spumante, plays Auld Lang Syne on the piano, and then eats lentil soup poured into one of the old coffee cups in the cabinet. Outside she can see the fireworks breaking open over the skyline.

After the night sky quiets and dims, she slowly walks to her bedroom, plumps up her pillows, and lies down. Julia's mind wanders from the past to the future in endless circles as she tries to fall asleep. She finally decides to take the sleeping pill she tried to avoid. Within a few minutes, she is sound asleep until she isn't. Julia can hear the piano playing. The notes ascend and descend the keys in a slow tempo. When she hears the right hand join in punctuating the chords, Julia sits up. She puts on her red robe and walks into the living room. Her mother is sitting on the piano bench. She raises her eyes up from the keyboard but keeps playing.

"Oh, Julia, you're up." Gracie is wearing the same scarf she wore on Christmas Eve, the night of the accident.

Julia doesn't speak but just stares at this vision of her mother.

"I came to say that I'm sorry for everything." Gracie blows a kiss at her and then disappears with the ends of the scarf evaporating into a breeze.

Julia shakes her head in disbelief. She walks back into her bedroom and takes one of the anxiety pills she holds in reserve. Then she pulls the covers over her head and falls into a fitful sleep. When she awakens, it is almost ten o'clock. Julia reaches for her red robe on the chair next to the bed and then looks down to see she has slept in it. In the living room, the book on the piano is opened to Beethoven's "Moonlight Sonata."

25

Sam's New Year

Sam is invited to dinner at his sister's house on New Year's Eve. He is glad to be going someplace non-threatening with good food. Gloria has been texting him since the banquet, and he finally turned his cell phone off this afternoon. There is no way he will spend tonight with her, but he isn't ready for confrontation. It is a quiet evening with Franny, Nick, and a few of his older cousins. They sit around the table talking about the big family parties they used to have when everyone still lived in New York.

"Remember when we helped Pa blow up all those balloons?" Franny asks.

"It was always my job to throw them off the balcony at midnight." Sam smiles. "Angie loved coming to our house on New Year's Eve."

"She brought her whole family...those brothers, oh *marone,* may they rest in peace," Franny kisses her fingers, looks up, and makes the sign of the cross. "Her mother was an angel like Angie."

"Her dad loved playing cards with us. We'd play until two in the morning. He said he looked forward to it all year…great guy." Nick takes another sip of his wine. "Things aren't the same anymore, that's for sure." All the cousins nod their heads.

Franny brings out a plate of pignolata piled high and coated with honey and colored sprinkles. Every spoonful of the treat pulls Sam back in time to his childhood.

Franny watches everyone enjoy the dessert and shakes her head. "Now all of our kids put their kids to bed at their regular bedtime, even on holidays. We never did that. What's wrong with letting them stay up with the rest of the family? It's a special occasion."

"They don't know what they are missing." Nick repeats himself. "It's not like it used to be…*familia.*"

Sam decides to drive home before midnight to avoid all the drunken drivers. His sister ladles some lentil soup into a plastic container and reminds him to eat it at midnight. "Remember, it will bring you luck in the new year."

When Sam arrives home, he settles into the couch and turns on the television. He falls asleep with his dog Yogi in his lap. Yogi starts barking at the sound of fireworks coming from the neighbor's backyard, waking him up in time to watch the New Year's Eve ball drop on Times Square. Sam peers out the window and watches the last rocket stream white light into the black sky. He pours his soup into the old heavy ceramic bowl he had kept from his parents' house and microwaves it while he watches throngs of strangers jumping up and down in the crowded streets.

"Yogi sit... C'mon boy, stop all the barking." Yogi settles back down next to him. "Look at those people on TV. Why would anyone want to be there?"

Yogi just gazes up at him and then nestles his head back down onto Sam's lap. Sam stares at the television for a long while, listening to the nonsense coming out of the drunken emcee's mouths. It strikes him that he has been living this past year as a spectator of his own life.

"Yogi, tomorrow's going to be a new year, pal, a new year. Maybe I should be jumping up and down like those nuts on TV. At least go to a ball game instead of watching it from the couch."

Sam walks into his bedroom and curls up on Angie's side of the bed. He whispers, "Tell me what to do," into the air and closes his eyes. He is overcome with exhaustion and slips into a deep sleep but not before he hears the first refrain of a gentle melody enveloping him. He sleeps all night peacefully in this cocoon of soothing sound.

In the early morning, before the sun is up, Sam dresses in his warmest clothes and heads to the beach. He watches the sunrise as he drives and turns on the car radio. A song he had heard a million times before but never listened to the lyrics is playing. Sam absorbs the uplifting words and cranks up the volume. He drives with the exuberance of a teenager and speeds up as he rounds the curve into the parking lot.

The wind barrels onto shore, and Sam wraps his scarf around his mouth so that he can breathe. Luckily the sand is packed down hard from the low tide, and he doesn't wobble walking the shore. Even though it is a struggle to fight the wind, he manages to go his usual five miles and is invigorated by the time he gets back to the car.

"I really could use a hot cup of coffee," Sam says to himself, but he knows he can't go back to the new coffee shop and risk running into Gloria. Instead, he exits the parkway at Merrick Road and stops at the first diner he comes to. It is busier than he thought it would be on the morning after New Year's Eve. Sam finds a small empty booth where he can look out the window at the cars passing by. The waitress brings coffee right away, and he orders a huge breakfast of eggs, pancakes, and sausage. Just as he finishes his last pancake, a tall man with a noticeably large beer belly walks up to him, holding two pieces of baklava, and squeezes into the bench across from him.

The man blurts out with a hearty laugh, "Sammy, don't you recognize me?"

Sam takes a few minutes to study the unshaven face, bald head, and bright smile sitting across from him.

"It's me, Pete. I know...I got fat, but man, you look great."

It all comes back to Sam in a flash. "Pete Russo, my God...what's it been? Twenty years?"

"Maybe more. I think I still had that curly mop of hair last time you saw me."

"What are you doing here? I thought you lived in Florida."

"I do. I do. I don't know what the hell you people are doing up here still. It's so damn cold."

"So, what are you doing here?"

"Eating!"

They both laugh with the familiarity of old friends.

"No, just a high-priced mutt. Angie loved him. Named him Yogi after my favorite Yankee." Sam feels the leather on the door handles. "This is some nice rental."

"I like to go first class, why not, right? Not going to spend my money when I'm six feet under." Pete turns to Sam. "Oh, sorry man, no disrespect."

"None taken." Sam grabs his seat belt and buckles in as Pete accelerates up the block. "So, where are we going first?"

"First stop, that pizza place on Francis Lewis Boulevard for lunch."

"How did everything go with the real estate agent?"

"Good, they already have someone interested. Maybe I'll be able to unload the place before I leave."

"That would be great, but then you wouldn't have an excuse to come back."

"Yeah, but man, you should come down to see me in Florida. We've got plenty of room. The MLB teams have spring training right nearby in Jupiter …and we could hang out on the beach. It would be like old times."

For their first fifteen minutes together, Pete races through a history of the past twenty years since they last saw each other. He weaves in and out of stories as much as he does the traffic, stopping suddenly and continuing in another lane or thought. Pete is still the high-energy friend that pulled Sam along on adventures. He is enjoying the company of his old friend more than he anticipated. Yesterday Sam eased his conscience about not seeing Gloria by using Pete as an excuse. But this morning, he came to a new realization. This friendship isn't an excuse at all, but is still a part of him.

"Maybe I should come down to Florida... you still play golf?"

"All the time...I belong to this great club. Live right off a pond near the seventh green...Of course, every once in a while, an alligator is sunbathing on my patio."

"So, what do you do?"

Pete takes his hands off the wheel and swings his arms back. "Get out my nine iron and whack the son-of-a-bitch. They run like hell."

As Pete finishes the sentence, they bounce in and out of a giant pothole on the expressway. Sam reaches to grab the steering wheel, but traffic comes to a dead stop, and Pete slams on the brakes just in time.

"Better slow down, cowboy."

"Yeah yeah...Shit, glad this isn't my car...hope that didn't wreck the suspension." Pete stares at the long line of cars crawling along the road ahead. "I don't get you guys who stick around here. Look at this traffic, crap all over the highway, potholes every two feet...New York's turned into a dump! Man, this is no way to live."

"I thought you missed the pizza?" Sam tugs his seatbelt tighter.

"Okay, you know me...I'm just exaggerating to make a point."

Both men start laughing. "Yeah, I remember...we have to take everything you say and divide it by ten."

Sam notices that Pete is also wearing his St. John's baseball cap. "Hey, why don't we get off here and take the side roads to campus first?"

"Yeah, okay...maybe we can see the new field they built for the team."

As they slowly weave their way through neighborhood streets, Sam feels the pull of time. The two of them were recruited out of their high school to play for St. John's. He can see Pete standing on the pitching mound, looking like Catfish Hunter with his long curly hair sticking out of his cap. Both of them were tall and lanky and sported mustaches. Their future wives, Lorraine and Angie, always nestled together in the stands waiting for them to go out after the games. Every day was brimming with anticipation back then. He wonders how they all drifted so far apart in the years after college. Yet now, in this moment, he feels bonded like a magnet to his old friend.

Sam points down a narrow street for Pete to turn. "So, how's Lorraine?"

"Oh, she's great, great. But she was glad to get rid of me for a week."

"Why, won't she miss you?"

"Oh, well, she says I'm too loud, and she needed to rest her ears, ha…you know she needs her space and since I semi-retired this year well…I guess I'm a pain in the ass sometimes."

"Who's running the business?"

"My boys took over…they got some app thing going now. If you need your lawn cut, you just get on the app and bang…we send a crew over."

"You make enough money cutting lawns?"

"Hell no, it's chump change for now…we still do commercial landscaping…but it's the way of the world…the whole thing is exploding. My boys have been hiring like crazy."

"Wow, maybe my father was right…get a business degree."

"Your dad was a hard-ass, wasn't he? Remember when you told him you wanted to be a teacher?"

"I know, I know. You were there for dinner. My mom had just given him a piece of pie, so I thought that with you there and all, he would have to control his temper when I told him I changed my major to become a teacher."

"Holy shit, I could see the steam coming out of his ears!"

"He came around, though, eventually. He was worried I wouldn't be able to support a family."

"Man, you did better than me...I'm just a goddam ATM machine...you changed the world...really, I'm serious."

"Thanks, Pete...sometimes I wonder if I did enough for my own kids and all."

"C'mon man, you cranked out three good kids, all doing great." Pete laughs. "Aren't they?"

"Oh, yeah...wonderful...so is Lorraine still a great cook?"

Pete lets go of the steering wheel and spreads his arms. "Look at me...yes!"

"I talked to her this morning. She's so sad to hear about Angie. She said to convince you to come down for a visit...she really meant it. And you're quiet, not like me!"

"Is she still teaching?"

"Kind of...substituting every few days. She can't stop...she really loves it."

"I know what that feels like...hey, there's the entrance to campus...turn in!"

"Look at that, Lou Carnesecca Arena, man those were great games. Made me wish I played basketball instead."

"Yeah, those Big East games against Syracuse were crazy. Let's walk around for a while."

Pete rubs his bare hands together. "It's cold out."

"Pete, you've gone soft in Florida. It's almost fifty degrees…we'll just be out for a couple of minutes."

Pete gives in and parks the car in a spot marked for official vehicles only, and they step down onto the pavement. It is still winter break, and the campus is empty except for a flock of seagulls sitting in the parking lot. They head off towards the baseball fields.

"This brings back a lot of memories, doesn't it?"

"Yeah, like having hair on my head under this cap."

Pete and Sam stand at home plate and exchange old sports stories as if they happened yesterday. Both men warm in the other's presence, thankful that time didn't erase their friendship. They walk back to the car, rejuvenated and protected in the bond they share.

"Ready for that pizza, Sam?"

"Yeah, hey, look, the church is open. Warm up the car…I'm just going to run in and light a candle for Angie."

"I'm coming in with you. I want to tell God he's a damn son-of-a-bitch for taking Angie from you."

"No, wait here. I told him that already."

27

Unburdened

Martina looks at her cell phone. It is ten minutes past eleven. Julia is never late for her therapy appointment. As she is about to call, Martina sees Julia fourteen stories below on the street racing towards the door. Martina muses that there is no mistaking this woman for someone else, even at a distance.

"Sorry, I'm late. I opened an email just as I was leaving and needed to finish reading it."

Julia unbuttons her coat but doesn't take it off. Her face has a look of bewilderment, and she collapses into her favorite chair, then spins around to face the window.

"That's fine, no problem. How are you after our holiday break?"

There is no answer. She can hear Julia's quickened breathing as she sits motionless, staring out the window. Martina asks a more straightforward question, "Do you want some tea, coffee?"

"A shot of whiskey maybe…sorry…I'm just a bit…well, not a bit…a lot… mystified, overwhelmed…pick a word…my God."

"Can you share with me why you're feeling so…unsteady?"

"I haven't told anyone yet…well, I just read it myself…Jesus, this is like a twisted version of *Who's Afraid of Virginia Woolf*…totally absurd!"

"Julia, you're going to have to let me in on this if you want me to help. Obviously, this is overwhelming you."

"Okay, okay, okay…just let me have a moment. Maybe if I say it out loud, it won't seem so bad." Julia spins around on the chair, pulls her arms halfway out of her coat, and faces Martina.

"I don't know if I even told you about my granddaughter and her big plan. Well, no matter…she gave me one of those ancestry test kits for Christmas, and we mailed it out a few days later. I got the results in an email this morning… I'm one hundred percent Italian!"

"What do you mean? You are Italian, aren't you?"

"Yes, on my mother's side. But, my father had a face like a piece of toasted soda bread, the pasty son-of-a-bitch. He wasn't Italian. He was Irish, or Scottish…I knew that much about him." Julia suddenly relaxes. "Oh, my God…he's not my father…thank God, he's not my father."

She stands abruptly, buttons her coat back up, and rushes to the door. "I've got to go. I'll call."

Martina is left stunned and tries to detain her. "Wait let's unpack this!"

But Julia skips out the door smiling like never before.

28

The Darkness Falls Again

Julia scrambles to her car and calls Andrea hoping her daughter will pick up. The call goes directly to voice mail. Impulsively Julia decides to drive straight to her daughter's office at Mercy Hospital. She makes a U-turn on the busy boulevard, tires screeching as she speeds off. The garage is packed, and Julia anxiously drives in circles all the way to the roof parking. She skips the elevator and runs down the staircase to the Physician's Office Building. Julia has only been there a few times and frantically searches the directory for her daughter's name. Finding it, she doesn't wait for the elevator and runs up the three floors, panting and out of breath by the time she reaches the door. The receptionist behind the glass doesn't look up and says, "Name please."

"Julia DeRosa, Dr. Cooper's mother," Julia hoarsely answers while nervously pacing.

In a monotone voice, the receptionist asks, "Do you have an appointment?"

Julia clears her throat and raises her voice to a rumble. "Excuse me! Excuse me…did you hear what I just said? Dr. Cooper's mother!"

The receptionist lifts her head and peers over her bifocals. "You're not on her schedule."

"This is an emergency…tell my daughter I need to see her now, right now!"

"She's with a patient. Please take a seat. I'll call her nurse." The receptionist turns her back to Julia as she spins her chair around to file a paper.

This insult puts Julia over the precarious edge she has been perched on, and she screams, "Don't tell me to sit down. Who the hell do you think you are anyway sitting there on your lazy ass…I need to see Dr. Cooper now!"

Andrea recognizes her mother's voice through the walls of the exam room. She comes running out, leaving her patient to an intern. "Mom, calm down, calm down, what on earth is wrong?" She glares at the receptionist, who is sitting dumbfounded at her desk, then puts her arm around Julia's shoulder and leads her into her private office. "Mom, what's going on? You're scaring me now."

Andrea has Julia sit in the chair next to her desk. She scratches her chair on the floor as she pulls in closer to her mother.

Julia is half laughing and half crying. "That ancestry test came back! I'm Italian…I'm one hundred percent Italian! I always looked like my mother, but this…this is wow…I don't know."

"So-o-o…you always said you really didn't know what your father was for sure."

"I lied…I knew…I knew he came from an Irish/Scottish family in Chicago."

"Okay, okay… here, have a cup of water." Andrea starts processing this information herself and then asks, "Why didn't you ever tell anyone that?"

"Because I hated him so much…I never wanted to ever acknowledge anything about him…I really can't explain it…maybe I didn't want to care that much about him."

"Well, Mom…maybe it's a good thing?"

"I've gone from mad to relieved to just overwhelmed right now. I'm sorry to bother you…I didn't know where to go. I ran out of the psychologist's office like a maniac…oh, my God! She must think I'm a lunatic."

"Why didn't you stay and talk to her?"

"I just couldn't be with a stranger right now."

Andrea reaches over and hugs her mother. "Oh, Mom…it will be fine. This doesn't change who you are."

Julia relaxes her shoulders and sighs. "I'm sorry to bother you at work…really."

"Look, I have an intern working with me today. There's just a couple of appointments left. I'll have her cover the rest with the Nurse Practitioner…let's go home to my house. I'm driving."

"Are you sure?"

"Never been more sure…let's go."

Julia and Andrea walk arm in arm back to the garage. As they drive, Julia suddenly feels a wave of exhaustion wash over her and falls asleep in the car. Andrea looks over at her mother affectionately and decides that she can run into the pizza place near her house to get two calzones for lunch. She has been so hungry with this pregnancy and craving all the food she has avoided for years. Andrea parks across the street from the pizzeria and whispers, "Mom, I'll be right back."

Julia hardly stirs and, in her catnap, thinks she feels the vibration of the road lulling her to sleep. There is a gentle melody winding around in her memory. The car door closing startles her awake, and she comes to as Andrea pulls into the road.

"We stopped?"

"Yes, calzone stop. Hey, I saw Mr. Testa in there with some guy."

"Who?"

"You know…that retired principal from Bella's school."

"Did you say hello?"

"No, I just smiled at him. He looked like something was bothering him…he was rubbing the side of his face."

"That smells good…I'm so tired…maybe I have low blood sugar or something."

"Mom, I think you just had a giant shock to your system. You'll be fine, really…let's go home, eat and then look at that email."

"Maybe Bella can bring Artie over to help."

"Well, I don't think we need Artie, but sure. It would be good for Bella to have a friend nearby when she hears this."

"You're such a good mother…I have so many regrets…I could've done so much better."

"Oh, Mom, what are you talking about?"

"I was an absentee mom when your father died."

"C'mon, don't be so hard on yourself…think about it…you never left me alone. Nonni was there still, Aunt Rosie too. Our family was always bigger than just the two of us."

"I know, thank God for them…I did come out of it…but I should have been stronger." Julia turns to look out of the window and whispers, "Thought of myself more than you."

Andrea hears the heartbreak in her mother's voice and desperately wants to distract her. She knows that Julia can slip into a dark space when she starts recounting the tragedies in her life. This latest news is sure to rock her mother's fragile grip on serenity. She forces a smile as she glances at Julia. "You know I still laugh thinking about that yodeling coming out of your little studio in the house."

"That wasn't yodeling. That was my favorite folk singer! I guess her voice was a little high."

"Whatever, it was terrible! I used to tell my friends they could use that to torture people…Stop! Stop! I'll talk!" Julia and Andrea turn to each other and start giggling hysterically. Everything burdening Julia is released in an explosion of tears and laughter.

29

Ancestry

Andrea throws the calzones in the microwave before she takes off her coat. Julia sits at the table with her palms propping up her head. She is dizzy and feels like the blood is shaking in her veins. She can't tell if it's the four cups of coffee she drank this morning or because she hasn't eaten anything since last night. There is a cloud of confusion swirling in her brain. As a child, Julia had always wished that she was adopted. It was the only logical way to explain her father's treatment of her and her mother's acceptance of it. But this revelation is a fractured version of her childhood fantasy. The haunting visit from her mother on New Year's Eve makes sense to her now, yet she feels foolish sharing it with her daughter. Andrea would blame the midnight vision on an aberration caused by the sleeping pills. So Julia teeters between two worlds. The reality in front of her eyes that she tries to cling to and the one that exists under the surface. The one that keeps pursuing Julia in her dreams.

Andrea watches her mother's eyes dart back and forth as if she were talking to some invisible person. Julia jumps as Andrea places the plate under her nose. The smell, so familiar, jolts Julia back into the conversation with her daughter.

"I'm starving. Maybe that's why I'm so jumpy."

Giving her mother an out, Andrea replies, "Maybe we really should check your blood sugar."

"This smells like Nonni's kitchen. Let me just eat a little... I'll be okay."

Andrea has already finished half of hers. "Sorry, Mom, I'm just so hungry this time. I don't remember being so famished with Bella."

"When is Bella getting home from school today?"

"You were going to pick her up at three." Andrea looks up to catch her mother's exasperated expression. "We can both go now."

"I completely forgot! Oh my, what a day."

"Well, it's been a day, hasn't it? Let me make you some coffee, and then we can take a look at that email."

"Make it a decaf espresso. I don't need any more jolts to my system today."

Just as Julia is about to take a sip, Bella and Artie come barging in through the back door. "Grams! You're here!"

Everyone stares at each other in a circle of confusion. Andrea suspects the worst of her daughter arriving home early from school with Artie.

"Why aren't you in school?" Andrea raises her voice an octave but tries to keep her face calm.

"I saw the email alert from Ancestry. I told my teacher that I had a family emergency, and she let me come home."

Julia is still confused. "How did you know?"

"Artie and I set up your account, remember? I have all your passwords. I was checking every day during study hall for the results."

"How did you get home?" Andrea is wary of Bella's explanation.

"I called Dad. He just dropped us off."

"Why didn't you call me?"

"I did…no one at your office knew where you were, and you weren't picking up your cell phone. We were going to call you to come over, Grams. I thought you might need us."

Julia stands and embraces Bella. "What did I ever do to deserve you?"

Artie looks around the kitchen. "Do you have any more of that food?"

Andrea marvels at the scene that is unfolding in front of her. "I'll order a pizza right now. I guess I better call Phil too."

By the time the pizza arrives Bella and Artie have found DNA matches and over one hundred hints. Many of the names are familiar, but there is a long list of 'names' that are only initials and numbers that seem to be in some kind of logical code. Aunt Rosie's son's family tree is public and shows all of her cousins from Astoria and their children. But there is also a private family tree with members whose DNA matches hers and an email contact. Julia stares at all the information and is again overwhelmed.

"Maybe this is some mistake. The more I think about it, the more I can't really believe it."

"Science doesn't lie," Artie mumbles through a full mouth of pizza.

"Well, someone did…" Julia rubs her forehead. "I don't know if I want to know all this."

Bella puts her arm around Julia. "Grams, I never thought in a million years that something like this…well, I didn't want to hurt you, that's for sure."

"Oh, honey, you didn't do anything wrong…I'm going to be fine. It's just a lot to take in when it's not what you're expecting."

"That's called unintended consequences. We learned about that in our Government Class, remember Bella?"

"Oh God, Artie…this isn't some public policy issue," Bella snaps, then quickly apologizes. "I mean, sorry, this is really personal."

Andrea nudges Julia under the table and motions towards the sunroom. "Let's take a break, Mom. Bella, maybe you and Artie want to watch a movie."

Artie stands up. "I better get going home. My mother thinks I'm still in school."

"Can I drive you home, Artie?" Andrea asks.

Artie blushes and puts on his coat. "No, no thanks. I can walk…you probably want some time for you know…girl talk."

Bella walks Artie out the door. "I'm sorry, Artie, I didn't mean to yell at you like that."

"It's okay. That was kinda' stupid of me to say, really. See you tomorrow."

Artie looks inside the kitchen to make sure Andrea and Julia can't see him, grabs Bella around the waist, and kisses her. He turns quickly and runs down the driveway with his curly light brown hair bouncing away. Bella smiles broadly and walks back into the house.

Julia and Andrea are staring at the laptop screen when Bella comes back in and sits next to them. "I hope Dad's test doesn't come back with any surprises."

"We've had enough drama for today," Julia answers. "What should I do? Email this person, a stranger?"

Andrea closes the top of the laptop. "Yes, enough drama for today. Let's just do nothing for now."

Bella chimes in, "But, think about it, that person "RGarden1" who manages the private family tree also got an email alert today saying they have a new match."

Julia panics. "You mean they know about me?"

"Well, Grams, we used an alias also, "Paint4u," so technically, not you specifically. They just know you exist, and they would have to email you. That's if they even check their alerts. Not everyone does...you know, people ignore these things all the time."

"God, I feel like fuckin' Little Orphan Annie."

"Mom, language, jeez...Bella, why don't you go do your homework? Grams and I have a lot to talk about."

"Let her stay, Andrea. There's nothing left to hide. I promise not to curse anymore."

30

Secrets

Andrea slips out of the kitchen to call her office and Phil while Bella and Julia move into the sunroom. They tilt into each other as they sink into the soft cushions of the sofa.

Bella leans over to whisper in Julia's ear, "Grams, tell me the truth. Am I adopted?"

Julia is stunned by the question. "No, Bella, no. Whatever made you think that?"

Bella continues whispering and turning around to see if Andrea is listening. "Well, Mom's pregnant. I mean, why didn't she have another kid after me? It doesn't make any sense to wait fourteen years. And there are no pictures of me in the hospital."

"You came so fast and early. They probably forgot the camera."

"What about the cell phone?"

"I don't think they had a cell phone that took pictures then. Why don't you ask your mother?"

Bella crosses her arms and shifts her weight away from Julia. "No…I can't talk to her about this…I mean, what if I'm not adopted, and then she would be upset that I even thought it."

"Stop saying you're adopted…you're not! My God, has the whole world gone mad?"

Bella hangs her head, and Julia quickly softens her tone. "Oh, honey, remember that wish you had when you were little to have a brother? Your wish is about to come true."

"You're not lying to make me feel better?"

"I said no more lies, and I meant it. Every time I look at you, I see your grandfather Mike's eyes, and your hands are just like my grandmother's…so delicate."

"What about my big feet?"

"Those you get from me." Julia and Bella laugh in relief.

"Bella, seriously, your Mom had you right before her residency started. She wanted to wait until it was over to have another child…but then, she had trouble getting pregnant again. There's no explaining it sometimes…everything happens for a reason, I guess."

Bella leans in to whisper one more time, "Are you're sure my dad is my dad?"

"Yes…stop worrying…let's just be happy that you are about to become a big sister," Julia pats Bella's hands.

"Yeah, it's great…just a little embarrassing thinking about you know…my parents, well you know."

"How do you think you got here?"

"I know, I know…never mind." Bella feels the heat rising in her cheeks. She jumps off the couch and goes into the kitchen to get another slice of pizza.

Andrea meets Bella at the pizza box. "This pizza is so good. I'm just so hungry all the time. I've missed pizza."

"Yeah, Mom, what happened to all your kale chips and hummus?"

"Temporarily on hold...hey, what were you and Grams talking about?"

Bella turns away from her mother. She can't help feeling embarrassed by her mother's pregnancy and her talking about it so much. She still hasn't told any of her friends except for Artie. She knows she will have to tell them soon since her mother's condition is obvious.

Bella talks into the open freezer, "Did Dad's ancestry test come back?"

She takes out a quart of ice cream. It used to be in the house only during the holidays, but now it appears every week. Sometimes there is even soda in the refrigerator and potato chips in the pantry. Bella thinks that is at least one good thing about her mother's pregnancy.

"I don't know. Ask him tonight. Did Grams seem okay to you?"

"Yes, she seems kind of worn out, though. We have to help her write to that person RGarden1."

"Yes, Dad would be good at helping you write the email."

"Why? Because he gives people bad news all day?"

"Oh Bella, don't exaggerate. Radiologists have to write a lot, explain things to people...really, sometimes...Can I have a taste of that ice cream?"

"Mom, jeez...how much are you going to eat?"

"I'll get my own. Maybe Grams wants some." Andrea calls into the sunroom, but Julia doesn't answer. She has fallen asleep again and is curled up on the couch with her head propped up on a pillow. Andrea covers her mother with a blanket and goes back into the kitchen to talk to Bella, but the kitchen is empty except for a dirty spoon and a half-eaten bowl of ice cream in the sink.

31

Pen Pals

When Julia wakes up, the interior of the house has fallen into shadow. She surveys the room and tries to recognize where she is as the day's events suddenly lurch back into her mind. She can hear Andrea's voice coming from her office and music weaving down the staircase from Bella's room. Julia wants to get up, sneak silently out of the house and drive home, but she realizes her car is still parked at the hospital garage. It must be close to dinner time, but no one is cooking, and Phil isn't home yet. Julia is tired of being a burden on her family. She speaks aloud to herself, "I've got to get my act together." She closes her eyes and remembers what her yoga teacher told her last time she arrived at the class looking bedraggled, "Julia, just breathe." She pushes up from the couch, pauses for a minute, then lies face up on the heavily padded rug on the floor and starts practicing pranayama.

She relaxes from her toes up to her shoulders and takes a long deep breath filling her lungs, holding her diaphragm for three pauses, and completely and slowly exhaling. Julia repeats this several times, focusing on her breath, and starts to settle down. Now feeling more relaxed, she practices the ocean breath she just learned last week. In slow motion, she starts making a guttural "ah" sound on her exhale. Unfortunately, Julia is still not that good at it, and today her low tones are interrupted by a squeaky sound. Suddenly the lights in the room flash on, and she hears Andrea screaming, "Bella, Bella, call 911!"

Julia opens her eyes and squints into the bright lights shining directly in her face. Andrea is bending over her, still screaming.

Julia looks at her daughter's frightened face. "What's wrong? Who needs an ambulance?"

Bella comes flying down the stairs with the house phone in her hand to find her grandmother sitting up on the floor and her mother's face changing from panic to laughter.

"Oh my God, Mom! I thought you were taking your last breaths!"

"Help me off the floor, will you? I was only practicing my new breathing technique from yoga class."

"It sounded just like the death breath…I'm sorry, but you were sleeping on the couch when I left you. I came back in to check on you, and you're doing this rattly breath on the floor…oh boy, I really got scared for a moment."

Bella shakes her head in disbelief at the scene in front of her.

"Mom, I'm going back upstairs since the Grim Reaper isn't coming tonight…are you cooking supper?"

"No, Dad should be home any minute. He's getting something from that Thai restaurant you like."

"Okay, great. I have to finish some homework, so Dad and I can work on that email tonight."

Julia stands and brushes lint off her black pants. "What email?"

Bella stops on her way up the staircase. "Dad and I are going to help you write to that ancestry person."

"I didn't decide that's what I wanted to do."

"Grams, you said no more lies…let's just find out the truth."

"But not knowing something isn't the same as lying."

"Maybe…let's write it, and then you can decide if you want to send it."

"I guess you're right, Bella. Before your mother freaked out, I was lying there thinking…it's not all about me anymore. It's about all of us. I'm just anxious about it."

"Mom, there's nothing to be worried about."

"What if I upset that family? What if they don't want to meet me? This isn't a good time for me to be rejected again."

"Grams, you still have us no matter what."

Phil walks in at that moment with three big bags of food that he places on the kitchen table. "Yeah, Julia, do you think we really would pawn you off on another family? We're not that heartless. We care about other people."

"Phil!" Andrea claps her hands at Phil like she is training a dog.

"Oh, Julia knows I'm joking."

Julia walks over and opens the bags. "Funny, Phil, but I forgive you because this all smells delicious."

"I know, this is my 'go-to' food…not your pizza. I grew up eating Pad Thai in London."

"Bella, help your Mom get some dishes. I'll be down in a minute…just want to change." Phil leaps up the first three stairs and quickly disappears from view.

Bella opens the cabinet and slams it closed with a pile of dishes in her hands. "Bella do this, Bella do that…how about Bella does what she wants?"

Andrea pauses folding napkins. "Honey, what's bothering you today?"

Bella doesn't want to tell her mother the truth and stares at Julia, signaling to keep their earlier conversation quiet.

"We're all tired, Andi. Leave your teenage daughter alone. She sounds a lot like you used to."

"Okay, let's just try to have a nice dinner…I hope Phil got that Tom Kha Kai soup…not too spicy."

They all sit at the round table under the bright light of the chandelier and pass the food. Phil demonstrates how he is an expert at eating noodles with chopsticks and laughs with his mouth full of food. Bella brightens, and Andrea glows in the light of pregnancy.

In a tone entirely opposite the one earlier in the day, Bella teases her mother. "Mom, I think you're eating for four."

"Wouldn't that be something? When is your sonogram, Andi? I have to put it on my calendar," Phil says.

"Next week, Thursday at noon. I'll be twelve weeks."

"That's right…hey, Bella, let's do this email right after supper. Are you up to it, Julia?"

"Yes…as long as I get to decide when to push the send button."

"Definitely… sleep on it."

"Dad, did your ancestry test come back?"

"Yes."

"Yes, what?"

"Oh, it's got a list a mile long of people named Cooper in England, a few from Scotland, Ireland, I think Germany. No big surprise. Goodness, if I eat another bite, I am going to blow up. This stuff is addictive."

"Are you going to contact anyone?"

"No, so what if I'm related to some bloody twit in Liverpool…I don't really care."

"What if you're related to royalty? A duke or something?"

"Then I really don't give a rat's ass."

"Oh, Dad…wouldn't it be fun to find out?

"I'll give you the password if you want…I just don't have time for it."

"Let's take care of this thing for you first, Julia. C'mon, let's go in the office and gather around the laptop."

Andrea stays behind and walks into the living room to watch the news. She wants to give the three of them some time together. They will all have to get along better with the new baby coming, and this little project might just be the thing for them. With their sarcastic remarks, the three of them can wear out a saint, and Andrea knows that she is far from perfection. When they get along, they are warmer and funnier than anything on television or in the movies. But when sparks fly, Andrea ends up being the referee. Her friend, a family counselor, suggested finding a project for them to work on together, and Bella's "Big Plan" for her mother was a perfect fit. Phil agreed to go along with the ancestry test and to show interest. This unexpected result in her mother's report has added a new dimension to the plan. Andrea was relieved when Phil stepped in after her telephone conversation with him this afternoon and volunteered to help write the email. Andrea knows he is trying to be more sensitive, but it doesn't come naturally to him. She can hear them in the office talking without raising their voices. That is a good sign. She gets up and leans on the wall next to the door to listen in just to make sure.

"Dad, do you think this email is too cold?"

"What part?"

"The 'it has come to my attention' part."

"What do you think, Julia?"

"Yes, why don't we start with 'I have recently learned'…better?"

Together they write an email that asks questions about Julia's father but tries very hard to be non-threatening to that family's dynamics. The recipient is probably already in shock if she also opened the email, "You have a new family link."

Early the following day, Julia takes out her iPad and reads the email one more time. She decides to make the first move and presses the send button. She doesn't want to be caught unawares and on the defensive. That's one lesson she's learned the hard way in the past few years.

32

Genetics

Lorraine began working on the family tree two years ago when her daughter-in-law gave everyone an ancestry kit for Christmas. The initial excitement was soon replaced with disinterest by everyone except Lorraine. But now, with most of the work completed, she rarely checks the website. She would like someone else to manage the family tree, but since she retired and everyone else is too busy, she continues to be the holder of the password. Usually, she only adds someone from the endless list of fifth and sixth cousins during the hottest days of summer when her New York body can't bear the heat of Florida. Lorraine rarely opens the emails from the website anymore. It's always a hint for another distant cousin that her husband has no real connection to and information about the family that she already knows. Birth records, wedding licenses, and voting records really don't reveal anything surprising or particularly interesting about the family. The whole thing has become more of a grind than a diversion. But today, for the first time, a "hint" from the website is quickly followed by an email from someone named "Paint4U." Lorraine logs onto the website first before reading the email and is shocked to see a match for a first-degree relative for her husband. It says, "likely sister." For her father-in-law, she does a double-take when she sees "likely daughter."

Lorraine immediately goes back to her inbox and reads the letter.

> *Hello, I have recently learned that I genetically matched with several members of your family. I was not anticipating this connection when I sent my kit to the ancestry company last month, and I am very surprised by the results. Obviously, I am not aware if you have knowledge of this and if anyone in the family knows of my existence. If it is not a burden or inconvenience on your family, I would very much like to communicate further. My name is Julia, and I am in my early sixties. I was born at Flushing Hospital in Queens, New York, and lived in Astoria and Long Island. My mother's name was Grace (Esposito) Hansen. If any of this information sounds familiar to some-one in your family, I would love to hear from you. Until then, best regards, Julia DeRosa*

Lorraine is bewildered. This would mean that Pete's father had an affair right around the time her husband was also born. Lorraine can't believe it's true. It makes no sense. He's such a loving husband even now with his wife, Bibiana, affectionately known as Bobbie, suffering from the early stages of dementia. He is so patient and kind. Lorraine decides to wait for Pete to come home to break this news to him. He is having such a good time with his old friend Sam and doesn't want to ruin it. In the meantime, Lorraine does a little more research on her own. She scrolls through Google looking for any information about this woman. On the second page, she finds a shop on Etsy called "Paint4U" and clicks the link. Staring at her is a woman standing next to an easel in an art studio. She looks just like Pete's sister, except she is tall and even more beautiful. She has gray curly hair with wisps of black and dark eyes with a smile that reveals heartbreak.

* * *

Pete closes the real estate deal on his parent's house two days early. It's cold in New York, and he decides to change his flight. Lorraine sounded like something wasn't quite right last night when she told him to invite Sam to come home with him.

"Sam, I'm going to take off a day early. Everything is set with the house, and this weather is killing me. The flight's practically empty...why don't you come back with me?"

Sam doesn't answer right away. He is not one to make quick decisions but finally says, "I've got the dog."

"Take that damn little rat on the plane. Lorraine loves dogs. You can just shove it under your seat."

The past few days with Pete and the holidays with his sister have made him realize how much he misses being around friends and family. And the gloom of winter is hanging over him like a cloud. If he goes to Florida, he can visit his sister and see his son in Tampa. Sam remembers what he promised himself on New Year's Eve and answers, "You're right...I can put Yogi in the carrier we, I mean I, have for taking him to the vet...what's the flight number?"

That night Sam hugs Angie's pillow and finally puts it over his head to stop the music that is pulsing against his eardrum. When he finally falls asleep, he dreams he is five years old on the playground at his elementary school in Astoria. His shoes are scuffed under his too-short pants. On the swing next to him is the little girl with dark hair. Her long legs reach towards the sky as she flies back and forth next to him. He wakes up, his hair damp from sweat, guilty and tired from longing for something new.

The flight isn't until two o'clock. Sam calls the vet and arranges for Yogi to stay in their kennel for a few weeks. He packs his summer clothes and puts his golf clubs in the carrying case. When Pete rolls up the driveway, Sam is ready to fly away.

"Where's that barking squirrel of yours?"

"I decided to put him in the kennel. I think he'll be happier there instead of all these new places."

"Okay, but Lorraine loves those little dogs. I won't let her get one."

"Why not?"

"All they do is yap all day."

"Yeah, that's true. I guess I'm used to it. Did you tell Lorraine I was coming?"

"Yeah, yeah…she's getting the guest house by the pool all ready for you. You'll love it…nice and private. You can skinny dip at night."

"Well, I don't think so…but, this is awfully nice of you."

"No problem, man. Lorraine did sound a little weird on the phone, though."

"About me?"

"No, no…she's great with that. No, she was asking some weird questions about my father."

"I hope he's okay."

"That old geezer…he's tough as nails. But, no, it's something else. I don't know…women, who the hell knows."

Pete and Sam spend most of the ride talking about the golf courses near Pete's house and the spring training games they want to see.

"We can see the Mets for ten bucks…box seats! Drive a little and see the Yanks…same deal. Let's get a drink before we get on the plane, okay?"

"Sure, sure…"

Pete curses all the way to the car rental return at LaGuardia Airport. The place is one big mess of potholes covered with plywood planks, handwritten signs pointing the wrong way, cops directing traffic yelling, "No Stopping!" They loop around the airport in endless circles and finally get the car returned and themselves through security. Pete spots a bar near their gate, and they sit down and order.

Pete raises his glass of scotch. "Here's to old friends."

Sam clinks his beer on Pete's glass. "And new beginnings, *salud!*"

33

Landing in Jupiter

Sam and Pete's flight lands in West Palm Beach an hour before sunset. They throw their luggage in the back of Pete's Chevy pickup and head north along the ocean on Route A1A. Pete settles in on these now-familiar roads and slowly drives as the daylight drifts away into a magenta sky.

Sam lowers the window to breathe in the sea air. "This isn't like Jones Beach…the ocean looks so calm."

"It gets stirred up sometimes…you know, hurricanes."

"I hate to admit it, but we never got farther south than Orlando. Took the kids to Disney once. This is so different."

"Orlando sucks, crowded, hot as hell most of the year…might as well walk around New York in the summer with a pair of mouse ears on."

"Yeah…we were there in the summer. Angie almost passed out one afternoon from the heat. But the kids loved it."

"Yeah, yeah, don't get me wrong…my kids loved it too…now the grandkids. But man, you pay big bucks just to stand on a line and sweat like a pig on asphalt."

"Ha, that's a good way to put it…are we near your house yet?"

"Ten more minutes or so…I hope Lorraine doesn't have something bad to tell me."

"It's probably nothing…maybe a pipe burst or something."

"I don't know…she usually just handles everything. Something's up…I can tell."

The house is in a gated neighborhood surrounded by neatly trimmed hedges at least eight feet high. There are bright spotlights along the walkways, and Sam notices the perfectly manicured flower beds and the thick blades of Florida grass mowed like a carpet. It's a balmy sixty-five degrees when they pull into Pete's driveway. Lorraine peers out from the corner of an immense picture window. The house is a modern white stucco with a clay tile roof. When they enter, Lorraine greets Sam with a warm hug and a squeeze around the waist for Pete.

"You haven't aged a bit since the last time I saw you, Sam. Still that handsome fella."

"Oh, you look wonderful yourself. Thanks for inviting me… really, thanks."

Lorraine gives Pete an urgent look as Sam takes in the high ceilings and obvious luxury surrounding him.

"Wow, this place is great…look, the pool is covered…nice.…"

"You can't live in New York like this. This place would cost five million there…see why I love it?"

"Yeah, wow…but you probably don't have many school principals living here."

"You'd be surprised, my friend…no damn income tax, and I pay less than a thousand in property taxes."

"You're kidding?"

"No, hey Lorraine, let's show Sam his little cabana."

"C'mon, Sam. You must be tired…you can get settled in, and I'll have Pete grill something for supper in a little while."

"Thank you again, Lorraine. This is really so nice of you to let me stay."

"Nonsense…Oh, Sam, I'm just heartbroken about Angie…we were practically twins growing up. I should have never let all this time slip by."

"It's all of us, getting caught up instead of catching up…not just you." Sam looks Lorraine in the eye. "All of us."

"I know, I know…take your time, go for a swim if you want. I have to get Pete up to speed about a few things."

Sam takes the cue and opens the door to his cabana. Everything looks brand new. The sheets are white and crisp with an embroidered duvet and overstuffed pillows. He marvels at the pebble floor in the bathroom and all the shower heads and hoses for just one person. Sam feels like he is staying at a hotel he can't afford. He slips his shoes off and sinks into the bed. In a few minutes, he is fast asleep.

Pete rolls his suitcase into the laundry room, and Lorraine follows him. Her voice comes from behind him.

"Pete honey, I didn't want to tell you while you were away…but I've got some news."

Pete feels terror course through his body. Lorraine had that little scare with a biopsy last year, and he is frightened that she has some bad health news. Having just spent the past few days with Sam, he fears the same fate. He doesn't know what he would do without Lorraine. He stops emptying his suitcase and turns around.

"Are you okay? It's not another biopsy, is it?"

"Oh, Pete, honey…no, no, I'm fine."

"Thank God, you've got me so worried. I could just hear it in your voice the other night."

"I should have told you, I guess…but this is just well. You're not going to believe it."

Pete pulls Lorraine close to him. "What? You're pregnant?"

"Pete, stop joking…this is serious…but someone else was."

"What are you talking about?"

"You know how I do that genealogy site? I got an email from a woman two days ago saying she thinks she is your sister…well, I mean, I got a message from the website too saying they had a new family link."

Pete stares at Lorraine incredulously. This was not anything like he was expecting.

"A sister?"

"Your father apparently fathered a child, this woman, when your mother was still pregnant with you or around that time. She's the same age as you!"

"C'mon…this is some joke, right? Where's the camera?"

"I wish it was…she's from Astoria, born at Flushing Hospital. The email says she didn't know any of this until she did her ancestry test."

"So, she matches with me?"

"And your brother and your sister. I googled her…wait, look at this picture on my phone."

Pete swallows hard after seeing the picture. "Holy shit, that could be Tina's sister!"

"Pete! It is Tina's sister and yours!"

"Holy fuckin' shit, that old geezer."

"You're going to have to talk to him…find out if he knows."

"Me?"

"Thank God your mother doesn't remember what happened yesterday anymore. This would kill her."

"Kill her? I'm going to kill him…the bastard myself…what the hell?"

"Oh, Pete…maybe he never knew, those things happened back then…women 'in trouble' usually took care of it themselves…well, we just don't know, do we?"

"Things like that happened…but Christ, not in our family!" Pete walks into the kitchen with Lorraine close behind. He opens the refrigerator and pops the top of a beer, silently twisting the can around in his hand.

"Honey, she wants to talk to us."

"Who?"

"This woman, Julia DeRosa."

"Did you answer her?"

"No, no…I wanted to wait for you to get home."

"Did you tell the boys?"

"No, I haven't told anyone."

"Oh man, can't a guy just come home with his friend and relax? It's always some shit storm raining down on me."

"Honey…maybe this isn't so bad for us, really. I've been thinking about this for two days straight now. Can you imagine what that poor woman is going through? Let's just talk to your father tomorrow and find out what we can."

"Yeah, yeah, you're right. I just need a minute…what do you want me to grill?"

"I bought some ribeyes for you and Sam. Make me a turkey burger…I'll make a big salad."

Sam wakes up to the smell of the barbecue. He walks outside to the patio and sits down under the umbrella. Tiny lights all along the rim cast a bright pattern on the table. Lights along the bottom of the pool infuse the water with a blue haze. The moon is almost full and sheds a warm glow down onto the golf course that rises at the end of the backyard. Sam thinks he can almost hear the sound of waves crashing in the distance. Pete comes onto the patio from out of the kitchen with a steak platter, followed by Lorraine holding a big wooden salad bowl.

"I hope you like mangos, Sam…I put them in the salad."

"I'm sure I will."

"What are you drinking, Sam?"

"Whatever you're having. This is really a great spot. So peaceful."

"Well, let's break open that bottle of Chianti." Pete's voice trails off, and he flips the steaks onto the grill and quietly stares at the flames.

"Sounds great…you okay, Pete? Tired?"

"Oh, yeah…I just might need that whole bottle of wine tonight."

"Pete, don't bother Sam with this."

"Something wrong? Hey, you guys need some time? I can take off…drive to my sister's condo."

"Sisters...huh." Pete laughs.

Lorraine puts the wine glasses on the table. "You're not going anyplace, Sam."

"There's no point in keeping this a goddam secret, Lorraine. Sammy, my man, I just found out that I have another sister."

"What?"

Lorraine, who has been bursting to talk to someone about this news, retells Sam the whole story as they start to eat.

"Wow, that's really unbelievable...Astoria. Do you recognize the name from the old neighborhood? Are you sure it's true?"

Lorraine takes out her cell phone. "Look at this picture."

Sam is startled as he is hit by a wave of sound. It feels like the low note of a gong being struck. It reverberates in his ear and gradually dissipates. The disorientation ebbs slowly as he studies the photograph on the cell phone.

"I know this person...I don't know how, but I feel like I've always known her." Sam looks up at the shocked faces of his two friends.

"Oh, man...pour me another glass of wine...this day just made another left turn."

34

Waiting

Julia has been a bundle of nervous energy since she sent the email two days ago. Still no reply. She searched the internet with Bella's help to see if she could find out anything about her newly found relatives, but nothing popped up. Any effort to calm herself down this morning has been fruitless: no pill, no herbal tea, no walks along the river have worked. She keeps pacing back and forth in her tiny house and imagines a gamut of scenarios.

Julia's mind races. *These people probably hate me. I just ruined someone's life. Maybe they are in the mob and are going to send a hitman to take care of me, the problem.* Then her mind swings like a pendulum. *Maybe they have been searching for me all this time. My mother might have told this man. She could have rejected him. Oh damn, I wish one of them needed a kidney...then they would have to meet me.* Julia gets her yoga mat out and lays down on the floor, staring at the ceiling. Her body will not cooperate, there's no calming it down, and she shouts, "This goddam live-in-the-moment crap is bullshit!"

Julia forces herself not to call Andrea. She doesn't want to cause any more stress on her pregnant daughter. She still has a few days until her next appointment with Dr. Blanding and is almost desperate enough to call her ex-husband. No one from her last job at the museum has called her in months, and she knows she has been brutal to her oldest friend. Misspoken words have put a wedge between her and the world.

* * *

Linda is bundled up on this crisp winter morning for a solitary walk on the boardwalk at Jones Beach to try to clear her head. The past few nights, she has been dreaming about Julia. She doesn't understand why, and it is making her anxious. When they were college roommates, Julia talked about psychic connections and how there was an energy in the universe. Linda always placated Julia when she spoke about universal forces and concentrated on her own strongly held religious beliefs. But now, as she has grown older, Linda is questioning herself and wonders what she really believes. She hasn't abandoned her faith but knows that there is more going on in the universe than she or her religion can explain.

Linda's dreams are in a smoky gray haze. In them, Julia is a child, but she also has crow-like features. Her arms are stretched out, and she is pretending to fly. There is a whoosh of sound and wind every time Julia flaps her arms. The air pulses and pushes Linda farther back from Julia. She keeps calling out,

"How do you know when it's time to fly?" Linda is worried it is a harbinger of danger for her friend.

When Linda gets back to her car, she does something she swore a month ago that she would never do again. Deep down, she knows that forgiveness is a gift for the one who forgives. She dials Julia's number.

"Julia, hi, it's Linda…how are you?"

"Oh, Linda…"

Linda can hear Julia start to cry on the other end of the phone.

"Julia…my goodness, what's wrong?"

"You don't know how much I needed to hear from someone, a friend. I'm so sorry for how I've acted this past year. I've been terrible…oh, thank God you called. It's almost like you knew I needed you."

"Don't worry…we just had a little rocky patch. I shouldn't be so sensitive. Where are you?"

"Home."

"Do you want to meet at our coffee place? I'm just fifteen minutes from there."

"Yes…I'll get in my car now…see you in a few…oh, thank you for calling…I have to tell you something."

Every bad feeling that Linda has had about Julia is suddenly erased. She keeps saying the word karma over and over in her head like a mantra. Her life has been a calm and fortunate one compared to most people. She can't stop thinking about the two of them in their dorm room talking about their plans and dreams for the future. Julia has been worn down by broken promises, the unfairness of fate, and Linda resolves to be a better friend. She wonders what there is about Julia she doesn't already know.

Julia hugs Linda for a long time when she enters the coffee shop. "I know I have been rude...just awful. I'm so sorry...I don't know what gets into me sometimes."

"It's okay, Julia...it's water under the bridge. Forget it."

As Julia pulls away, Linda notices that Julia isn't her usual put-together self. She is only wearing a quick coat of lip gloss, baggy pants, and an oversized sweatshirt.

They find a booth towards the back of the café and slide to the spots closest to the wall.

"What made you decide to call me?"

"You're not going to believe this, well, actually, you probably will. I have been dreaming about you for the past few nights...weird dreams."

"What about?"

"Well, it's all in black and white...you look like a crow, sorry...but you're a child in this raggedy black dress and barefoot. And you are running around me in circles, not disturbed but not happy either...determined maybe, but flapping your arms like you are trying to fly...and there's this pulsing sound...like a rumble every time you flap your wings."

"Are you saying anything to me?"

"Yes...I keep asking you how do you know when to fly?"

"How to fly?"

"Uh-huh, it's pretty ominous...like you are in trouble."

"Oh my...like I have to escape?"

"Yeah...it's pretty scary...that's why I called. I just had to make sure you were okay."

"I'm okay kind of…trying to handle things…those rumble strips in the parking lot made me think what my life has been like the past week…a bumpy ride in slow motion."

"What happened?"

"It's a long story, but I just found out my father was not my real father. Bella gave me this ancestry kit for Christmas… she was trying to cheer me up with activities like I'm a teenager or something…she meant well."

"So, what happened?"

"The results came back with those 'hints,' and I genetically matched with this family, father, two brothers, and a sister. I have no idea who they are or where they live…nothing. All I know is they are Italian because I also discovered that I'm not half Irish and Scottish like my father but one hundred percent Italian."

"Wow…my God…that's unbelievable!"

"I know. I still can't get my arms around the whole idea."

"Could you email them? Was there some link?"

"I did two days ago.…their family tree is private, no names…you have to send a message through the site…I haven't heard back. I've been pacing up and down the halls in my house like a zombie. I can hardly sleep."

"This explains a lot about what you told me about the way your father treated you."

"It does…but not my mother. I don't think I will ever know the whole story. No one in my family knew anything about it. I called my two cousins in California to ask them if Aunt Rosie ever mentioned anything, and they said no. They were just as shocked as me."

"What about your birth certificate?"

"It says Dennis Hansen and my mother Grace Esposito Hansen…it's obviously a lie. I feel like I'm floating in some nether land…like I will never really know who I am."

Linda didn't mean to laugh out loud, but she did. "Oh, Julia…you're not floating anywhere… you are definitely a force to be reckoned with!"

"You sound like my son-in-law. He said that these people don't know what they are in for…am I really that bad?"

"No…no…you are just…what's a nice way to say it? Dynamic?"

"I know…sometimes I get so excited or worked up I just blurt things out without thinking. So working on that…that's how I got myself fired at the museum…saying things impulsively."

"I thought you were laid off with the big budget cuts."

"Technically, yes, that's what they said."

"What could you have possibly said to get fired at the museum? I thought they loved you there."

"Well, there was this new curator, and they were deaccessioning some smaller works by some of the Abstract Expressionists…you know it was a meeting, maybe five of us there…so he put up a slide of this god-awful little painting by some once famous abstract expressionist…oh, I'm embarrassed to even admit to it now."

"How bad could it be? Julia…c'mon just tell me."

"I said it belonged in Duchamp's toilet."

Linda burst out laughing, and Julia soon joined her. "Oh my God, Julia…that's very clever, really."

"Well, the curator was a humorless buttoned-up jerk. A misogynist just like that artist. I should have known better, but you know, the stress with the divorce going on…I should have kept my opinion to myself."

"Did they end up auctioning it?"

"No, the board president, some guy from the Upper East Side, said, 'No museum in their right mind would ever sell it.'"

"Are you sure you weren't just laid off?"

"Maybe, maybe not…I was old too…don't forget that. They probably thought I was just some old cranky biddy…disposable."

"Julia, don't feel that way…look at all the great paintings you have been doing since then. You really are so talented."

"I guess… like you said…it's all water under the bridge now." Julia suddenly shifts her weight and smiles broadly. "Oh my God, I forgot to tell you the good news!"

"Please!"

"Andi is pregnant! She's due this summer."

"Oh, what a blessing, congratulations…my goodness, a second grandchild. That has got to take the sting out of all this."

"It does, it does… And that burden, of having to explain my rotten father to another child…it's gone, he wasn't my father…that anger…it's not our inheritance anymore. I really hope these new relatives are kind. I mean, who wouldn't love Bella?"

"You could use some warm and fuzzy relatives."

"People like my grandmother…I miss her every day. Would that be too much to ask for?"

"Oh, your grandmother…I loved her. She was always trying to get me to eat, *mangia, mangia.* She cared so much for everyone."

"Enough about me…how are you?"

"Except for the weird dreams, good. Although I have this one friend, well acquaintance, really. She is driving me crazy with text messages."

"What about?"

"She had one, maybe two dates with this guy, a widower I know from church. Well, he just dropped her like a cold fish, and she's trying to get me to call him."

"What are you going to do?"

Linda crumples up her napkin and throws it on the table. "Nothing...I'm out of the matchmaking business. I should have never introduced him to her. I was just trying to help the poor guy; he was so lonely."

"Love takes its own course, doesn't it?"

35

The Rooster Comes Home to Roost

Sam and Pete wake up early and play nine holes of golf before the course is crowded. Sam has one of his best games in a long time and shoots three over par. Without tearing up the grass, Pete can't get the ball off the tee or make any of his easy putts. His attempt to take his mind off the task of talking to his father later this morning hasn't worked. Lorraine is picking up his mother for the morning, and he is supposed to go over to his parents' condo. They stop at the restaurant in the club for a quick breakfast. Sam can't believe how the course was so well-groomed. With a quick glance, he can see everything in the restaurant is also top-notch.

"Sam, I hate to ask you this... but, would you come with me to take care of this business with my old man this morning?

You're better with words than me. I'm just afraid I'm going to lose it and start yelling at him."

"Sure, sure, I owe you some support."

"I just don't know what to say to the guy...I never talked to him about this stuff."

"Yeah, I can see that. I never discussed anything with my father either."

"The only thing I remember him saying was something about those Kennedys and all their girlfriends. He said, 'Men like that can't help themselves.' I don't even know what the fuck that meant!"

Pete slurps his coffee and dunks his toast in his over-easy eggs, and continues to eat with urgency. He pats his stomach when he is done and curiously watches Sam cut his pancakes with a knife.

Pete can't keep still and starts talking to Sam, "Different with our boys...isn't it?"

"Yes, maybe we should just pretend he's one of our sons and give him the old man-to-man."

Pete slams down his coffee cup. "Like, hey Pop, I heard you like to cut the neighbor's grass..."

"Goodness, no, Pete. Let's just give him the straight facts and see what he says."

"Okay, I'll start, but you step in when I start to lose it."

"That's a good plan...we'll team tag him, good cop, bad cop."

They stop home to shower and head off to take care of the business of the day. Lorraine left a note to tell them she is taking Pete's mom to the beauty parlor and then out to lunch with her younger sister Carmella. The last line of the note says, "Take your time. Stay calm."

The condo is only five minutes from Pete's house in the same development. It is one of over a dozen tall pink concrete buildings that face the ocean. There are very few people walking along the shore. Almost half of the condos still have their hurricane shutters closed.

Sam is surprised by the emptiness of the place. "Where is everyone?"

"It's cold out today. They're inside watching TV or at the diner eating an early bird lunch. A lot of these are rentals too."

"I never knew sixty-eight degrees was cold."

"Welcome to Florida!"

Pete knocks on his father's door and then walks in, calling, "Hey Pop, it's me. I brought a friend."

Pete's father comes out of the kitchen holding a plate of orange wedges dressed in gray sweatpants, a button-down long sleeve shirt, and sneakers that have Velcro tabs. He still has a full head of curly gray hair and is shorter than Sam remembers him.

"Pop, look, it's Sam, the third baseman from St. John's."

"Hey Sammy, how are you? You had quite an arm."

Sam reaches out to shake hands. "Hello, Mr. Russo. Nice to see you again."

"Mr. Russo, c'mon Sammy...call me Enzo."

Pete is still hovering by the door. "So, Lorraine took Mom and Aunt Carm out for a few hours."

"Yes, I'm glad. Your Mom hardly ever wants to go out to eat with me, but she always goes with Lorraine. Sit down...want some orange? You can't get an orange like this in New York, Sammy…Coffee?"

"No, Pop, we just had breakfast at the club…we're good."

Enzo bends over and sucks all the juice out of an orange wedge. The television is blasting the local news, and Pete clicks it off. Sam looks around and sees the walls are lined with amateur paintings of turtles, seagulls, and palm trees.

"Who did all these paintings?"

"I did. I take a painting class at the senior center while Bobbie plays cards with her girlfriends. It keeps my mind sharp."

"They're pretty good."

Pete sits close to his father and puts his hand on his arm. "Pop, I have something to ask you about."

"Yes, I made a will."

"God, no, not that. Something else…we got an interesting letter a few days ago."

"From who?"

"This woman. Do you remember a few years ago Pete Junior's wife had us all spit in those containers?"

"Yeah, yeah…what was it for?"

"That ancestry test. You know they tell you where you're from and who your relatives are?"

"Yeah, why did we need to do that anyway…we know everyone, right?"

"Well, Pop, a funny thing happened…this woman, the one who wrote the letter, said her genes, you know DNA, show that she is related to us."

"Is it one of Bobbie's cousins?"

"No, Pop, it's not Mom's side of the family."

"So, I got another cousin?"

"Dad, you don't know, do you?"

"Know what?"

Enzo finishes eating his orange and gets up to go to the sink to wash his sticky hands. Sweat is starting to bead on Pete's forehead.

Pete talks to his father's back. "Pop, you have a daughter."

Enzo is drying his hands on a checkered dishcloth and turns around quickly. "Tina, I know, what do you think I'm some kind of idiot?"

Pete gets up and opens the curtains. "Why you got these closed? It's like a morgue in here."

"The glare bothers my eyes in the morning."

Sam motions to Enzo to sit back down and says quietly to him, "No, another daughter."

"What are you two talking about?"

Sam takes out the copy of the email that Lorraine left for them to show Pete's father. He decides the best thing is to hand it to Enzo and let him read it.

Pete is still standing by the window, looking out at the horizon.

Enzo's face turns red when he reaches the part of the letter that mentions the name Grace. He whispers, "She never told me."

Pete looks at his father staring at the letter and starts pacing and huffing. Then, finally, he bursts. "What did you do, Pop? What the hell did you do?"

"I don't want to talk about it," Enzo yells back.

"Does Mom know?"

"There's nothing to know."

"Well, there is now!" Pete bellows.

Sam stands up and says, "Hey, Enzo, how about a walk on the beach. I could use some fresh air. What do you think?"

"Yeah, yeah...let me get my jacket."

"For Christ sakes, Pop, it's seventy degrees out. You don't need a jacket."

"Says who?"

Enzo puts on his green nylon windbreaker, wraparound sunglasses, and a Yankee's baseball cap. Pete watches his father move slowly towards the door. He finds it hard to believe looking at him now that he was the type of guy who would have an affair. He is taken aback by his father's acknowledgment and decides to stay in the condo while Sam and his father go for a walk. He watches from the patio as his father goes down the wooden staircase one step at a time, holding the handrail.

Sam also puts on his Yankee baseball cap. "Are you okay walking on the sand?"

"Yeah, yeah, just let me get to the flat part...I'll be fine."

"You don't have to tell me anything if you don't want to...I know this is pretty upsetting news after all these years."

"I wasn't that kind of guy...it wasn't like that."

"I'm sure."

"I kind of put it out of my mind...like it never happened. Bobbie can never know."

"I don't think, judging from what Lorraine has told me anyway, that she would put two and two together."

"I love my wife...it wasn't like that...I made a big mistake. Didn't you ever make a mistake?"

"Well, Enzo…no, but I was tempted a few times."

"That jackass son of mine, he probably has done worse than me…and that big mouth of his."

"He's a lot of bluster, but he's really a great guy. You may not think it, but he's a lot like you. He'll go the extra mile for a friend."

"Do you know who this woman is?"

"I have to be honest, Enzo…Lorraine found a picture of her, and she looks like someone I know…but I don't know why."

"What does she look like?"

"She looks like a Russo, mostly gray with a little black curly hair…stunning actually."

"Her mother was a looker too."

They kept walking in silence until Sam could tell he was getting tired. "Let's head back."

"Yeah…okay, it's cold out."

"What are you going to tell Pete?"

"Nothing. It's nobody's business. I'm not airing my dirty laundry now… But I would like to meet this gal. Just me, though."

"Maybe someone calls her first?"

"Lorraine could do it…she's good with people."

36

Across the Miles

"What do you mean he wants to meet her but not tell any-one? How is he going to do that?" Lorraine is in the water at the edge of the pool with just her head sticking out.

"He wants you to call her and set something up," Pete confides.

"Me? Why not you?"

"He trusts you, Lorraine."

"Oh, this poor woman. I'm not going to be part of this plan of your father's. He can't keep this secret to himself forever."

"I know, I know...I don't know what he's thinking. Besides, I want to meet her. I mean, I have a sister. The boys have an aunt."

Lorraine comes out of the pool and wraps herself in a pink towel. "Your mother really wouldn't understand what's going on. It shouldn't stop us from meeting her."

"How was she at lunch?"

"She was cheerful. You know she always orders what I order. That's fine…I mean, she still knows how to fake it in public. I guess I am kind of filling in the blanks for her. It's funny, though, how much she remembers from the old days when she's with Aunt Carm."

"Yeah, but she won't remember someone new…we will just tell her she's a new friend if it comes up."

Sam is standing at the far end of the pool in his bathing suit and jumps in. He swims over to Lorraine and Pete. "This water is so warm…feels great. What a treat."

"Sammy, what do you think about what my father said?"

Sam climbs the ladder out of the pool and stands there dripping. "I don't know. He was pretty shook up. Maybe give him a few days to think about it. I mean, he's a smart guy. He knows he can't meet her and not tell anyone."

"Yeah, honey, Sam's right. He's an old Catholic guy, he's probably ashamed of himself and now after all these years finding out he had a child, well…."

"Well, nothing, he should be ashamed! What the hell was he thinking? There better not be more brothers and sisters popping up. Son-of-a-bitch!" Pete storms into the kitchen, and Lorraine follows him.

"Calm down, honey. Don't be so hard on your dad. We don't know the whole story. We all do things we regret."

"Yeah, yeah…I guess you're right…but geez, not like this. I just can't believe it still. You think you know someone, and then pow…the shit hits the fan." He grabs a beer from the refrigerator and takes it back out to a lounge chair by the pool.

Sam pushes off the edge of the pool. "Maybe there's a bright side, Pete. She sounded so nice in that email, and she kinda' looks like you…how bad could it be?"

Lorraine returns with some chips and places them next to Pete. "You know, honey, maybe I should call her. I hate to leave her hanging. Just to tell her we got the email, and well, it's been a bit of a shock. Acknowledgment goes a long way."

"Yeah, but find out if she's after our money."

"Oh, Pete, for goodness sakes!"

* * *

Julia is on her way home after seeing Linda. She is in such a good mood she stops at the art store and buys a few large canvasses. She spots a children's clothing store down the block and strolls through the store, looking at baby clothes. On one of the shelves, an assortment of stuffed giraffes, pandas, and unicorns nestle in a woven basket. She lifts each one out just to feel their softness against her skin and then gently puts them down. Julia doesn't buy anything; old superstitions die hard. Her family has never had baby showers for fear the evil eye, *malocchio*, would bring great sorrow. But Julia still relishes the anticipation of a new grandchild.

She arrives home content and makes herself a small plate of her favorite snacks and a cup of green tea. She settles into her favorite chair to watch a YouTube video on television about a new painting technique she wants to try.

"Thank God Bella taught me how to stream things. This is terrific," Julia speaks to herself.

As she takes a sip of tea, her cell phone starts to vibrate. The screen lights up, "Unknown Caller," so Julia lets it go. Lately, almost half of her calls have been spam. She forgot how Bella told her she could fix that problem, so she just lets the phone ring. She takes another sip, and the phone rings again with the same "Unknown Caller." Frustrated, Julia puts the phone in the kitchen and returns to her video. But then she hears that little beep that signifies voicemail, and she walks back into the kitchen and stares at the phone. Julia's serenity shatters as she realizes that this might be the person she emailed on the ancestry website. She stands still for a long time until she finally taps the voicemail symbol on her phone.

"Hello, Julia. This is Lorraine." The voice has a definite Long Island accent. "Umm, thank you for contacting me. We were very surprised to hear from you. Give me a ring back at this number."

Julia runs back to her chair and eats all the chocolates she had put on her plate. She rubs her palms on her forehead. "Do I really want to do this?" Then she races back into the kitchen and rummages through the cabinet. She takes out the bag of chocolates and eats three more pieces. Finally, she pours herself a small glass of Anisette, gulps it, and returns the call. It is a Florida area code.

Lorraine is sitting alone at the island in her kitchen. The men have gone out to drive around the properties Pete's landscaping company takes care of. She sees the phone light up with Julia's name, puts down her iced tea, and answers hesitantly.

"Hello, is this Lorraine?" A voice that has a raspy timbre is on the other end.

Lorraine pauses to catch her breath. "Yes, you must be Julia."

"I don't know where to start...thank you for reaching out to me." Julia is careful with each word she speaks. She does not want to alienate these newly found relatives.

Lorraine gauges her voice to try not to sound too emotional. "It's been a bit of a shock to everyone. You sound like you're from New York."

"Yes, Queens, lived on Long Island for quite a while... you too?"

"Yes, my husband's family was originally from Astoria and then moved out to the island."

"Oh, my...this is so surreal."

"It is. I guess, if the DNA test is right, I'm your sister-in-law. My husband, Pete, Pete Russo, would be your half-brother."

"Oh my, can I ask...is his father still alive?"

"Yes...he wants to meet you, but it's a little complicated."

"Well, yes, I can imagine it is...so unexpected."

"Unexpected is an understatement."

"I hope I haven't caused any problems with your family."

"No, no, don't feel that way. It's mostly getting used to the idea."

"I know...I've gone my whole life not knowing...it's kind of turned me upside down."

"Here's the thing, Enzo, your father, wants to meet you, but he wants to keep it to himself. Only my husband and I know so far. He's 92 years old, and his wife doesn't know, but that's another story. She's not well. I think we have to work on getting him to tell the rest of the family before you come down here."

"Oh, of course, sure...but tell me, did he know about me?"

"No, he admitted to knowing your mother, Grace, but he said he never knew about you. It was something long forgotten really…no, I didn't mean it like that…hidden is a better word."

"Oh, I would love to speak to him…I really don't know anything about it…my parents died years ago."

"I'm so sorry."

Julia pushes a little. "What do you want to do…I mean, about meeting?"

"This sounds a little crazy maybe, but we have a good friend, Sam, who is visiting us now, but he lives on Long Island and is flying back next week. So we thought maybe he could fill you in on everything until we get things straightened out here. Would that be okay?"

"Oh, well…of course, take your time. I'm very grateful that you got back to me. So, this Sam will contact me?"

"Yes, next week. He's a lovely man. He'll explain everything… Are you married?"

"No, not anymore…."

"Children?"

"Yes, a daughter and granddaughter."

"That's wonderful…we'll work things out eventually, I'm sure."

"Thank you, Lorraine, thank you."

Julia puts down the phone, stunned. It isn't the warm fuzzy embrace she hoped for, but it isn't a denial either. She laughs, "I hope this Sam isn't their hitman."

37

Dream a Little Dream

Dr. Martina Blanding arrives at her office early to prepare for a totally booked day. The sun breaks the sky open in a glorious sparkle over the city. The view of Long Island Sound is beautiful from her perch on the 14th floor. Moving from behind her desk, she takes her place in the leather armchair opposite the plate glass window. Martina worries her clients think she is gazing out into space instead of listening to them. Having the sky close to her helps her concentrate. She can't explain it, but it does. There will never be blinds on these windows. "So much subtext to think about," she says aloud.

It's now almost ten o'clock, and she stands up to adjust her skirt. Martina spies Julia and her floral scarf swaying in the breeze as she walks away from her parked car. In a minute, Dr. Blanding will be greeting her biggest challenge of the day.

"Julia, thank you for leaving that message last week. I was worried about the way you rushed out of here."

Julia is tentative. She doesn't know how much she wants to share with Dr. Blanding. She has hidden so much from her: the apparition of her mother, the pulsating sounds that come over her in waves, the obsessive worrying, and now even her friend Linda's dream. Sitting opposite Dr. Blanding, she brushes back her hair, feels for her earrings, and adjusts her scarf. Her anxiety level goes up one more notch.

"Would you like to share what happened last week, Julia?" Martina turns to her side and cups her hand along the side of her face to block out the sun.

"Do you have a headache? The way you're holding your head...."

"No, no, it's just the sun in my eyes...."

Julia laughs. "Your scrunched-up face...well, I thought you were mad or annoyed at me."

"Sorry, sorry..." Martina swivels to the side, blocking the sun.

"I guess that's a lesson. Things aren't always what they appear to be. Isn't that right, Martina?"

"Yes...yes, is there some sort of cryptic message in what you just said?"

"Not so much cryptic...obvious, really. I mean my whole life... I lived with this one reality...a pain in my heart, this feeling of being less than, you know... from my father, and now it turns out he wasn't even my father."

"Well, how do you think all this impacts you, the adult Julia? Are you still less than?"

"I guess I don't know...what if this real father, this new family, doesn't accept me either? For all, I know I am yesterday's news to them...ready for the recycling bin."

"So, you contacted these people, and they got back to you?"

"Yes, just the other day. I found out they live in Florida. But they are sending a friend of theirs to meet me...not a family member. Like they have to investigate me first...or put me on hold like when you call the cable company."

"Julia, try to remember your own power...what is another way to look at it?"

Julia sits there for a moment, embarrassed to have someone barely older than her daughter helping her to navigate through the strong current that always seems to drag her away from everything she loves. There are so many obstacles to letting this therapy work.

"Julia, you're staring...say something...whatever you are feeling."

"Okay...okay...I'm embarrassed to be here sitting on this couch...to need someone, you... practically a kid... help me. I'm sorry, I'm sorry...you have helped, but I am just so frustrated with not being able to handle things myself."

"Don't be embarrassed, Julia. Think of me as a guide, not a mentor. Like someone in a museum pointing you in the right direction. You have to find your own way."

Julia relaxes and smiles. "You're the queen of metaphors, aren't you?"

"Maybe I learned a little of that from you...now Julia, what is your power?"

"Could be something my friend Linda told me the other day."

"What was that?"

Julia lifts her head and takes a deep breath. "That I am worth the trouble."

"Well, yes…you are a complicated person."

"That's a nice way to say it."

"Julia, your complexity is your strength and your weakness."

"That doesn't sound like a good thing."

"No, no, it is. The way you look at the world doesn't allow you to see life through rose-colored glasses. It's really part of your creative profile.…"

"I guess, maybe…when I let my imagination go wild is when I get myself in trouble."

"Give me an example of one of those out-of-bound thoughts."

"Well, I keep imagining this Sam they are sending to meet me is really a hitman. I was googling where to buy a flak jacket. Am I being ridiculous?"

"No, accept the fact that you're going to have these kinds of, let's call them flights of fancy. That is the power of your creativity at work. So, what you want to do is keep that thought in the background but control the event."

Julia reaches for her purse. She feels like she should be taking notes but realizes that would look ridiculous. "What do you mean?"

"Do not under any circumstances be alone with him or tell him where you live. Don't get in a car with him. Instead, meet in a public place…maybe a cafe with a lot of other people around. Somewhere you feel safe."

"I can do that…that's a good idea. I was obsessing on some stranger pulling into my driveway…I could see the headline: 'Elderly woman in Astoria murdered in her own home by mysterious stranger'…oh my, it sounds preposterous when I say these things out loud."

Both of them laugh at the absurdity.

"Meeting this man could be life-changing for you, Julia. Don't be afraid of what he has to say."

"You're right…and I could definitely use a change. But it still makes me suspicious that they are sending an envoy instead of someone from the family."

"That is a legitimate fear. Maybe you could bring your daughter?"

"No, no, not Andi…I don't want to stress her out. Really, I think your first suggestion is just fine." Julia wiggles herself into a perfect posture. "You know, really, I can do this."

Martina taps her hand quickly on the arm of her chair. "That's good affirmation…you have the power to control your own life, Julia."

"And honestly… if I understand everything you are saying… it's also okay if I dream a little dream that this will be a wonderful experience."

"Yes, powerful and imaginative."

"Well, call me a wonder woman then!"

* * *

"Mom, did I wake you up?"

Julia looks at the clock next to her bed: 6:30 a.m. "No, no, Andi, I was just lying here reading for a bit before I got out of bed."

"What are you reading?"

Julia stumbles on her words since she is still groggy from the sleeping pill she took last night.

"Mom, oh, I'm sorry...I did wake you up, didn't I?"

"It's fine, fine...I wanted to talk to you today." Julia sits up and clears her head for a minute as Andrea starts peppering her with more questions. "Yes, yes, Andi, I have the list of questions to ask this man that you emailed me."

"It's very important, Mom, to ask about the medical history, don't forget."

"I won't, but really do you think he's bringing a DNA analysis with him?"

"Just ask, okay?" Andrea shakes her head. "Now, where are you meeting him?"

"I can hear your earrings jangling...don't shake your head at me, Andi...I'll try to find out what he knows."

"I guess this baby won't have to worry about hereditary hearing loss."

"Very funny...So, I offered to meet him at that coffee shop I go to with Linda out on the island. He insisted that I didn't need to drive so far and is meeting me at that diner on Astoria Boulevard."

"What did he sound like?"

"It was just a bunch of text messages."

"Okay, well, that one near Grand Central Parkway? You go there a lot, don't you? So they know you, right?"

"Yes, I go there after my yoga class for breakfast. I'll ask Callie, the hostess, for a booth where she can keep an eye on me. They are lovely there."

"What did you want to talk to me about?"

Julia can hear the signal blinking in Andrea's car. It's her cue that Andrea is about to turn into the hospital parking lot and the call is about to end. "I don't know if you have time now...I was wondering how Bella was feeling about all this. So many changes for her this year."

"A bit moody...she can be hard to read sometimes. Hey, why don't you come stay with us this weekend? Phil and I are on call, so we will be in and out depending on what pops up at the hospital."

"Can't Bella come here?"

"She has something going on at school. I forget what night...but you could just be there to keep her company when she is home."

"Okay, sure...should I pick her up after school on Friday?"

"Yes, that would be great, thanks, Mom. Four o'clock."

"So, I'll call you later tonight to tell you what happened?"

"Yeah, gotta' go."

Julia gets out of bed, and a flash of last night's dream appears in her mind. She can hear an earworm repeating and repeating, then the shock of recognition. It was Handel's *Sarabande in D minor* that her mother used to play. It was slow, stately, and foreboding but somehow soothing in its predictability. Each note is in a logical sequence. Then she remembers the vivid touch of her hand being held on a beach, heading towards the horizon line, an uncanny feeling of security. Julia tries to shake off the sound and images. Her mind whirrs with the thought that her mother might have visited again last night.

She runs into the living room to check the piano, but there is no music on the stand. Everything is like it's been for days.

In the kitchen, however, the cabinet is open, and two coffee cups sit squarely on the counter. Napkins are neatly folded in triangles and stacked in the shape of an eight-pointed star in the center of the table.

This is not how Julia wanted her day to start.

38

Table Talk

It took Sam three days at home to work up the nerve to contact Julia. He is uncomfortable being the go-between for the Russos, but he couldn't say no after all Pete and Lorraine have done for him. Finally, he texted Julia, and they agreed to meet at a diner in her neighborhood, the same one where he lived as a young child.

Since he touched back down on the runway at LaGuardia, all the dreams he'd been having returned. Florida was only a brief reprieve. Every morning he wakes up cradling his pillow, fearful of losing the memory of Angie but yearning to move on...to listen to the sounds and images that sail through his mind each night like a quiet storm. This morning when Sam wearily climbs down the staircase to walk Yogi, he notices that all of Angie's magazines that he left on the coffee table are piled neatly in the basket on the side of the couch. He has no memory of cleaning up and moving them.

"I must be losing my marbles, Yogi…c'mon, let's go for a walk."

Yogi jumps off the couch and follows Sam into the kitchen. As he bends down to put Yogi's leash on, he spies a piece of paper with Angie's writing on it under the table, wedged against the wall. He gets down on the floor and reaches for it. It is one of her favorite dessert recipes on an index card. Angie had written in red pen, "Julia Child says, 'Don't be afraid!'"

* * *

Julia takes a long time getting ready this morning. She wants to look like her best self. Last night she stood in front of the mirror and snipped her split ends for an hour while she rehearsed imaginary conversations. She practiced keeping a steady demeanor. Next, she went through her closet, trying to find the outfit that would say, "I want to know you." This morning she is still second-guessing herself but finally goes with the business casual look…slim black pants, a long blouse with a small floral print, and her favorite teal sweater. Then she worries her boots are too high and decides on her stylish flats even though there is a coating of snow on the ground. With one last look in the mirror, Julia feels confident and ready to confront this stranger.

She spins on one foot and laughs nervously. "Who wouldn't like me?"

* * *

Julia arrives at the Astoria Diner fifteen minutes before their ten o'clock meeting time. It is a place filled with familiarity. Fifty years ago, Julia studied the same baklava, giant black and white cookies, and cheesecake slices behind the glass case at the cash register. Her grandmother never let her leave without bringing a treat home for later. The counters, tables, and chairs are all refurbished versions of what had always been there. Julia already knows that she will order the Greek omelet for breakfast without looking at the menu.

"Callie, can I have a booth in the back…but one where I can see the parking lot?"

"Of course, how are you, hon? You look nice…no yoga today?"

"No, I'm meeting someone for breakfast."

"Oh, a man? Should I make myself scarce?"

"No, absolutely not. If I wave, come right over."

"Oh, one of those Tinder meet-ups?"

"God no! It's hard to explain…I mean, I don't expect any trouble…just you can't be too careful nowadays."

"I hear you, sister. I'll keep an eye on you."

"Thank you, Callie…can I have a cup of coffee while I'm waiting?"

Julia settles in with one eye on the parking lot and the other on the front door. She realizes she doesn't even know what she is looking for and jumps every time a man gets out of a car. Her hand involuntarily shakes as she lifts the cup of coffee to her lips. The cup rattles in the saucer as she puts it down. Julia presses her left hand on top of her right on the Formica table and steadies herself.

Callie drops an order off at the table next to Julia and walks over. "Are you sure you're okay? Let me wipe up that coffee. You seem a bit frazzled."

Her presence calms Julia down. "Yes, do I look that nervous? He's ten minutes late."

"No man's worth sweating over…I'll be right over there if you need me."

"You're right. I just wish he would get here so I can get this over with."

"Okay, well, that's not a good attitude."

"I'll explain someday. Really, I'm fine."

"Can I get you something else?"

"In a little bit…when he gets here."

Callie puts her pencil back behind her ear and sits at her perch near the hostess stand. Julia continues to search the parking lot. A late-model dark blue minivan with a lot of college stickers on the back window pulls in. Julia looks away and searches in the opposite direction. But then she hears that now-familiar pulsing melody slowly starting to amplify. She looks around. No one else seems to hear it.

Sam stays in his minivan for a few minutes before he walks in. His head is also reverberating with sound. It is like the buzz of cicadas in summer, but it's still winter. It makes no sense. He feels dizzy and blames the sensation on being tired from traveling. He hasn't slept through the night since he arrived home.

"What the hell, now?" Julia whispers to herself as the sound drones in her head. She looks down into her purse for her lipstick. When she looks up, standing before her is a man she recognizes. It takes her a minute to place him, and then she stands up, relieved, and reaches out to shake his hand. "Sam…Sam Testa, hello."

Suddenly the noise in their heads stops and is superseded by an intense curiosity. They laser focus on each other.

Sam looks at Julia incredulously. "You know me?"

"Well, yes, but not really…not personally. My granddaughter, Bella, goes to Immaculata High School. I was at the gala during Christmas break." As she is speaking, Julia remembers that she had the same sensations that night.

"Bella Cooper? You're Dr. Cooper's mother, from the advisory committee?"

"Yes…but, how did you recognize me?"

"Oh, Lorraine, Lorraine Russo… found a photo of you on some website and showed me." Sam brushes his hand through his hair above his ear. "Maybe that's why you looked so familiar…from school."

"Well, this is a small world, isn't it?"

"Yes, sorry I'm late…I was driving around looking for a parking spot, then I remembered this diner has a lot."

"I'm sorry…I should have told you. Well, texting and all. I didn't think of it…You've been here before?"

"Yes, I lived a few blocks from here until I was about seven years old. My father used to take me here every once in a while. Looks like the same family still owns it."

"Are you hungry? Did you eat?"

"Starving actually, I don't cook much." Sam could feel his stomach getting ready to growl.

They continue to stand in the aisle until Julia signals him to sit down. All the negative thoughts she had about today slip away as if they never existed. She waves at Callie to come over and take their order.

Julia notices Sam waits for her to sit down first, then puts his napkin on his lap. "Callie, this is Sam. We are ready to order."

"Hey, good lookin', what can I getcha?"

Sam blushes. "Do you still have that breakfast special...the one with the pancakes and all?"

"Sure thing...and the usual for you, Julia?" Callie winks at Julia as she leaves the table.

They sit quietly for a moment until Julia realizes that Sam is waiting for her to say something first.

"So, I'm so used to hearing your name, Mr. Testa...it feels funny calling you Sam."

"Please, not Mr. Testa...that name is retired." Sam's eyes smile as he speaks.

"This is so strange. Of all the people, who would have ever guessed that you would be the connection to my real father? Bella is not going to believe this!"

"She's a terrific kid. Well, so is your daughter. She worked hard on that committee. Very dedicated."

"I've only heard good things about you too. I'm embarrassed to say what I thought." Julia starts to laugh.

"Is it something terrible?"

"Yes! Oh, my goodness...it was so unnerving that Lorraine said they were sending a guy," Julia makes parentheses with her hands as she says the word guy, then continues, "Like a goom-bah, to meet me...well, such a stereotype I know...but we are Italian, and she has such a strong New York accent ...oh, I can't even say it."

Sam breaks into a broad grin. "No...oh, my! I see where you're going! Good thing I didn't walk in with a briefcase!"

"Oh, all of this has gotten the best of me. I guess I'm still in shock finding out about the person I thought was my father," Julia pauses and looks at Sam, listening to her intently. Finally, she looks away from his stare. "And learning my real father is alive. It's overwhelming."

"Don't apologize, Julia. This will all work out. I promise...they're good people." Sam reaches out and touches the top of Julia's hand. They both stare at their hands and feel a pulse of electricity connect them in a surge of emotion.

39

Into the Unknown

Shocked by the sensation, Sam quickly pulls his hand away. Equally caught off guard, Julia looks towards the kitchen. He checks the time on his watch, and she adjusts her sweater. Both are trying to decipher the signals that are disrupting their senses. They withdraw back into themselves and shift their weight nervously in their seats.

Julia looks over Sam's shoulder and breaks the silence. "Oh, look, our food is coming."

"They have great pancakes here…I'm really starving."

Callie slaps the plates down on the table. "More coffee?"

"Yes, please," they say in unison.

"Oh, are you addicted to caffeine like me?" Sam asks.

"Yes, I'll even drink this diner swill… the food's delicious, but this," Julia holds up her coffee cup, "is not exactly Starbucks."

"It's not that bad.…"

"You're kidding, right? It tastes like they used the water right out of that big pothole in the parking lot."

Sam almost spits his coffee out. "Oh my, if you aren't Pete's sister, nobody is!"

"What do you mean?"

"The way you just said what's on your mind...no holding back. Although Pete uses a lot of expletives."

Julia realizes that her attempts to try to be reserved have already failed. She tries to backpedal. "I meant to say the coffee is not what I usually drink, you know, at home."

"You don't have to explain, Julia. I'm just after the caffeine, not the flavor so much."

"I guess I have to admit to being a coffee snob then."

"There are worse things to be, right?"

"Yes, like the unwelcome daughter. Or as Bella says, 'NPE.'"

"NPE? What's that?"

"Not Parent Expected. There's some Facebook page she told me about for those of us with misattributed parentage, another new term I recently learned."

"I guess Enzo had an NDE last week then...not daughter expected."

Julia shakes her head. "Honestly, Sam, did he not know about me?"

"Truly, he didn't know. I was there with Pete when he told him. We gave him a copy of your email to read. You can't fake a face like that. He was shocked."

"You were there? Are you related somehow?"

"No, no, just old friends from St. John's...baseball buddies."

They fall silent again. The space between them is marked by the clinking of forks on plates and cups on saucers. Julia tries to focus on the things she had rehearsed last night in the mirror but falls back into an anxious patter.

"It's upsetting in so many ways. I can't picture my mother having an affair…I mean, she was a good Catholic girl her whole life…or at least played the role, I guess."

"Pete feels the same way about his dad. Can't figure it out."

"What is Enzo, this father of mine, like?"

"I have to be honest, my best recollections of him are from my college days. Pete and I hadn't seen each other in a long time…that's another story. But he's like a lot of guys from his generation…tough on the outside."

"You mean like a soft-boiled egg?"

"Yes, that's a good way to put it. He has a heart of gold underneath it all."

"Lorraine said that his wife is ill. Is that why he doesn't want anyone else to know?"

"No…well, maybe that's part of it, she has dementia…early stages. That's a lot for him to handle."

"Oh, I'm so sorry to hear that."

"Like you said about your mother, a good Catholic man who is embarrassed by his behavior right now. I think he'll come around."

"Yes, being Catholic is a blessing and a curse."

"Amen to that."

"I can't believe I just heard a principal from a Catholic high school agree with me."

"Ex-principal. Let's say sometimes I feel like no one upstairs is listening."

"Are you as bad as me then? I tell people, 'Oh, I'll pray for you,' and I never say a damn prayer. Why go through the motions when you can't feel it anymore? Honestly, I wish I could."

"I guess we are two lost souls then…God help us!"

Julia watches Sam break out into a warm smile. In that moment, she feels he has an innate understanding of everything she is feeling. Julia stares at him as he lowers his head and finishes his breakfast. She asks herself, *What is it about this man?*

Callie sees the empty plates, but curiosity is what draws her back to the table. "Dessert? We have some great desserts."

Julia, who never orders dessert, breaks her own rule just to stay longer. "Yes, Callie, why not? I'll have a small, tiny piece of baklava. Have something, Sam."

Callie takes a good long look at Same. "We have freshly made apple pie today, just for you, hon."

"That sounds great…yes, thank you."

"More coffee?"

Julia and Sam glance at each other. His eyes twinkle as he replies, "What's dessert without a good cup of coffee?"

Callie leans down and whispers in Julia's ear loud enough for Sam to hear, "If you don't want him, I'll take him."

They watch as Callie walks away, and they both laugh uncomfortably. This time the silence is broken by Sam. "I know this is difficult for you. I'm kind of stuck in the middle. I guess I need to bring back a message…what do you want me to tell them?"

"I was really hoping they had a message for me."

"Understood."

"How long do you think it will be before I can talk to some-one? Maybe a video call?"

"Hopefully, Lorraine has talked some sense into Enzo by now. He can't talk to you without one of them setting up the call. Pete is biting at the bit to meet you also. You have a big family in Florida."

"Yes, well, I have a small family now... So many losses..." Julia remembers what her daughter told her about Sam's wife. "Oh, I'm sorry. I shouldn't have said that to you."

"You know about my wife?"

"My daughter told me...that night at the gala."

"Oh, yes...it's been a tough couple of years. We were married a long time. But don't feel bad...I don't hold a monopoly on that. Did you say you were married?"

"Twice. My first husband passed away when Andrea was a teenager and the second one, well, a tragic mess...divorced for two years now."

"I'm the one who should be saying he's sorry then."

"It's all over now. Time to move on...I try to put one foot in front of the other every day, but unfortunately, I fail miserably sometimes."

Sam reaches out and touches Julia's hand again. This time he doesn't let go.

40

The Weekend

Julia and Sam stand in the parking lot and exchange contact information. Both slowly walk to their cars. Sam turns around and stands by the driver's door and watches Julia's signal blink as she turns away. He wants to follow her but knows how creepy that would seem. He decides to wait a few days and then call her to ask how she was doing. It is as good an excuse as any to talk to her again. The rest of the day stretches before him like an endless desert. He doesn't know where to go, what to do. Finally, he slides into his car and heads towards the ocean. It is the only place where his mind calms, and he can try to figure out a path forward.

There are a few winter stalwarts, like Sam, walking along the shoreline. The other few pace up and down the boardwalk. Sam remembers he threw his wool cap and scarf in the trunk two weeks ago and finds his gloves under the car seat. It is cold, but fortunately, the wind is calm at Jones Beach. The waves roll onto shore in tiny rivulets and break in a lilting hush on the sand. In Florida, Sam missed the scent of the cold saltwater. Here he inhales the air in long deep breaths. He whimsically says to himself, "I must have been a sailor in another life."

As he walks, he thinks about Julia. There is something more about her that seems familiar besides the connection to his high school. He would have remembered meeting Julia, even if Angie were alive. And today, when he touched her hand and looked down at those long slender fingers, there is an echo of memory that he can't shake. Sam searches to make the connection. Like most men, he has a file cabinet full of memories. People, places, and things are carefully placed in the right compartment. And even though he walks for miles, this memory will not unlock.

When Sam gets home, he puts Yogi's leash on, and they walk down the street to the one empty lot at the end of the block near the woods. He pulls out his cell phone and dials Pete.

Pete answers at the first ring. "Hey Buddy, what the hell took you so long to call me?"

"Sorry, I just had a lot to do when I got back home."

"Yeah, yeah...so what's the story with this Julia?"

"She's a lot like you...well, the nice version."

"She's bald and has a pot belly?"

Sam laughs into the phone. "Yeah... that's it."

"C'mon, stop pulling my chain. I've been dying here for you to call."

"She's a lovely person...sophisticated, with this little rasp in her voice...says what's on her mind but without your cursing."

"Does she need money?"

"It doesn't appear that way. She had a credit card…tried to pay the bill at the diner where I met her."

"Any crook can afford to pay for two plates of scrambled eggs."

"Pete, I don't think it's a problem. She had a nice car, really nice clothes."

"Are you sure she's not some kind of nut?"

"C'mon Pete, be serious. She's been shaken by the news like any normal person would be."

"Sorry, I guess I'm shook up too…what did she say? What does she want to do about this?"

"Really, she hoped to at least meet your father. But for now, she would be happy with a video call with some of your family. She can't figure out her mother…there's some story there that no one knows except your dad…but she wouldn't pressure him, though."

"Lorraine has tried to talk to him, but he's stubborn as a mule. I think maybe I ought to go over there and put my foot down."

"Maybe you should let Lorraine handle it."

"Wait, let me get her on the phone…she's just out by the pool."

Sam can hear Pete bellowing in his husky voice, "Lorraine, come here. Get on the horn! Sammy is calling."

Sam watches Yogi sniff along the ground and then look up at him and wag his tail. He lets the leash out as far as it will go to Yogi's delight. "Go ahead, boy, we're not going anywhere yet."

"Hello, Sam? Did you have a good trip home?"

"Hi Lorraine, yeah, yeah…the flight was right on time…so how are things going with your father-in-law?"

"He doesn't really want to talk about it. All he talks about is you and how great it was to see one of Pete's *nice* friends." Lorraine emphasizes the word 'nice.'

"Pete is lucky to have both his parents still with him."

"Yes, he should stop complaining so much about his father."

"So, Julia wanted to set up a video call, FaceTime or something…do you think it's possible?"

"Yes, Pete just told me before I got on the line. I had a little brainstorm."

"Okay…what?"

"Well, like I said, Enzo really respects you. He keeps talking about how you were a principal and a teacher, how you turned out to be a stand-up guy."

"That's awfully sweet of him…the feeling is mutual."

"So, I was thinking if I told him that you would be with Julia during this video call…then maybe he would do it. He might feel like you would protect him."

"Oh no…I don't know about that, Lorraine. I'm not comfortable with that at all."

"I know…it's a big ask…think about it, won't you, Sam?"

"I will, but all Enzo really wanted was to talk to Julia on the phone…by himself."

"Well, he's going to have to compromise."

Sam stands still while Yogi runs around him on his leash. There's a space in the conversation and muffled voices. He hears Lorraine give the phone back to Pete.

"Sammy, that Lorraine…she's always got a good idea…think about it, pal, okay?"

"Well, I don't know, Pete."

"I'll call you in a couple of days. It's the last thing I'll ever ask you to do."

"You realize that you have to get Julia to agree to me being there, don't you?"

"You're practically family…explain it to her."

"Maybe Lorraine could call her first."

"Okay…that's true…woman-to-woman."

Sam can hear the wheels spinning in his friend's head.

Pete continues, "So, are you sure this is for real? She's not some phony? I don't mean to keep asking, but this is all still coming at me from left-field if you know what I mean."

"I understand, Pete. All I can say is that in person, she has a strong resemblance to your sister…there's no doubt."

* * *

Julia drives home and runs into her house to call Andrea's cell phone. She tries several times. It either rings and rings or goes straight to voicemail. Next, she tries her friend Linda, and again all she reaches is voicemail. She doesn't leave messages. The news is too big not to hear the reaction on the other end of the line. She finally gives up and decides to wait until later this afternoon. Bella will be the first one she will tell when she picks her up at school. Julia bundles up and takes a walk along the East River. Her mind finally stops spinning when she rests and sits on a bench looking across the water at Manhattan. It is one of the few quiet places in the city where the park widens and the bridges are off in the distance. The thing she fears most is losing the control she has worked so hard to regain. As she sits there, she isn't so sure meeting her Florida family is worth it anymore.

By the time Julia goes back inside her house, she has just enough time to throw some things into her overnight bag and head to Bella's high school. Bella is waiting for her inside the school lobby and comes running out to the car.

"Hi, Grams, you're on time for once!"

"Never mind that. I have to tell you what happened this morning!" Julia carefully checks her side-view mirrors and pulls away from the curb.

"Grams, you drive like an old lady, do you know that?"

"No, I don't, I'm careful, that's all." Julia thinks one day she might tell Bella how and why she didn't learn to drive until well into her twenties, but not today.

"Listen, you're the first one to know. I couldn't reach your mother today."

"I know how that is...sometimes I just call Artie's mother when I need something."

"They really overwork her at that hospital."

Bella turns to look out the window so that her voice is barely audible. "Do you think so, Grams? Or does she do it to herself?"

"Maybe she is trying to get everything done before the new baby arrives."

"Maybe, but I'm still here." Bella's voice is tinged with anger.

"Oh, Bella, that's why I'm here...she hasn't forgotten you."

"I guess...hey, what did you want to tell me?"

"This is truth stranger than fiction. The Sam that our new Florida family sent to meet me was not just any Sam...it was Mr. Sam Testa, your old school principal!"

"Mr. Testa? Really?"

"Really...I was so relieved when I saw him standing there in front of me at the diner. You know I was expecting...well, I don't know who."

"Did he recognize you?"

"He said I looked familiar. He had a picture they found of me on that Etsy Shop that you set up."

"As soon as I told him about you and your mother, then he knew why I looked familiar to him."

"What did he say about me?"

"Only good things...he is such a gentleman, so caring."

"Yeah, I wish he was still the principal. Everyone loved him." Bella laughs. "The bad kids miss him the most. This new principal just sends everyone home, no second chances...Is Mr. Testa a relative then? That would be so awesome."

"No, just a close friend of my half-brother, your half-uncle? I don't even know what to call him...Pete Russo."

"When do we get to meet them?"

"Not sure yet...working on it."

"I wonder if they have a pool in Florida. I think everyone there does."

"Oh, Bella...a pool?"

"A girl can dream, can't she?"

Julia and Bella pull into the driveway and head in through the kitchen door. There is a note on the table: *Will be late tonight, don't wait up. Dad might be home before me. He can get his own dinner. Love, Mom/Andrea*

"It seems like they have been on call a lot lately. Grams, I have to be back at school by six-thirty."

"Well, I better make you something to eat now. What's going on tonight?"

"A thing." Bella looks down and makes a circle with her finger on the table.

"What thing?"

"A play at school, a musical."

"Why do you have to be there so early?" Julia looks through the cabinets for something quick to cook.

"I'm playing my violin in the pit orchestra."

Julia stops her search and puts her hands on her hips. "You are? Did you tell your parents?"

"No, it's not a big deal. I mean, no one can see me." Bella is still staring down at the table, scribbling with her finger.

"But they can hear you. Bella, why didn't you tell them?'

"I don't know...they are so busy all the time. It didn't seem like, as they say, a priority."

"Well, I'm going. I'll drop you off and bring a book to read until it starts. I can get a good seat and maybe see your violin bow moving up and down."

"Oh, you don't have to." Bella smiles, secretly relieved that someone from her family will be there.

"I do. What musical is it?"

"Hair!"

Julia is bent over with her head in the refrigerator. She straightens up. "I assume the cast will be wearing bathing suits then."

Bella and Julia fall on each other laughing. "No, it's that corny one...Oklahoma."

"I love that one…I didn't know that I would have an evening out…I need a distraction tonight."

"Can we just get pizza delivered?"

"Sure, I'll order a salad too."

Bella goes upstairs, and Julia tries to reach Andrea one more time. No answer. Julia decides to leave a message in case Andrea comes home to an empty house: *At the high school. Bella is playing violin in the pit orchestra tonight. Thought it would be fun to go.*

41

Beauty and the Beast

Julia changes into the new clothes that she brought with her. She always packs a 'just in case' outfit when coming to Andrea's house. Her daughter and son-in-law make it a habit of running late. Plans to eat dinner at home switch to a quick bite at a local restaurant. But no one in this neighborhood goes out to eat in their leisurewear. Earlier in the week, she did some anxiety shopping, even though she knew she should be cutting back on spending, and bought a new silky blouse, slim-fitting pants, and a sweater. In her rush to leave to pick up Bella, she threw the new outfit into her overnight bag, tags and all.

Bella comes downstairs dressed in her black orchestra outfit. Julia looks at herself in the mirror in the downstairs hallway. "Well, there are some benefits to anxiety. This fits perfectly."

"Grams, you're styling...wow, that looks nice."

"Thanks, Bella. Are you ready?"

"Yes, let's get this over with."

"Why the attitude?"

"They make us do this because we are in the orchestra. It's not a volunteer activity."

"But, aren't you enjoying it at all?"

"We're all crowded into that pit, and the boy sitting next to me sweats. His hair is plastered to his head by the end of the play, and he stinks."

"Oh, Bella…your mother was right. You are kind of moody."

"No, I'm not."

"Okay, you're not. I'm going to have a good time being the proud grandma."

"Maybe you can drop Artie and me off at the ice cream place after."

"If that will cheer you up, then yes."

"Look, I'm smiling…let's go."

Julia parks the car in the lot, and Bella jumps out with her violin. She turns around to wave and runs towards the side door of the auditorium. Julia walks towards the small crowd that is gathering at the front door to buy tickets. She passes the same beat-up minivan from the diner and looks around. Sam is walking through the front entrance.

Julia catches up to him in the lobby as he takes off his coat. "Sam? Sam, is that you?"

He is dressed in a sports jacket, dress pants, and a tie, hair is neatly combed, brown leather shoes polished. She catches a whiff of aftershave.

"Julia, what are you doing here?" Sam is equally surprised and delighted to see her.

"Bella is in the orchestra tonight. I have a good excuse...but what about you?"

The corners of Sam's eyes crease into a smile. "I'm chaperoning, maybe selling tickets. They called me this afternoon to help out."

"Oh, do you do that often?"

"Not really....I offered to last time I was here, but this is the first time anyone called me. I miss the kids. It's great to see them."

"I bet it..."

Julia is jostled, her words cut off by a blonde in a white puffer vest, tight leggings, and fur-trimmed boots elbowing her way over to Sam. He recognizes Gloria as she grabs him by the arm. "Sam, there you are! I told Ryan to call you for tonight. Isn't this wonderful? We are chaperoning together."

Gloria's grip tightens as she drags him towards the ticket booth. "There are a few things I have to tell you about selling the tickets. Let me show you before a bigger crowd gets here."

He tries to get away from her, but she pushes him forward through the thickening crowd, talking in run-on sentences into his ear. Julia watches Gloria wrap her arms around Sam's waist. By the time he frees himself from Gloria's clutches, Julia is gone, escaping into the auditorium and taking a seat without buying a ticket.

* * *

At the end of the musical, Julia finally locates Bella as the orchestra stands and takes their bow. Bella spots Julia, points with her bow, and mouths, "Stay there...I'll be right out." As the crowd filters out of the auditorium, Julia hunkers down. She doesn't want to stand and look for Sam like a foolish schoolgirl, so she curls into her seat, waiting for Bella.

Sam scans the auditorium and the groups of parents and students leaving but can't find Julia. Gloria stuck to him like glue throughout the whole evening, following him into every conversation with former students, standing next to him to pass out programs, and timing her appearance at the coat check perfectly when Sam was leaving. He wants to apologize to Julia, but once again, Gloria is at his side, asking if he wants to go get a bite to eat.

"Sorry, Gloria, I have to go home and walk the dog." Sam is relieved that at least he isn't telling a lie.

"Can't she wait an hour?"

"He, she is a he…Yogi."

"Well, he's just a dog. What does he care if you are a little late?"

"No, I really have to go." Sam turns and runs to his car to get away from Gloria.

She calls after him, "Come to the bagel place tomorrow morning. I'll save you a seat."

Sam half raises his hand to say goodbye. He mumbles to himself uncharacteristically, "Damn that woman."

As the last few people trickle out of the auditorium, Bella shows up with Artie and two more friends. "Grams, do you think we will fit in your car? Can you drop us off?"

"I guess we can squeeze in." Julia was hoping to join Bella and Artie, but now it is apparent that she will be driving home alone, maybe to an empty house.

"Great…c'mon everyone, my grandma is driving."

Julia drops the foursome off at the local ice cream shop, and they tumble out of the car. "Call me when you are ready to come home, Bella…not too late."

Julia slowly drives back to her daughter's house, trying to decide what she should say to Andrea about Bella when she arrives. Phil's car is parked in the driveway blocking Julia's usual spot. She can see him standing in the kitchen with his tie loosened and his coat draped over his shoulder. She cracks open the door and calls in, "Phil, can you move your car?"

"Come in for a minute Julia, I have to tell you something." Phil speaks in a heavy voice.

Julia is instantly in panic mode. "What, what's wrong? Where's Andi?"

"She's okay, she's okay."

"The baby?" Julia is standing right in front of Phil. He is so tall that she is peering up into his chin.

Phil holds her arms to steady her. "Fine, fine…only a little hiccup this afternoon. She's staying overnight for observation, that's all."

"What do you mean? Why are you lying to me? She said everything was perfect when she had the sonogram in January."

"It is…uh, a little complication. Her blood sugar was off, and she fainted, really nothing serious."

"What about the baby? Is the baby alright?"

"Well, Julia, we didn't tell you right away because Andrea wanted to make sure everything was okay. One was smaller than the other, and that sometimes could be a sign…."

Julia looks at him in disbelief. "What do you mean one was smaller than the other…what are you talking about?"

"She's carrying twins, Julia."

"Twins?" Julia collapses in the kitchen chair. "Why didn't she tell me?"

"I wanted to, believe me. I didn't see any reason to protect you, as Andrea said. But she wanted to be sure that both babies were developing normally before she told you…spare you the anxiety."

"Does Bella know?"

"No."

"Oh my God! Am I so crazy that no one can trouble me with anything?"

"You said it, not me."

"I'm fine…perfectly fine. Bella is going to be as shocked as me."

"I know. Just go easy on Andrea. She's had a hard day."

"Of course, Phil. Can I go to the hospital?"

"Yes, she was asking for you."

"Are you sure she's going to be okay?"

"Absolutely positive. She has to watch her diet and slow down. No more calls or late hours."

"You have to pick up Bella and her friends. She's calling the house in about an hour or so. I'm going to stay at the hospital."

"You don't have to do that, Julia. Really, go give her a squeeze and come back."

Julia stands to go. "No, I have to stay. She's my daughter."

"You're going to leave me home alone to tell Bella?"

"Yes, she's your daughter."

Julia goes upstairs to pick up her overnight bag and then heads to the hospital.

* * *

Andrea is lying in bed propped up with two pillows behind her back. She has her laptop sitting on another pillow on her stomach. The room lights are turned up bright. "Mom, you didn't have to come. I didn't realize how late it was. Today has turned into a blur."

"I didn't want you to be alone." Julia bends over the laptop and hugs Andrea. "You're not still working, are you?"

"Just finishing my notes so someone can cover for me for a few days. Almost done."

"You should take the whole week off, get some rest."

"What did Phil say?"

"That you fainted and that you are having twins! My God, Andrea, why didn't you tell me? I mean, how do you go from not being able to have another child to twins?"

"I'm old. It happens to us geriatric mothers."

"Thirty-eight? Maybe if I was pregnant, that would be geriatric."

"It would be a miracle birth."

"Yes, well, then I would have to start a whole new religion, wouldn't I?"

"Oh, Mom, look...I'm sorry I didn't tell you right away. I was worried about you with everything going on. Finding out you have a new father and all."

"Stop worrying about me so much, Andi. I've lived through it all and survived. One more kick in the pants isn't going to take me down."

"You seem so fragile lately."

"I know, I know. I have to admit I've been a bit moody, as you like to say. But I think I've really turned a corner. You don't know how much this baby…I mean, these babies are making me stronger."

"Really, Mom?"

"Really. Don't you see Andrea? You, Phil, Bella, and now these new ones are my second chance."

"What do you mean?"

"Dr. Blanding and I talked about it quite a lot these past few weeks. She said it's okay to acknowledge and feel the pain, but it is hope, strong family bonds that keep us going."

"I thought you hated Dr. Blanding?"

"I did, at first, but something happened. I don't know…she really has helped me."

"I can't believe you're admitting that."

"Me neither." Julia laughs and then turns serious. "Why didn't you at least tell Bella?"

"She's been so hard to talk to lately. So I kept putting it off."

"Take the week off and spoil yourselves a little, watch one of those shows together or something, let her stay home from school for a day….really Andi, think about it."

"Maybe…I'm so tired I would probably fall asleep in front of the TV." Andrea closes her laptop and puts it on the table next to her. "Hey Mom, I almost forgot, what happened today at the diner?"

42

Awakenings

The sun is rising on a chilly morning as the hospital rustles with activity. As the nursing shifts change, she can hear voices in the hall giving instructions for the day. Julia's neck is stiff after sleeping in the chair next to the bed. Andrea is still sound asleep. The peaceful look on her face reminds Julia of when she used to stare at Andrea as a baby sleeping in her crib. That same feeling of needing to protect her, of loving her, has never diminished in all these years. Julia knows that her love of Andrea and Bella and now these two new babies are the only true things in her life. "Even Phil," she says aloud.

"Mom, are you awake?"

"Andi, I thought you were still asleep."

"I was just resting my eyes. Who can sleep here, really? They were poking me every few hours to check my blood sugar. Why don't you go get yourself some coffee in the cafeteria?"

"Look at me, I'm a wrinkled mess...maybe if I put a bag over my head...No, I'll wait for Phil to get here, then go home...How do you feel?"

"Much better, really. I checked my chart...I just need my OB to sign off on my release, and then I can go home."

"Are you sure you feel well enough to leave?"

"Yes, positive. I have to watch what I eat, that's all. No more orange juice, but I can eat an orange."

"What on Earth are you talking about?"

"My body is working overtime with these two babies. I have to be careful not to stress it with too much sugar at once, like a big glass of juice. Don't worry, Mom...it happens sometimes. I can handle it."

"No cookies?"

"No, no cookies...all the broccoli I want, though."

"That seems cruel...my grandmother would be going crazy if she heard this. I can still hear her voice when my cousin Dom was born. He had a big red birthmark on his stomach. 'You see that birthmark? I told Rosie to *pincha' her cooley*, but she no listen.'"

"Pinch her *cooley*?"

"Yes, She believed a baby would be marked if the mother denied herself anything. So you should *pincha' your cooley* so the birthmark wouldn't be on the baby's face but on the rear end. At least it was on his stomach. Of course, you could never convince her it wasn't the shape of an Italian ice."

"Mom, that's absurd. It's a miracle you came out halfway normal with all those crazy superstitions."

"You say crazy; I say colorful."

"You know you really never talk much about your childhood."

Julia stands up and looks out the window. "I've told you the good parts."

"Well, Mom, you don't have to protect me. I think you can trust me to handle things."

Julia spins around to face Andrea. "Look who's talking...."

"Touché...you're right. I guess we both can do better trusting each other."

"Yes, but don't get all serious on me now...I want to enjoy this news...twins...it's unbelievable."

"Yes, I hope I'm not sorry for what I wished for!" Andrea laughs.

"It'll be fine...you can do this. We're all going to help."

Phil steps into the room. "You're not including me, are you? I don't think I remember how to change a nappy."

Andrea turns her attention to her husband. "Phil, was Bella up yet? Did you tell her anything?"

"She called last night and said she was getting a ride home with Phoebe something. I was in bed when she got in, and she was asleep when I came here. You see, Andi, I saved the long chat for you."

"Mom, why don't you go to our house until I get released? Bella might not be up until noon...but just to be safe."

"Yes, sure."

Julia picks up her bag and quickly combs her hair. She kisses Andrea, hugs Phil, and sleepily walks to her car. Her cell phone is sitting on the car seat. There are three missed calls from Sam Testa. No voicemail.

It's barely seven-thirty, and Julia impulsively taps the number. It rings four times and goes to voicemail. Julia clears her throat. "Hi, Sam. Just returning your call. It was nice to see you last night."

She feels like she sent an appropriate message, not too needy sounding even if it is still early in the morning. Sam told Julia yesterday that he was an early riser, so calling before eight isn't too out of line. Julia drives back to her daughter's house, looking at the screen of her phone, waiting for it to ring. By the time Julia pulls into the driveway, she is talking to herself. "What is wrong with me? I can't fall into that trap again. I have more important things to worry about."

Julia decides to lay down on the couch in the sunroom and wait for Bella to wake up. The exhaustion hits her as soon as she puts her head down, and she falls into a deep sleep. She dreams of long ago playing outside in the dusty brown schoolyard. Images appear in vivid colors. She feels the motion of being on a swing. Air swishes through her hair. Her dress presses against her skin as she rises above the dust and the noise of the other children. Looking towards the sky on the upward curve of her sweep, she sees a luminous blue. Then she is back at the bottom of her arc in a fuzzy dust cloud. Up again so high at the peak, she feels like she will swing over the top. Finally she lets go of the ropes, flying into the air, landing squarely in the schoolyard. In front of her, there is a scruffy little boy with hazel eyes that crease in the corners as he smiles. He reaches out his hand.

Julia wakes up with a start. "Oh my God! It's him…it's him!"

43

Crimes and Misdemeanors

Julia sits up on the couch, disoriented, when Bella comes clopping down the stairs in her oversized slippers.

"What are you doing, Grams? You're a mess!"

Julia looks down at her clothes and catches the reflection of her hair in the window. "Oh my, I look like I just came out of the spin cycle."

"Worse…where's Mom and Dad?"

"They're going to be here soon…what time is it?"

Bella stands in front of Julia with her arms crossed. "How can you say they're going to be here soon if you don't even know what time it is?"

"Give me a minute, Bella. I just had this really strange dream. I can't think straight."

Bella runs into the kitchen and yells, "God, Grams…stop acting so weird!"

Julia follows her, tripping in shoes that are half on. "Bella, I'm sorry. Your mother will explain it all when she gets home."

"Is something wrong?"

"No, let's have some breakfast and a lot of coffee."

"Why can't you tell me?"

"She wants to tell you herself, that's all."

Julia is saved by the sound of cars pulling into the garage. "See, they're home." She mutters under her breath, "Just in time."

Andrea walks into the kitchen in yesterday's clothes with Phil behind her, carrying her laptop and purse.

"Mom, what's going on? Why is Dad carrying your stuff?"

"Give your mother a little space, Bella. She has to rest." Phil drops everything on the bench by the door and heads straight for the espresso machine.

"Phil, I'm fine, really. Let's have a little breakfast and talk for a while, then I'll go upstairs and lie down."

Julia recognizes the look of fear on Bella's face and puts her arm around her. "C'mon Bella, help me make something… Eggs, Andrea?"

"Sure, Mom…that would be perfect."

Phil is already drinking his first cup of espresso. "Who else wants something? Latte?"

"Decaf for me, Phil…c'mon Bella, Grams can handle the eggs. Sit down."

Bella slides into the seat next to her mother. "Are you sure you're okay? The baby?" Bella's emotions are swirling around her in a teenage storm.

"Nothing serious. I fainted last night at the hospital. I didn't even fall. I felt it coming on and landed on a chair. Look at me; I'm fine."

"But why did you faint?"

"My blood sugar was off, that's all. It happens to some women at this stage in their pregnancy…a little early for me."

"Why?"

"Well, here's the good part of the story. I'm pregnant with twins!"

There is a long silence. Bella gets up as if to leave the room. "Twins, oh my God. I'm going to spend my high school years working as a nanny."

Everyone is shocked. Phil raises his voice. "Don't walk away, Bella. Don't upset your mother."

Bella stomps up the stairs shouting, "Did you ever think of me when you two came up with this grand plan of yours? You can barely take care of me, and now there are going to be two more! And why are you telling me this just now?"

Phil looks at Andrea. "Well, that went well."

Julia rushes over to her daughter. "Don't take that to heart. She's acting out. Something else must be going on. Let me go talk to her."

"Maybe that's the problem, Mom…I keep asking you to do the things I should be doing."

"No, no…I can tell something else is going on. She's taking it out on you…believe me, I recognize that."

"I'm just so tired, Mom. Is it terrible that I can't deal with this now?"

Phil sits next to his wife and puts his arm around her shoulder. "Here, drink this decaf. Let's get you right first, and then you can worry about Bella. Your mother's right. Bollocks, I can't believe I'm saying that, Julia."

"Thanks for noticing, Phil."

A moment later, Julia's phone starts to vibrate. She pretends not to notice, but everyone can see it light up on the table.

"Mom, is that your phone or Bella's?"

"Mine. Just ignore it."

Andrea picks up the phone and sees the name Sam Testa on the display.

"Mom, why don't you answer? It's Mr. Testa."

"It's a long story; besides, I'm going up to talk to Bella."

Andrea raises her eyebrows. "Should I answer it?"

"Oh God, no!"

"You never really finished telling me what happened yesterday."

"I will...later."

Julia takes her double espresso and climbs up the stairs. She kicks off her shoes into her room and knocks gently on her granddaughter's door. "Bella, Bella...it's just me...can I come in?"

"If it's just you."

"It is, I promise."

Julia opens the door and quietly shuts it. Bella is in her bed facing the wall. She doesn't turn around. Julia moves a pile of clothes to the side and sits down on the edge of the bed.

"Don't say it, Grams...I know, I know I'm a horrible person."

"Bella, you are the least horrible person I know. Everyone is on edge this morning. Really, you wouldn't be normal if you didn't lose it every once in a while."

"So you're super normal?"

"Very funny... I guess you're not that upset."

Bella quickly reverts to a whine. "It's just at school. These kids have been saying things."

"Kids always say things."

Bella draws her knees closer to her chest. "Like your mother is some sexy Catholic? And worse about Dad. It's so embarrassing."

"That's it?"

"No, there's more. Even before this, these two girls Brooke and Ashley...everything I do they make fun of...first they say my curly hair looks like well...never mind, it's terrible." Bella sits up in the bed. Tears are beginning to well in her eyes.

"What could they possibly say about your beautiful hair?"

She looks down and whispers, "That I belong in *pube-lic* school... and then when I straighten it, they still say something nasty."

Julia wraps her arms around Bella. "Oh...that's just nonsense."

"There's more...now. When I leave class to go to orchestra, they chant, *There goes the nanny.* When I told my friends that Mom was having a baby, I thought it was a good thing. Instead, it's turned into a disaster." She starts to hyperventilate.

"Oh, Bella, why do you listen to them?"

"Because I can't not. Everyone hears them, and everyone thinks it's so funny. I'm so embarrassed."

Tears start rolling down her cheeks as Julia cradles her in her arms. She speaks quietly to Bella.

"I had two girls too...Ann and Debbie. They were best friends, an evil duo really...teasing everyone, especially the girls who didn't dress in the latest fashion."

"Did they bother you?"

"All the time, you know my Nonni made most of my clothes. Sometimes I cried myself to sleep because of it."

"How old were you?"

"Around your age, maybe a little younger."

"What did you do?"

"My Nonni might have put a curse on them," Julia makes the evil eye sign with her hand and grins. "But, I found new friends, better people. They kind of faded away because I stopped focusing on them."

"Your school was so much bigger than mine, though. It's hard, Grams."

"I know, but try to ignore them. When I look back at it...the things they said...all totally ridiculous. It's just the stupid stuff we have to endure...I saw both of them at my fortieth high school reunion."

"Really? Did you say anything to them?"

"No...they both acted like we were all best friends. I don't know...maybe they were embarrassed about how they behaved," Julia sighs. "Or never even knew how cruel they were."

"You *really* didn't say anything?"

"No point in it, Bella. It took me a long time to realize those nasty things they said weren't really important. I'm giving you a head's up, so you don't waste your time worrying about that bullshit."

"Oh, Grams…don't let Mom hear you say bullshit!"

"Bullshit! Bullshit!" Julia jokes. "Really, even your mom got picked on at school."

"For what?"

"Raising her hand too much and being smart."

"Now that's bullshit! What did you tell her?" Bella wipes her tears on her sleeve and smiles.

"If that's the worst thing kids make fun of you for, you don't have much to worry about."

"OMG, Grams…did you really say that to Mom?"

"Yes, I guess I've mellowed a little, well maybe not, huh?…C'mon, why don't you go downstairs and talk to your Mom? She needs you as much as you need her, believe me."

Bella gets up and combs her curly hair, changes into her jeans, and goes downstairs. Julia watches from the balcony as her daughter and granddaughter start to talk. When she hears laughing, she returns to the guest room, takes a shower, and drives home. Once she is at her own kitchen table, she listens to the voicemail from Sam. "Julia, I really need to talk to you. Please call. Sorry I couldn't find you again last night."

44

On Hold

Julia decides to take a nap before she calls Sam back. Exhaustion has gotten the best of her, and Julia wants to be able to see things clearly when she speaks to Sam. She finds some carrot sticks and hummus in the refrigerator and makes herself a small lunch before falling asleep in her living room. Again, she dreams of being on a swing. This time she notices the little boy's ankles showing, his pants too short for his lanky body. And those eyes greeting her. She feels a warmth envelope her and the sound of music lulling her into a deeper sleep. When she finally wakes up, it is almost five o'clock.

Julia struggles to decide what to do. Can this man be the boy in her dreams, the boy she loved so much as a child? She feels like she is in a fugue state, unable to tell what is reality and what is a dream. Her heart hopes that it is true, but her logical mind finds it impossible.

In the past twenty-four hours, she has had so much drama she doesn't feel that she can take anymore, and she procrastinates returning Sam's call. Finally, she picks up her phone, puts it on speaker, places it on the table, and watches it vibrate. Expecting to reach his voicemail again, she is startled when she hears, "Hello, Julia…so glad our game of phone tag is over."

"Hello, Sam. Yes…sorry it took me so long to call back…just a lot was happening at Andrea's house today."

"Is everything alright?"

"It is now…no worries…so what did you have to tell me?"

Sam can list all the things he wants to tell Julia. He knows she feels a connection to him but hesitates to ask her about it. His first responsibility is to do this favor for the Russos and explain it to Julia. If that conversation goes well, he will try to broach the subject.

He begins, but an incoming call distracts him. It's his daughter Vi. He ignores it, but she calls again. And again.

Julia notices the interruptions. "The phone is clicking. Is someone else trying to reach you?"

"I'm sorry, Julia, it's my daughter in North Carolina. Maybe something is wrong. I think I better take this."

"Sure…give me a call tomorrow morning then. We'll start fresh." Although curious about what he has to say, Julia is relieved to have another day to think about what her dreams mean and her attraction to Sam. None of this is how she envisioned her life going forward only a few weeks ago.

Fumbling with the phone, Sam hangs up on both Julia and his daughter. He sighs and redials. "Hi Vi, is there something wrong?"

"I was going to ask the same thing myself! I have been trying to call the house for days, and no one answered. Then you weren't answering your cell phone! Caroline had to tell me you were in Florida!"

"I'm sorry. I've been out a lot since I got home, and I forgot to turn on the ringer on my cell phone…it was on silent all day."

"How could you go all the way to Florida and not tell anyone? Caroline had to call Aunt Lucy to find out where you were!"

"Okay, calm down, Vi. I'm sorry. It was spur of the moment."

"And why are you flying all the way to Florida instead of coming here? North Carolina is much closer. Your grandchildren miss you."

"I told you I was driving down for their spring break. Sorry, I didn't think anyone would care."

"Oh, Dad…don't pull a stunt like that again. You have to tell us where you are going. And turn on that darn cell phone. You had me and Caroline scared to death."

"You're right. Your mother always took care of all that…talking to you. I'll do better next time."

"Next time? Are you going somewhere again?"

"No, no, no…just saying if I go, that's all," Sam paces back and forth in his living room, waiting for the questions to stop.

"So, what were you doing in Florida?"

"I ran into my old friend, Pete Russo, at the diner on Merrick Road. We hadn't seen each other in years…well, one thing led to another, and next thing you know, I'm flying back to his house in Florida."

"Oh, yeah, Mr. Russo. He was a funny guy. The one with those three cute sons, right?"

"Yes…it was just nice to get away. You know his wife was best friends with your mother growing up."

"I kinda' remember that…they weren't at the funeral, though."

"No, you know how you lose touch with people. I don't even know why…."

"Kids, Dad…they take all your time. That's why. We were a handful."

"Yeah, maybe…anyway…It was good for me to get out of the house. Pete has this great place on a golf course near the ocean."

"I'm sorry, Dad. I shouldn't be so rough on you…but the way Mom died and then you weren't answering the phone…ya' know, made me very anxious, to say the least."

"Geez, I'm sorry."

"Hey, did you ever go out for coffee with that woman?"

"Uhm…no…it didn't work out."

"Wait a sec, Dad, I hear little Sammy calling me. I'm going to have to get off…Hey, when you drive down, maybe you should bring a friend. You never made that trip alone before."

"I can bring Yogi."

"Oh, Dad…Yogi is welcome…but think about it…one of your golf buddies or someone."

"Okay, and don't worry about me…I'm fine."

"Bye, Dad…love ya."

45

Stormy Weather on the East Coast

The air is moist with thunder. Lorraine and Pete stand by their car for a moment to watch the lightning strikes hit the water on the ocean before they head into their golf club's restaurant. They are celebrating the birthday of their oldest son, Pete Jr. They have gone out for a special dinner on his birthday since he was a year old. When he was very young, they used to take the day off from work and spend the entire day with him celebrating. Now, the tradition continues in a scaled-down fashion, but the bond with their first son remains strong. Pete Jr. is now running the family landscaping business, and his wife, Chelsea, does the accounting. Pete checks his watch, and Lorraine asks the maître d' for a seat facing the ocean.

"I love to watch the storms rolling in, don't you, Pete?"

"I guess. At least they blow over quick here."

Pete is dressed in his sports coat and the shirt Chelsea picked out for him as a Christmas present. Lorraine took the designer purse out of the closet that her daughter-in-law gave her, even though it's not her style. They sit down and sip their water. No need to check the menu; they have it memorized. The conversation they started in the car about what to do about Pete's father, Enzo, picks up where they left off.

"Well, Pete, I tried calling Julia several times, but she wasn't answering."

"Did you leave a voicemail?" Pete scans the front door for his son and daughter-in-law and then twists around to see if his favorite bartender is working.

"No, it's not the kind of thing you leave a voicemail about."

"Did you call Sammy and tell him you couldn't reach her?"

"Yes, he didn't answer either, but I left *him* a message."

"You think Julia wasn't picking up on purpose? She knows your number now."

"Oh, I don't think so. I mean, she must be busy...her own art business. That's so cool."

Pete thumps his fingers on the table. "Don't get taken in by that, Lorraine. We really know nothing about her."

"Oh, Pete, why are you so suspicious of everyone all the time?"

"I'm not. Just being careful. Hey, let's get a drink...you know how late Petey and Chelsea are all the time." Pete motions to the waiter to come over to their table.

"Good evening, Mr. Russo...Mrs. Russo. The usual?"

"Yeah, thanks...Marco. We'll get a bottle of something later when my son gets here."

"Marco, don't forget the cake when I give you the signal."

"I won't, Mrs. Russo. It looks scrumptious."

Marco comes back with a gin and tonic for Pete and a chardonnay for Lorraine.

"Look, Lorraine, maybe we should tell Petey about this."

There is a crash of thunder, and Lorraine jumps and then clears her throat. "No, absolutely not! Not on his birthday. Don't be in such a rush. This isn't something you can solve overnight."

"They're going to find out eventually."

Lorraine reaches out and touches the top of her husband's hand. "Just wait. You always want to fix things. Hon, I love that about you...but this isn't something you can bulldoze your way through."

"Yeah, yeah...that old man of mine might croak though before we figure this out."

"Oh, Pete!... Look, there's our birthday boy."

Pete Jr. leans over and kisses Lorraine and slaps his father on the back. Chelsea is all smiles and kisses both of them. "We made it in before the rain, did you hear that thunder?... Oh, it's so nice to have a night out without the kids."

Pete Jr. is a younger version of his father at age thirty-five, but with his mother's disposition. After ten years of marriage, Chelsea, a native of Florida, is still trying to figure out this big New York Italian family.

Lorraine puts her purse on her lap and reaches in to get a tissue just so Chelsea sees that she is using it. "How are my beautiful grandchildren?"

Chelsea tucks herself in between her husband and her mother-in-law. "Good, they are looking forward to coming over after school next Friday. They love your pool, well, and those snacks. Go easy on the potato chips this time."

"What about the beer?" Pete laughs. "Hey, happy birthday Petey, you're looking great."

Chelsea doesn't laugh but picks up the menu and studies it.

"Thanks, Dad, couldn't be better. Look at this weather. Remember what it used to be like in New York? Once it started raining, it would go on for days, couldn't mow a lawn for weeks…not here…stops as fast as it starts." Pete Jr. turns away from the window. "Hey, Mom told me your old friend Mr. Testa was in town."

"Yeah, poor guy…his wife, Mom's old friend, Angie, died last year."

"Yes…remember when we all used to go to the beach together? Mrs. Testa was like the world's best cook…she used to pack those giant cutlet sandwiches and those cookies!"

Lorraine smiles at her son. "It was like we were going out to a restaurant instead of the beach…she just loved taking care of people…only the good die young."

"Well, Lorraine…then I guess you're stuck with me for a while." Pete, Lorraine, and Pete Jr. laugh and continue their chatter.

Chelsea, bewildered at their humor, puts down her menu. "Hey, Mom." She always feels awkward calling her mother-in-law Mom, but they insist. "I got an email from our family tree site that there was a new match."

"You still have the password?" Lorraine asks, trying not to panic.

"No, but I still get those emails...they never stop. It's so annoying."

Immediately relieved, Lorraine answers, "Oh, well, I guess I better look tomorrow."

"I thought you were taking care of the family tree?"

"I am...but you know, it's not a rush...like you said, they bombard you with emails."

"I guess, but this last one highlighted the words, *There's a new branch to add.*"

"Well, I'll look. Every fifth cousin is a *new branch* to them."

"Give me the new password. I'll take care of it if you're busy."

"No, I'll look...hey, let's make a toast to the birthday boy."

The sky clears, and the sun sets on the small inlet across from the club as they dine on the catch of the day. The dinner dishes are removed, and on cue, the restaurant staff comes out singing, "Happy Birthday to Petey."

Lorraine says to Pete Jr., "I got your favorite chocolate mousse cake."

Chelsea kisses her husband on the cheek. "I guess I'm not baking you one."

The evening ends with an empty bottle of wine and wrapped boxes of leftovers. Cake is saved for the grandchildren. They all hug goodbye. As Chelsea and Pete Jr. walk to the car, Chelsea complains, "Your mother always has to be in charge of everything."

"What are you talking about?"

"Your birthday, the cake, where we go to dinner, and now she won't give me the password to our own family tree site!"

"Oh, Chelsea, stop being so sensitive. You know you're my number one."

"You just don't see it."

"Hey, if it's that important to you, I'll ask her for the password."

"No, don't start any trouble…they're babysitting for us next week."

"So, why do you want the password?"

* * *

After Sam hangs up to talk to his daughter, Julia checks her phone again. There are three calls from Lorraine Russo in Florida but no voicemails. She can't decide if she should return the call and wonders if Sam knows what it is about. Julia doesn't want to be rude and call during the dinner hour, so she decides to wait and maybe call around eight o'clock tonight, if at all.

She heads into the small third bedroom at the back of the house. It has windows that face the sun for most of the day, so she had transformed it into her art studio. In this cozy space, she continues working on her newest project. She is surprised at how many of the cards and prints she made from her paintings are selling. Bella had been right about setting up the website. Julia is earning a small income from the sales, and when she adds up her share of profits from selling the house on Long Island, her early retirement buy-out, and a small pension from the museum, she is sure she can maintain her independence. Julia never wants to be dependent on anyone again after her failed second marriage. Looking up out of her window, she thanks her grandmother for leaving her this house.

As the evening falls into darkness, she works until her stomach starts growling. She is so lost in her painting that she has forgotten to eat supper. After a hectic day, sitting alone with a canvas and brushes for a few hours was good therapy. Julia knows she won't sleep well tonight if she doesn't return that phone call. She will be tossing and turning all night, trying to figure out why Lorraine was calling. The advice that Dr. Blanding had given her popped into her head, "You can control the situation." Julia decides right then to be proactive and call Lorraine. "There's nothing to be afraid of...don't anticipate," she tells herself.

*　*　*

It is a little after eight, and Pete and Lorraine are in their car heading home from dinner.

Pete reaches over and takes Lorraine's hand. "Remember when Pete Jr. was born, God, that was the best day of my life."

"It was something, wasn't it? Who would ever imagine the two of us, now grandparents?"

"Yeah, it's really something...that was a nice dinner, wasn't it?"

"Yes, hon...but Chelsea seemed a little out of sorts. Did you hear her ask me for the password to the ancestry site?"

"No, why the hell did she want that?"

"I didn't realize it, but she still gets emails when there is a new hint or family connection."

"So?"

"So, she knows that there's a new *branch on the family tree*, but she needs the password to see it. Now she is going to start asking me about it."

"I told you we should've just told everyone instead of letting my old man take his sweet time."

The screen on the dashboard lights up, showing that a cell call is coming in on Lorraine's phone. Pete and Lorraine both see the name, and their conversation suddenly changes course.

"Jesus, it's Julia...are you going to pick up, Lorraine?"

"Should I?" She doesn't wait for an answer from Pete. "Hi, Julia, thanks for calling back."

"Sorry I missed your calls, had a bit of a hectic day."

"No worries...I'm in the car on speaker. Pete is here too. Is that okay?" Lorraine looks at Pete, but he can hardly see her expression in the half-light of the dashboard.

"Well, yes, I guess so." Julia is tentative and then says, "Hello, Pete."

"How ya' doing, Sis?" Pete's voice booms across the thousand miles.

"Good, good, thank you. This is some first introduction, isn't it?" Julia is surprised by Pete's thunderous voice.

"Didn't Sam fill you in on me? Tall, dark, and handsome?"

"Well, he did say you were quite the comedian."

Lorraine interrupts. "Listen, Julia...I had a little brainstorm. Enzo is really hesitant about this video thing, but I thought if Sam was on your end while we did it, he would be a lot more amenable to the idea."

"Sam? Why?"

"My old man likes Sam better than me!"

Waving her hand emphatically, Lorraine motions to Pete to be quiet.

"My father-in-law trusts him. I think he's a little afraid of the whole confrontation thing. He feels terrible, really...he had no idea about you. Having Sam there would be calming to him."

"You know I was just talking to Sam earlier this evening, but our conversation got cut short. His daughter was calling from Carolina, I think."

"Oh yes, both of his daughters live there...So, how do you feel about having Sam there?"

"I think it would be fine...just so you know, I would never say anything confrontational to him. Let's just start small...meet online and see where it goes from there."

"Hey, Sis, that's a great idea. I'm sure Lorraine will be able to set this thing up."

"Did Sam agree to all this?"

"Well, he wanted us to check it out with you first... So I think he'll go along."

"He's such a gentleman." Julia also is calmed by the idea.

Lorraine wants to keep the conversation going. She is driven by curiosity. "So, where did you say you are from?"

"Born in Astoria...we moved to the Island for a time, and then I moved back with my grandmother when I was a teenager."

Pete's antenna shoots up, and he talks over Lorraine. "Really, why did you move back?"

"Oh, that's a long story...so, I'll wait to hear from you."

"Okay, goodnight Julia."

"Sweet dreams, Sis."

Julia puts her phone down and recovers from the call. No one ever called her Sis before. Pete sounded overly friendly towards her; she isn't sure about him. His voice was so deep and husky that she was taken aback by it. And she thinks Lorraine sounded controlled but very open to meeting. It is hard to read people without the visual clues. Julia hopes she has the sweet dreams her brother wished her tonight and decides to wait until morning when Sam calls to worry about it. She really feels that she has made some progress in handling herself in a difficult situation.

* * *

When he reaches their driveway, Pete doesn't open the car door right away. "Lorraine, did you hear that?"

"Hear what?"

"The long story thing about moving back in with her grandmother."

"That's nothing. We moved back in with your parents for a while."

"That's different...something's up with her."

"Oh Pete, for goodness sakes, let's just let this thing play out. Besides, we have to decide if we should tell Petey and Chelsea before they figure something out."

"Let's get my father to do this right away. Then maybe we can tell everyone."

"She does have a nice voice, don't you think? I love hearing a New York accent. Makes me miss home a little."

As they walk into the house, thunder starts booming, and the sky lights up as bright as day.

"You see, Lorraine, that's a sign that something's up with her."

46

Say What?

It's Saturday morning, and the sun beams in through the slats of the Venetian blinds. Sam watches the shadows run across the bed. Finally, the days are getting longer, and there is some hope for warmer weather. He remembers that Julia is also an early riser. On impulse, Sam jumps in the shower and then plans to call to ask if she would meet him for breakfast. He could get to the diner in Astoria in less than a half-hour since there is no rush hour traffic. It is seven-thirty when Julia's phone rings. She is sitting at her kitchen table drinking her first cup of coffee. She doesn't look at the phone but picks it up and instinctively says, "Hello, Andrea."

"Julia?"

There's laughing on the other end of the phone. "Oh my, Sam...no one calls me this early in the morning except my daughter."

"I'm sorry. It's just that you said the other day that you're always up before seven."

"True…and what are you doing up so early on a Saturday?"

"It's the teacher in me…old habits die hard. I was always at work by six-thirty."

"Well, honestly… I simply can't sleep." Julia laughs.

"I was wondering, instead of talking on the phone…do you want to go have breakfast? I'll drive over to that diner if you like."

"Well, ahh…why not? But let's meet halfway. There's a café right near Roosevelt Field that my friend and I go to…the coffee is excellent."

"All right, are you sure you don't mind?"

"No, it's so beautiful out. It'll be nice to go somewhere fun with you."

Sam's heart flips a little when he hears Julia describe their meeting as fun.

"Great…see you in a half-hour or so then?"

He goes back into his bedroom and finds the new shirt his daughter Caroline bought him for Christmas. Never worn, it still has pins and plastic inserts in the collar. He puts it in the dryer to take out the wrinkles. Then he finds the can of hairspray for men he bought for one of his daughter's weddings, combs his hair perfectly, and sprays a cloud of mist filling the whole bathroom.

Sam catches his reflection in the kitchen window. "How do I look, Yogi?"

Walking into the garage, he sighs at the sight of his old beat-up minivan. He walks back into the house and gets the keys to

Angie's car, an almost new silver Camry. He has been starting it once a week to keep the battery from dying, but it hadn't left the garage except once when his children were home, and they used it.

Sam slides into the front seat and catches his breath. He whispers, "Angie, I love you. I hope you understand." He zooms down the block smiling, but as he turns onto the parkway, that pulsing sound starts pounding in his ears. Could it be Angie warning him or Julia calling? Unable to grasp the meaning, he turns the rock station on the radio up loud to mask the sound.

Julia looks down at the sweatpants she wears for pajamas and runs into her room to look in the closet. She is glad that she took her shower last night, but her hair is a tangled mess. She puts it up in a twist and picks out her best jeans. Even though the weather is warming, she chooses a turtleneck.

"At least I can hide my wrinkly neck."

Julia digs through her dresser and decides on a sweater with an exotic pattern, puts on her makeup in less than five minutes, and is out the door driving fast through the empty streets. She can feel her heart pulsing in her ears and does deep yoga breaths as she passes LaGuardia airport. Jets fly low overhead, drowning out any other sound. As Julia arrives, she searches the parking lot for a blue minivan but instead spots Sam standing by the front door of the café.

He pulls the door open for her as she approaches.

"Hello, we have a lot to talk about." Julia's body skims his arm as she enters the café.

"Oh, you mean Lorraine reached you?"

"Yes, and I spoke to Pete. They were in the car on speaker last night."

"They called you from the car?"

"No, I returned her call. They were just leaving a restaurant."

"Probably at the club. That's the only one Pete goes to."

"I don't mean to be rude, but you seem so different than him."

"What do you mean?"

"He's... I don't know...sounds like a Neanderthal." Julia pauses and then tries to correct herself. "In a good way, if that's possible."

Sam points to a table, laughing, "Oh, Julia...you don't know how much you sound like him!"

"What? What do you mean?"

"He's got a description, a name, an exaggeration for everything...you do it too. You two could be a comedy team."

"I guess I do exaggerate for effect sometimes...but I didn't think that was hereditary."

"Apparently, it is...you don't look anything like him if that makes you feel better."

"He was calling me 'Sis' on the phone...it felt so strange."

"Julia, he really is a wonderful guy. You know how we men are; we say stupid things sometimes when we don't know what to say."

"Well, yes, but I've known plenty that say stupid things on purpose."

"No, really, he's not like that. He's as broken up about this as you and wants to make things right."

"Okay, hey, we have to go place our order at the counter here. It's kind of self-serve, hope you don't mind."

"No, not at all…let me go get the coffee…what else can I get you?"

Julia lets Sam get her coffee and place her order. She hasn't had the luxury of a man taking care of her like that since her first marriage to Mike. She recognizes that he is not doing it to diminish her in any way, but simply because he is a caring and considerate man. Julia can't help but feel protected by him and understands why Enzo would feel the same way.

Sam returns with the coffee. She notices that his shirt has the creases of a newly opened package, and there is the subtle scent of aftershave. She doesn't know if she should tell him about the boy in her dreams as she looks at his hazel eyes. After over fifty years, it's so hard to know if it's the same boy from the playground. And she doesn't remember his name being Sam. Yet there it is, that feeling of having known someone staring back at her.

"So, Julia, what did you think when Lorraine suggested I be there with you?"

Sam's question brings her back to the present situation. "Well, it's a little unusual, but this whole thing is unusual. If you're okay with it, then why not?'

"Yes, I mean, I don't want to be the reason this doesn't work out for everyone… But, I mean if I said no."

"Do you think he'll agree?"

"Yes, Lorraine has a way with him. She's the only one he takes orders from," Sam laughs.

"Okay, so let's wait for Lorraine to call. Anytime is fine…the sooner, the better."

"I'm free all weekend…I'll text Lorraine." Sam takes a sip of his coffee and waits for Julia to talk again. He can sense she is anxious and doesn't want to pressure her.

Julia finally puts her cup down. "That is good coffee, isn't it?" and without waiting for an answer, goes on. "What is he, Enzo, like?"

"Well, I knew him when I was growing up…in high school and college. He's a sporty guy…loved baseball. Took me, Pete, and his brother to Mets games. The stadium was practically in our backyard. We sat way back in the cheap seats in the outfield trying to catch home runs…great fun."

"Oh, that's right…you said you were from Queens."

"Yes, we moved to Whitestone when I was about eight."

"Where did you live before that?"

"Astoria…near that bakery with the great Italian ice. Not far from the subway."

Suddenly Julia hears a commotion near her and looks sideways. A small group of women is standing at the edge of their table—everyone looking bewildered.

Linda is dressed in her beach-walking clothes. "Julia! You know Sam?"

Dina and Carol are behind her, and Gloria squeezes forward in her tight workout pants and bejeweled jacket. "Sam! Isn't this wonderful? Scooch over! Dina, go grab those chairs! Can you imagine running into you here?"

Julia speaks up sarcastically, "It's Kismet."

"What's Kismet?" Gloria grins foolishly and then ignores Julia.

Julia and Sam sit politely still. There is no way to stop what Gloria has put into motion. Gloria snuggles close to him and starts talking about their walking group that meets on nice days at seven a.m. at the tunnel at Parking Field Four at Jones Beach.

"Oh, Sammy, you should join us. We could use a guy in our group…speed us up a bit."

Sitting on the bench next to Julia, Linda whispers in her ear, "How do you know Sam Testa?"

Julia whispers back, "It's a long story…I'll call you."

Sam can't extricate himself from Gloria's grip and keeps sliding until he is halfway off the bench. Too polite to be abrupt, he finally looks at his watch and says he has to go home to walk his dog. Julia, likewise, waits a few more minutes, finishes her coffee, and excuses herself. "I have to drive my granddaughter somewhere…it was nice meeting you all."

By the time Julia is outside, she can't see Sam anywhere. She scours the parking lot for a blue minivan. Embarrassed and frustrated, Sam has driven away. Julia calls him on his cell phone, but he never connected it to Angie's car, and it pulses quietly in his jacket on the back seat.

47

The Corners of
the Mind

Lorraine calls to Pete, who is watching a basketball game, "Let's pick up your parents for five o'clock mass tonight, then bring them here for dinner."

"Why? You know they like to be home early for that show at eight."

"They can watch it here. I have an idea."

Pete gets up from the couch and turns off the television.

"What's wrong? St. John's losing again?"

"Yeah, there's never been any coach as good as Carnesecca...so what plan are you hatching?"

"I'll make your father's favorite meal, ravioli with that fennel sausage he loves...then you take your mother by the pool. Make sure you refill his wine glass too. That mellows him out. Then

I'll talk to him about doing the video call…maybe tomorrow before he can change his mind."

"Okay, I'm in…at least for the ravioli. Did you ask Sam if he would do it?"

"Yes, he texted me that they're both okay with the plan and Sunday afternoon works for them."

* * *

Sam is home watching the same game on television when his phone rings. He hopes it isn't Julia because he still doesn't know how to explain Gloria. All afternoon Sam has been trying to come up with a plan to get rid of her from his life. He finally decides to pick up the phone and is relieved that it is Angie's friend Linda.

"Sam, it was so nice to see you this morning."

"Yes…what's up?"

"Well, it's not really any of my business…but you know Julia's an old friend of mine."

"You must be the friend she said she meets there for lunch sometimes."

"Yes, yes, every few weeks…well, months sometimes," Linda admits.

Sam sits up straight in his chair. "How do you know her?"

"I was going to ask you the same thing."

"It's a long story."

"Oh…well," Linda pauses as she reconsiders what she is going to say. "I don't want to interfere."

Sam is becoming impatient. Self-control has always been his hallmark. But his annoyance festers. After all, Linda is the one who introduced him to Gloria. "So…what are you not interfering with?"

"Oh, Sam…you know I loved your wife, Angie. Of course, we weren't best friends…but still, you know, close for a long time. And well…I've known Julia for a long time too."

"Angie knew Julia?"

"No…no, that's not it. I just want to warn you about Julia."

"Warn me?"

"Don't get me wrong, she's a lovely person…but she's troubled, you know, depressed. We were roommates in college, and I've known her and her family since then. Our friendship has had its ups and downs…with her mood swings and all."

"Why are you telling me this?" Sam can feel his grip tightening on the phone.

"I didn't want you to go into something blind."

"She never mentioned any of this…but I just met her…she *is* a lovely person…she's certainly doesn't seem depressed, as you're saying."

"She didn't tell you then…about her father killing the whole family in a car accident when she was a teenager? And about her first husband?"

"No."

"Well, it's all very tragic, but I just want you to know…before you get too involved, that she, well…struggles with all that. Who wouldn't? … I'm just thinking of how Angie was so different, such a good-hearted woman…as a friend to Angie…I…just thought I should tell you."

"You were right, Linda…it really is none of your business." Sam stares at the phone receiver in his hand, then slams it down into the cradle.

* * *

Lorraine, Pete, Enzo, and Bobbie are sitting around the dining room table after church. Enzo is especially hungry since they are eating later than he is used to and is absorbed in his meal. Lorraine speaks loud in Enzo's direction. "Wasn't the priest's homily good this week? You know, talking about how we should be more open to other people's ideas and feelings?"

Enzo looks up from his plate. "Yeah, yeah…there wouldn't be so much trouble in the world nowadays if everyone did that…but I don't like eating so late. Next week take us to the early mass on Sunday."

"C'mon Pop…isn't it nice to have dinner with us?" Pete asks.

"Yes, but let's just do dinner early next time…no church."

Bobbie puts her fork down. "We have to go to church, Enzo. Are you taking us in the morning, Pete?"

Pete reaches over to touch his mother's hand. "Yeah, Mom…we'll go in the morning."

"Okay, I can't miss church." Bobbie continues eating.

Lorraine leaves the table when everyone is almost done with their meal and brings in a bowl of grapes piled high, oranges, and mangoes. She asks Bobbie if she would like something from the bowl.

"Fruit's not dessert!" Bobbie has been uncharacteristically losing her temper lately.

"You're right, Mom. I have some cake too. Would you like a piece?"

Before Bobbie can answer, Lorraine directs Pete. "Here, take your mother by the pool with her cake. Pour your dad a little more wine."

Pete stands and offers his mother his hand, then guides her to a chair by the pool, out of earshot of Lorraine and Enzo.

"How's that cake, Mom?"

"Good, Lorraine's a good baker, isn't she?"

"Hey, Mom, look…Lorraine put together this photo album for you. Want to take a look?"

"Sure, sure, Pete." Bobbie takes the photo album and opens it to the first page. There are pictures with names and dates on each one written in block letters.

"Who is that in the picture with you, Mom?"

"Oh, that's my little brother, Nino. He was such a good baby, always smiling. We're standing in front of the old house on 38th Street."

"You remember the street?"

"Why wouldn't I?"

"No reason…isn't this great how Lorraine put it together?"

"Lorraine made this?" Bobbie turns to the middle of the book.

"Yeah, Mom, she thought you'd like it, you know to help you remember things."

"I remember things!"

"Oh, I know you do. Mom…look, there's Pete Jr."

"Who's that girl with him?"

"Look, Lorraine wrote it down. That's his wife, Chelsea.…They've been married for ten years."

Bobbie raises her voice and shakes her finger at Pete. "Pete Jr. got married, and no one told me?"

Pete is worried that he agitated his mother and asks again, "Hey Mom, how's the cake?"

"Good, who made it?"

In the dining room, Enzo is watching Bobbie through the patio doors. Lorraine finally convinces him that a video call with Julia would be the right thing to do. He is relieved that Sam will be on the other end of the conversation. Underneath all his fear, he wants to meet Julia and make amends.

Seeing that Bobbie is fine, Enzo turns back to Lorraine. "Bobbie can never know, Lorraine. You have to promise me that."

"Of course, Pop. Sam says she's wonderful. How could your daughter not be?"

48

Worlds Collide

Julia is up early Sunday, waiting for it to be late enough to make a call. Before the beach-walker invasion at the café yesterday, Sam and Julia had decided to tell Lorraine that today would be a good day to try to connect. Lorraine emailed last night that the time is set at two o'clock this afternoon. Despite her desire to not stress Andrea out, she decides to call her daughter to ask if she could do the call from her house. Bella's help with the technology will alleviate some of Julia's stress.

"Andrea, How are you feeling this morning?"

"So much better, Mom. I'm downstairs sitting on the couch...I never thanked you for staying with me at the hospital."

"Oh, it was nothing... Hey, how are things with Bella?"

"Improved greatly. We had a really long talk yesterday, and I know what I have to do."

"What's that?"

"Well, Bella said something funny…she said that I was almost as good as you to talk to after our conversation yesterday."

"She still says the cutest things. You know Andrea, you really don't have to do anything special, just being there is enough."

"I know. I have to do better getting my priorities straight. Phil too…hey, you really didn't tell me much about Mr. Testa."

"Actually, that's why I'm calling. Just say no, like Nancy Regan, if it's too much trouble."

After Julia explains the situation, Andrea responds, "No problem, Mom, and you're right. Mr. Testa would be more comfortable here. He knows us. It's a much better arrangement. Bella can set you up in the sunroom with her laptop…even Phil could do that if she isn't home."

"I hope this isn't a mistake."

"What? Asking Mr. Testa here or meeting your real father?"

"Both, I guess…although Sam seems like such a genuine person."

"Mom, he is. I've worked with him on a few committees at school. He really listens to people. Hey, why don't you ask him to come early for lunch?"

"Well, if all of you are there. I would like to get to know him better."

"Okay, I'll have Phil pick something up at the deli for lunch after he takes Bella to mass this morning. Do you want to go with them?"

"No, tell Phil to pray for me," Julia teases. "I'll bring something from the bakery…you know, the one by the subway."

"Do you want me to call Mr. Testa?"

"Yeah, that's a good idea. Thanks, see you later then."

Julia spends the rest of the morning fretting about what to say to her new family, what she should wear, and trying to decipher why she is drawn so strongly to Sam. There is a list of questions on her desk, a pile of clothes on her bed, and an unfinished bagel sitting on the chair. In an attempt to memorize them, she runs through the questions while trying on clothes. It would look foolish to keep looking down at a piece of paper, but worse, if her outfit sent the wrong message.

"Maybe I should write these on the palm of my hand," Julia laughs to herself. She finally decides on the blouse with a small geometric pattern and a black cardigan with pearl buttons.

* * *

By eleven-thirty, she is ready and heads to her daughter's house for lunch and the inevitable.

Phil has been cleaning up after himself and Bella since Andrea has gotten home from the hospital. He runs over to the deli after church without one complaint and comes back with a giant plate of sandwiches, olives, salads, and a large bowl of assorted berries.

Phil places the platters on the table. "Look, Andrea...*Abondanza?* Right?"

"You've outdone yourself, Phil...can you get some plates and napkins?"

Bella walks into the kitchen. "I'll do it, Mom. I can't believe Mr. Testa is coming here. It's like having a priest come for supper."

"Not that bad!" Phil laughs.

"Dad, no…it's a good thing. He's so nice. He'd be perfect for Grams."

"Oh, Bella, I don't think your grandmother is interested in that kind of thing," Andrea scoffs.

Bella pulls the kitchen curtain to the side and looks out into the street. "Well, it's still exciting to have him here."

"Bella, did you set up the laptop in the sunroom for Grams?"

"Yes, do you think we could stay and listen?"

"No, I think your Grandmother wants to have some privacy for this first meeting," Phil answers.

"I guess…where are you going to be?"

"I have to go do some errands for your mother, and she has to go back upstairs and put her feet up after lunch."

Julia pulls into the driveway as Sam parks his car on the street. She runs into the house, not recognizing his vehicle. He watches her. He notices how confident her stride is, how she seems in control of every movement as if she has calculated each nerve to fire precisely on cue. He thinks about what Linda said and cannot connect that image of a fragile woman with the one he sees. When she is in the house, he opens his car door and walks up the path to the front door, and knocks. He has a box wrapped in string with a half dozen pastaciottis from the bakery near his house in his hand.

Andrea and Bella greet him at the door, "Mr. Testa!"

"Please, call me Sam, Andrea…well, Bella, you can still call me Mr. Testa, I guess." Sam grins at Bella.

"Come in, come in. My mother was telling me the story…my goodness, it's a small world."

"It is, Dr. Cooper."

"If I'm going to call you Sam, then you have to call me Andrea…I think you've met my husband Phil."

Sam notices how assuredly Phil grips his hand. "Of course, nice to see you again."

Julia is standing behind all of them, and Sam moves towards her. "Oh, Julia, I'm sorry things got so messed up yesterday. I barely know those women."

"I only know Linda. When I came out, I looked for your blue minivan…but you were gone."

"Oh, I had the other car…time to retire that clunker."

"Well, you're here now…come on in; lunch is on the table."

They sit together around the table and politely pass the food, and talk about the weather. The adults are still a bit uncomfortable, and conversation gives way to the sounds of chewing and forks scraping plates. Bella, who is delighted to be part of this serendipity she started with her big plan for her grandmother at Christmas time, is brimming with expectation. Earlier in the morning, she thought she could almost hear music playing in her ears when her mother told her Mr. Testa and her grandmother were doing this video call together. She is the first to restart the conversation. "Mr. Testa, where do you live anyway?"

Sam is grateful for this distraction. "Seaford, south of here."

"Why do you live so far away from the high school?"

"Well, Bella…my wife and I got our first teaching jobs in Farmingdale. I thought since we were moving out to the island, it would be nice to be near the beach."

"Your wife was a teacher?"

"Yes, second grade until she retired, maybe about ten years ago."

"Do you have kids?"

"Bella, this isn't the Spanish Inquisition," Phil cautions as he reaches for another sandwich.

"It's fine, really...two daughters in North Carolina. They teach college there, and my son is in Tampa, working for the Rays."

Phil stops mid-bite. "Okay, now you have my attention, Sam. What does he do for the Rays?"

"Promotion, advertising...things like that...you're a baseball fan?"

"Yankees...don't mistake my accent for someone who loves football, or as you say soccer...the most monotonous of all sports... grown men running up and down a field in packs like a bunch of wolves...ridiculous."

"But how'd you become a baseball fan?"

"My family moved to Manhattan from London when I was in my late teens. My father worked for one of the global banking firms. I just wanted to be an all-American lad, like my mates."

"So, your parents are still here?"

"No, they went back and left me behind for college...ta-ta...they were about as sentimental about it as the Queen mother."

"Dad, you never told me that!" Bella practically shouts across the table.

"I guess, didn't seem that important...can I make anyone a latte?"

"Yes, Phil...I'll have one." Julia can see that Sam is uncomfortable with the direction of the conversation and turns to him. "Sam, what did you say were the names of your grandsons?"

"Well, there's little Sammy, Lucas, and Mikey." Sam smiles as he says their names.

"Mike was grandma's first husband's name," Bella blurts out. "I never met him."

This time Andrea steps into the conversation. "Bella, if you're done eating, why don't you go check the internet connection on the laptop…So, how has retirement been, Sam?"

"Can I have dessert first?" Bella asks, trying to stay tuned into the adult conversation.

"Yes, bring the box Grams brought over… and the one from Mr. Testa."

Sam sees the name of the bakery on the box that Julia brought. "Look at that. Our apartment was right next door to that bakery. It was the best one in Queens."

"Still is. It's right near where I grew up too, well, live now." Julia reaches over to take one of the almond paste cookies. Sam watches her slender hands move across the table.

Julia takes out the list of questions she wants to ask her father, neatly folded in her pocket. She unfolds the paper slowly and places it on the table sideways so Sam can read it also. Each word is carefully printed and adorned with little loops on the serifs. He sees the letters, and a memory suddenly drops out of a box and slides into his consciousness. Sam is now fully aware of who this woman is sitting next to him.

Bella interrupts the moment. "Come on, we only have fifteen minutes. Let me show you what to do."

49

Everything Old is New Again

Lorraine sets up her laptop in the kitchen of Enzo and Bobbie's condo. Enzo paces nervously up and down the kitchen floor, the beige tiles clicking with each step. He has on a tie and shirt with his suit jacket from the last grandchild's wedding. Bobbie asked him earlier this morning why he was wearing a tie. He said, "To go to church." She had forgotten they went the previous night.

Yesterday Pete drove his father to the barbershop so they both could get a haircut. Pete also put on his best sport shirt for today's video call. For an hour this morning, he practiced counting to five before talking, as Lorraine suggested.

The volume on the television in the living room is purposely turned up. Bobbie sits in the recliner with the floral brocade, feet up. She usually falls asleep this time of day watching game

252

shows. Pete is still in the living room with his mother getting her settled in with a drink and a snack.

"Do you need anything, Mom? Just call me if you do. I've got to fix something in the kitchen with Pop."

"Okay, get me my blanket. I feel a little tired."

Pete gets the blanket and covers his mother. She looks ready to doze off. He watches her pick up the television remote, study it, turn it over, put it down, and then repeat the whole process. He moves it farther away from her before going back into the kitchen.

Enzo looks at the laptop on the kitchen table. "Why can't we just talk on the phone?"

"Oh, Pop…this is the way people talk nowadays. It's easy." Lorraine, sensing Enzo's agitation, tries to settle him down. "Come here…sit down."

Enzo sits up in the kitchen chair and straightens his tie.

"Look…see, you're very handsome on camera."

"But where am I going to see her?"

"In one of those boxes…it's all very intuitive…I mean automatic."

Enzo studies the screen and watches Lorraine arrange the chairs next to him, so they all will fit on the screen. "Are you ready, Pop?"

"I guess so…maybe this is a bad idea."

"We promised Julia, Pop. There's no turning back now."

"Well, I'm not going to say anything that I don't want to."

"You don't have to. Just hellos, and how are you. Sam will be there with Julia, and we will be right here next to you."

"What about Bobbie?"

"Oh, Pop…she won't know what's going on. Pete put on *Wheel of Fortune* for her."

"Yeah, she loves that show. I don't know how she can figure those words out when she doesn't know what she had for breakfast."

"The mind works in mysterious ways, Pop. She's happy…look at her, paying attention to the show…don't worry, I'll just leave the door open an inch."

* * *

"Now, Grams, do you see how you move the cursor to change the view? And this button to mute or stop the video?"

"Yes, I see…Sam. Do you get it?"

"I've got it. I used this video program at work before I retired…just a little rusty."

"I'm going to stay in the kitchen if you need me…I promise not to listen, really. I have some homework to do," Bella lies. She leaves the room and then props herself against the wall right next to the archway leading to the sunroom.

Julia sits straight and stares at the laptop as she waits for the call to begin. "Sam, after this…I have to talk to you about something else…if you can stay, of course."

"Yes…I do too…it's this…well, I can't even explain it."

"I know." Julia doesn't dare to face Sam with the call about to start. The screen opens, and she sees an elderly man surrounded by a man and a woman on either side. Julia notices the pelicans flying across the wallpaper behind them.

"Hello, Sis!" Pete booms.

Lorraine reaches behind her father-in-law and taps Pete on the back.

"Hello, so nice to meet you. Well, this is Sam...Oh, you all know Sam." Julia stumbles and then regains her composure. She is taken aback by what she sees on the screen. Her father appears so small and frail sitting next to Pete. Pete is what she expected, only larger. In her head, she calculates that he is at least twice her size. With her athletic build and look of authority, Lorraine is the only one who somewhat resembles what she imagined, except for the blonde hair.

"Thank you for sending Sam to set this all up. He is wonderful, as you promised, Lorraine."

Lorraine smiles appreciatively. "Julia, this is Enzo. I know you have a lot of questions for him."

Enzo stares at Julia and tries to feel a connection. He is stunned by how much she looks like his daughter and, at that moment, truly realizes this is not some mistake. Julia likewise stares back at him and waits for some sign of acceptance. After a few more moments, she says, "I'm sorry we had to find out about each other this way."

Enzo puts his head down. "I didn't know. I'm not that type of guy."

"I understand, I understand...but now that we know, I was hoping we could get to know each other."

Enzo reflexively bristles. "How? We live so far away from each other."

Pete tries to calm his father. "Pop, we can fly to New York, or Julia can come here."

"No...it's too much. I'm old." He waves his hand at the screen.

Lorraine laces her arm into Enzo's. "C'mon Pop...let's just talk a little. No one is accusing you of anything. Julia just wants to get to know you. Like I said, we can take it slow."

Enzo looks up. "What does Sam think?"

Sam is surprised by the question but quickly responds. "Lorraine is right, Enzo. I think if you get to know Julia, everything will fall into place."

"Okay...I didn't mean to be rude to you, Julia. I just wish your mother told me about you. I never knew! I never knew!" He didn't expect such an intense rush of emotion and is almost in tears.

"Pop, it's okay." Pete looks straight at Lorraine as he talks to his father.

Julia waits as she listens to Enzo take a few deep breaths. "I don't know why she didn't tell you, but we can't change that. I'm so sorry you didn't know. But when I look back now, I'm pretty sure she knew you were my father."

"Is she alive?" Enzo asks.

"No, no. She died young...when I was a teenager."

That news sends a reverberation of shock through him, and he wipes tears from his eyes. "Oh, no...I didn't know...I didn't know."

"None of it is your fault. I don't hold anything against you." Julia pauses and raises her voice a little. "I'm sure we can work everything out. Maybe our families can get to know each other."

Pete suddenly notices that the sound on the television is turned off. He turns around and sees his mother through the crack in the door, getting up out of the chair. Bobbie runs through the kitchen door. "Is that Gracie? I hear my friend Gracie!"

Enzo yells, "Shut it off! Shut it off, dammit!"

Julia's screen goes blank. Bella peeks out from behind the wall. "What was that?"

50

Strained Relations

Pete slams the lid down on the laptop as Lorraine jumps out of her chair to talk to Bobbie. Enzo runs into the bedroom, cursing as he walks. "I knew this was a bad idea, dammit."

Bobbie watches her husband run past her. "Why is Enzo shouting? I thought we were going to church."

Lorraine puts her arms around Bobbie's shoulders and leads her back to her chair in the living room. "We already went, Mom."

Bobbie looks at her and has a brief moment of clarity. "Oh, yeah…that's right," then returns to what she was saying when she burst into the kitchen. "I thought I heard my friend Gracie talking…she has such a beautiful voice…You know she doesn't call me anymore."

"Mom, Pete was just watching a video on the computer on how to fix the faucet."

Bobbie appears puzzled and then continues, "We were such good friends, Gracie and me...I don't know what happened."

"I'll look for her number in your telephone book, Mom."

"Yeah, do that...when are we going to church?"

Lorraine finds the remote on the floor next to the chair. "In a little while, Mom...here, let me put your show back on."

Bobbie stares at the television and pulls the blanket over her shoulders. She lifts the handle of the recliner, her feet go up, and in a few minutes, she is quietly breathing with her head turned to the side in a deep sleep.

Pete comes into the living room with beads of sweat on his forehead. "Pop won't open the door to the bedroom."

They walk out onto the patio, and Lorraine holds her head in her hands. "We can't just leave them like this. Do you realize what just happened?"

"My father was a real son-of-a-bitch. Mom's friend? That's who he decides to play around with?" Pete starts to sweat through his shirt in the outside air.

"No wonder why he kept saying Bobbie could never know. Oh my God!"

Pete takes the shirttail out of his pants and wipes his forehead. "Let's hope she forgets this like everything else. Poor Mom, she doesn't deserve this. What the hell is wrong with him?"

"I know, I know...Not only that, Pete... Mom's become too much for Pop to handle alone, well, for anyone anymore...being here today makes it so obvious...what a mess."

"I don't know what to do, Lorraine. Man, the shit hit the fan this time. What the fuck! Can we leave her here?"

Lorraine looks out at the ocean. "No, let's wait for her to wake up and take her home with us for now."

"Oh, Jesus fuckin' Christ...what about Julia? Now, what do we do? Do you think she heard Mom?"

"I don't know how she could have missed it...Pete, calm down...we have to call your brother and sister."

"And tell them about Julia?"

"No, well...I don't know...First, we have to get your Mom more help. After today, I see the situation is out of control."

"We can't just leave that goddam bastard here alone either...what a fuckin' mess." Pete grips the railing on the deck tightly. He feels a pain shooting down his left arm and can't catch his breath. He turns towards Lorraine.

She notices he is sweating heavily and swaying, and she steps toward him. She reaches out, thinking to steady him just as his eyes roll back and his head droops. Lorraine sees her husband's knees wobble, his body going limp as he collapses onto the concrete patio.

She shouts into the house, "Pop! Pop! Call 911! Get out of your goddam room!"

Bobbie wakes up and sees Pete lying on the patio. She watches Enzo open the sliding glass door, and Lorraine runs in to open the front door. She shouts, "Why is Pete sleeping on the patio?"

Lorraine runs back out to the patio and puts her ear to his chest as paramedics sweep into the condo.

"Step back, everyone, please." The first paramedic pushes Enzo and Lorraine aside, and she speaks to Pete, who is moving his leg a little. "Sir, are you in pain?"

Pete lifts his hand to say yes, but can't speak.

Another paramedic dashes in with a gurney, a medical bag, and a portable EKG machine.

"Okay, sir, you're going to be okay. You might be having a heart attack. I'm going to place an aspirin under your tongue. Try to chew it."

There is a flurry of activity, machines beeping, oxygen and Pete is on the way out through the front door into the ambulance within five minutes.

Lorraine looks at Pete being driven away, then her in-laws in the doorway. She doesn't know what to do; she can't leave them like this. Lorraine decides to get them in the car with her and drive to the hospital. On the way, she calls Pete Jr.'s house.

His wife, Chelsea, answers the phone.

"Chelsea, Chelsea…is Petey there?"

"No, he's at a baseball game with the kids. What's wrong?"

Lorraine realizes she doesn't have time to start going down the list of relatives to call. "Okay, well, I need you to come to the hospital, St. Vincent's…they are taking Pete there. It looks like he had a heart attack…I have Mom and Pop with me…You need to come get them."

"Oh my God! Oh my God! I'll be right there…oh my God!" Chelsea, hopping on one foot, puts on one shoe then the other as she talks. She is out of the house in a minute and on the phone, trying to reach her husband. He doesn't answer, so she speed dials her sisters-in-law, and the message spreads through the family like wildfire.

51

Pandora's Other Box

Bella quickly emerges from behind the pillar leading into the sunroom.

"Grams, what happened, what happened...who was that lady? Who's Gracie?" She furiously taps on the laptop keyboard, trying to rejoin the meeting, but the connection is hopelessly fractured.

Julia sits planted on the couch, stunned. Barely noticing Bella, she gasps for air.

Sam tells Bella to run into the kitchen and get a glass of water for Julia. Bella is back in ten seconds with water sloshing above the rim. He takes the glass and puts it up to Julia's lips. "Here, take a sip...you're okay. Everything is going to be okay...take a deep breath...there you go...Bella, maybe you should go get your mother."

Julia chokes on the water. "No! No, don't bother Andrea...I'm fine, fine...just give me a minute."

"Are you sure? You look a little pale." Sam is staring at her intently.

"Yeah, Grams. Mr. Testa is right...you don't look too good."

Julia puts the glass down on the end table and stands up. "Under no circumstances bother your mother...and I thought you were studying, Bella."

"I was going to, but...."

"Never mind, that's not important." Julia turns to Sam. "Was that Enzo's wife?"

"Yes. Bobbie...I don't know what she was doing there." Sam is as confused as Julia and looks at Bella. "Who is Gracie?"

"Bella, go up to your room for a while, hon, please just for a bit, no hiding behind the door...I have to talk to Mr. Testa alone."

Bella is scared enough to listen and runs up the stairs to her room. When Julia hears the door close, she answers Sam's question. "Gracie was my mother."

"Your mother?"

"The sound of my voice on the phone, once I got older, would sometimes make my Aunt Rosie cry...she missed my mother so much. I thought she was over-sentimental...maybe not."

"You have that little rasp. It's well...distinctive ...but Bobbie has dementia...how would she remember that?"

"I don't know...but she did...my God, do you realize what this means?"

"Wow, his wife's friend...I would never imagine Enzo doing something like that. None of this makes any sense...wow." Sam shakes his head and lets out a loud sigh.

Andrea has been standing at the bottom of the staircase, listening. She walks into the room. "People with dementia lose their short-term memory first, but for many, their earliest memories stay intact for a long time. It's all very confusing for everyone."

"Oh, Andi...what are you doing up? You're supposed to be resting."

"Resting, Mom...not staying in bed all day...remember what we said about protecting each other from the truth?"

"Yes, but, Andi...How long have you been standing there? This is too much for you!"

"Long enough...Mom, I know you...you feel guilty now. You've done nothing wrong...absolutely nothing."

"Maybe not...but I had envisioned this beautiful family portrait. Instead, I feel like the damn lonely screamer in that Edvard Munch painting."

Andrea sighs at her mother's words. "It's very possible it's not what you think."

"Yes, Julia. Andrea is right. Listen...let me call Pete in a few hours after things settle down. I'll find out what happened."

"Oh, Sam...I don't want to get you mixed up in this mess."

"It's not a mess...it's a misunderstanding. Let me help. I spent most of my life straightening things out between people."

Hearing her mother's voice, Bella shouts from upstairs, "Can I come down now?"

Andrea calls back, "Yes, Bella."

Bella runs down the staircase, sits next to Julia, and hugs her tightly. She says the words she rehearsed in her room, "You know Grams…you have us. We love you. Do you really need anyone else?"

52

You Have to Eat

Lorraine manages to get her in-laws into the Emergency Room, and they sit down on the hard plastic chairs. She walks up to the reception desk to ask about Pete. The woman at the desk, barely an adult, tells her to wait until a nurse comes out to get her.

"Can't you tell me how he is? Is he breathing?"

"You'll have to wait. I'm sorry...just take a seat. Someone from admissions will want your insurance information first."

Lorraine paces the waiting area, where her father-in-law comforts Bobbie who is crying. The sight brings tears to her eyes. She can't understand what he did years ago, but she can understand this -- despite all the imperfections that this day has brought to light.

As Lorraine passes the front doors, Chelsea arrives at the emergency room entrance. She will have to explain what happened in as little detail as possible for now. Lorraine walks up to the admission desk one more time to ask about Pete's condition, and again she is given the same answer, "Sit down, please, and wait."

Chelsea runs up to Lorraine. "Mom, what's happening? How is Dad?"

"I don't know. No one will tell me anything. He was moving a little when they wheeled him out. Everything happened so fast."

"I couldn't reach Petey…but I called as many people as I could on the way over. Do you want me to take Poppa and Nonna home?"

"No, can you take them to your house?"

Enzo stands up. "I'm staying…take Bobbie."

Lorraine answers, "Pop, are you sure? This could be a long time…just sitting here waiting."

Enzo is adamant. "No, this whole thing is my goddam fault. I'm staying."

Chelsea watches this conversation. "What happened?"

"Pete just got riled up…you know how he gets. He stepped outside, and boom, he fell over on the patio. Thank God an ambulance is always parked close to the condos."

Lorraine is saved from further explanation as a line of relatives pours through the Emergency Room door. Her second-oldest son, Pete's brother and sister, their spouses, and the cousins that live nearby all arrive in a panic. In less than an hour, the Russos have taken over the waiting room. Another cousin comes with a bag of subs from Jimmy Johns and a box of coffee from Dunkin' Donuts. The decibel level rises in the waiting room. Soon, waxed paper smeared with mayo, coffee creamers, sugar, and little stirring sticks are strewn on all the tables in the waiting room. One daughter-in-law picks up the trash and stuffs it into a plastic bag.

A nurse, in a blue cap and scrubs, finally emerges from behind the pneumatic doors that lead to the patient treatment area. "Is there a Mrs. Russo here?"

She surveys the crowd. "Oh my…I didn't know this was a picnic area."

Lorraine rushes out from between Pete's sister and brother. "Yes, yes…I'm here! How is he?"

"Come on in. You can bring one other person."

Lorraine takes her father-in-law's hand. "C'mon, Pop, let's go."

Enzo struggles to keep up. They arrive in a wider space with glass-paned rooms, and she pushes open a door across from the nurses' station.

Pete is sitting up in bed with an oxygen mask on. He pulls it to the side. "Hey, I gave you a little scare, didn't I?"

Lorraine starts to cry and hugs him as a doctor walks in.

"Mr. and Mrs. Russo, and…" she gestures towards Enzo.

Lorraine steps in. "This is Pete's father, Enzo."

"You're a doctor?"

"Yes, sir…I'm a doctor…a real doctor." She tries not to react to this question that older men ask her daily. "Mr. Russo, you're a lucky man. The EMTs got there quickly and were able to stabilize you. Unfortunately, you had a minor heart attack."

"It didn't feel minor…it hurt like hell."

"I'm sure it did. We'll need a few follow-up tests to determine if you need additional treatment. So, we're going to admit you. Plan on being here a day or so."

"Oh, thank God!" Lorraine collapses into the chair next to the bed.

"I understand there's a crowd outside for you. Once you're in a room, just two visitors at a time…but you need to rest."

Lorraine smiles. "I'll give them the news. They'll go home after they hear Pete is okay."

"It's a good thing. So many people care about you. Mr. Russo…you're a lucky man. Take this as a warning, so you stick around for them."

After the doctor leaves, Enzo approaches his son. "You scared the shit out of me, Pete."

"Hey Pop, I scared the shit out of myself."

They both laugh, and Enzo embraces his son. "I'm sorry I caused all this."

"Oh, Pop, my doctor told me last year to lose weight. Cut down the booze. I didn't listen…It's not your fault."

"If I didn't get everyone so upset, this would have never happened."

Lorraine steps up to the bed and puts her arm around Enzo. "Pop, let's forget about all this for now and go tell everyone that Pete is going to be okay."

As she leads Enzo out of the room, he leans in confidentially. "Yeah, let's forget about it…do you think there's any sandwiches left?"

"Yeah, Pop, come on…let's get you something to eat."

53

What Now?

The day started with so much expectation but is now shattered by false hope. Julia, Sam, and Andrea quietly watch Bella close up her laptop and push it into a backpack. Bella's cotton blouse sparks as it grazes Julia's sweater in the dry stagnant air. They drift from the sunroom to the kitchen table and nibble on the leftovers from lunch. Wimpy pickles curl limp in their hands, bread is crusted over, the salad is soggy with vinegar. It seems like everything has gone in the wrong direction. After a while, Bella excuses herself and heads back to her room to text Artie. After getting up several times to look out the window for Phil, Andrea goes into her office to finish some patient notes. Julia and Sam are left alone at the table, seeking each other silently.

Julia puts her coffee cup down. "Maybe I should go home."

"Let me drive you. You've had a rough day." He reaches for her hand and holds it softly.

"That sounds inviting, but how would you get your car?"

"I can take the train back. We're right near the station...or better yet, I'll try the Uber account my son set up for me. You really had a shock this afternoon...let me do this one thing for you."

"What about your dog?"

"Oh, Yogi? I met this great kid, Aidan, working at the vet's office. He's watching the dog today...I can just text him; I'll be late...no worries."

Julia rolls an olive around on her plate. "Well, I don't want to bother Andrea, and God knows where Phil is...but...."

"But, what?" Sam's voice is filled with expectancy.

"Nothing...maybe we can go for a walk when we get there. I always feel better getting a little fresh air. It clears my head."

Sam stands up and brushes the crumbs from his lap. "Me too. Come on, why don't we say our goodbyes and get you home?"

Julia calls up to Bella, and she slides half her body out the bedroom door and waves. She is on the phone with Artie and giggles as she closes the door. Andrea thanks Sam profusely and returns to her work after kissing Julia. It is late afternoon, and the sun breaks through cumulus clouds casting shadows on the lawn. Sam takes Julia's car keys, opens the passenger door for her, and squeezes into the driver's seat.

Sam's knees are scrunched against the steering wheel. "I hope this seat goes back...a lot!"

For the first time this afternoon, Julia smiles. "Welcome to my clown car."

Sam takes his time to adjust all the mirrors and checks for the location of the turn signal and lights. She studies his careful movements, how he's deliberate about everything he does. As they glide onto the highway, she whispers, "I dreamed about you. Your eyes are the same."

Sam doesn't turn his head. He is afraid of being overwhelmed and stares forward. He inches his right hand closer to hers. "I've been dreaming about you for months now…well, not you, I didn't know it was you, but it is you…it's so hard to explain."

"It's like we've been tumbling down some vortex towards each other."

"Yes, I don't understand what is happening."

"Do you hear it too? The vibrations?"

"Yes."

They decide to wait until the car is parked safely in her driveway to continue talking. It is too much to take in while navigating through the traffic. The only words Julia speaks after this revelation are "19th Avenue across from the park."

Sam knows the way instinctively. In the driveway, he runs around the car to open the door for her. She reaches out to take his hand. "How did you know for sure?"

"When you put your note on the table…your handwriting…those little curls on the ends of the letters. That's when I knew it was you."

"What a strange thing to remember after all these years."

"I know…I used to sit next to you and watch you write…but I couldn't remember your name…just these…I don't know how to describe it…visions…and dreams."

"Let's go for a walk."

They cross the street and walk hand in hand along the metal railing that runs against the East River. The sun forms low, narrow rays as it seeps between the buildings in Manhattan. They stop to look across the water at the skyline. Julia is always pensive when she sees this view at sunset.

Julia turns to face Sam. "I'm afraid to want this."

He reaches out and draws her close to him. "Tell me what you dreamed…please, Julia."

Julia starts to walk again and wipes her eyes with his handkerchief. "I was on a swing, and when I jumped off, there was this little boy with hazel eyes, the same ones as yours, reaching out to me."

"I dreamed of you on the swing too…and this music…but I couldn't make any sense of it until Lorraine showed me your photo. That's when something inside told me I had to meet you."

"But your name, Sammy? I didn't remember that at all."

"My real name is Anselmo. Only my family called me Sammy. After college, when I was looking for a teaching job, I changed it to Sam, you know…more *American*."

"Oh my, Anselmo is a beautiful name…you would think I would have remembered that." Julia shakes her head and draws her palms up against her face. "Everything is so complicated."

"I know, I know…but maybe this, what's happened between us, doesn't have to be."

"You don't know me now…you remember that innocent little girl."

"Let's go back to your house and talk. Come on, we'll order a pizza and catch up on the past fifty or sixty years."

Julia smiles broadly and turns around to head back to her house. "Is pizza going to solve everything?"

"Well, I've seen it work miracles at teacher meetings."

"I hope the Russos are eating pizza then."

"They probably are…let's worry about that tomorrow."

Julia sees the sparkle and the creasing in the corners of Sam's eyes. She's surprised to feel love, trying to make itself comfortable in her closed-off heart again. Only a few hours ago, she'd been sitting next to Sam on the couch when Bella had asked, "Do you really need anyone else?" She reflects on how naturally they all seem to fit together, like a puzzle that was just solved. A thought reveals itself. "Maybe this is all I need."

* * *

Early the following morning, Andrea looks out the window and notices a silver Toyota parked across the street, a red ticket under the wiper. Overnight parking is not permitted in this exclusive neighborhood. She tries to remember what car Mr. Testa had been driving and can't.

When Phil comes downstairs at seven, she asks him, "Did you see Mr. Testa come back and get his car last night?"

"No, but I don't know what kind of car he was driving."

"There's a Toyota across the street with a parking ticket on it."

"Oh, Andrea, that's impossible. You've gone as crackers as your mother now."

"Have I?"

54

Once Upon a Mattress

Light is pouring into the room through the spaces in the curtains. Julia squints at the clock next to the bed. It is eight-thirty. She feels the weight of Sam's arm around her waist. Her hand is entwined in his. The stark light of day ushers in a new reality. She is afraid to move.

Last night started with a slice of pizza and a bottle of red wine. For a long time, they sat in her kitchen and talked about their present-day lives. Sam scrolled through photos of his grandsons on his phone, careful to omit the ones with Angie in the frame. Julia showed him her studio at the back of the house. There were canvasses lined up along the floor of paintings she was working on.

Sam studied each painting carefully. "These flowers are surreal...the colors...how do you do that?"

"You can't make a flower more beautiful than it already is, so I try to change them, make them into something you still recognize but not exactly what they are...does that make sense?"

"Kind of like the way you add a little curl to your letters." He smiled.

They went into the living room, sat next to each other on the couch, and Sam poured them a second glass of wine. Julia didn't turn on the lamp next to her as the sun set but lit the lavender-scented candle she kept on the coffee table. Her rose quartz necklace sparkled in the light from the flame, and Sam reached out to touch it.

"This is beautiful, like you."

She drew him closer. Every touch between them sparked desire. Julia could hardly remember feeling so deeply for someone. It had been so long since her first husband died. After her failed second marriage, she banished any thought of romance. Love was reserved for her family. But the night moved on as if being together was preordained. She couldn't believe it when she said, "Let's see if we fit better in my bed."

* * *

As Julia was replaying the night and questioning what she had done, Sam tightened his grip around her waist and kissed the back of her neck. She didn't turn around.

"Sam, maybe you should go get your car."

Sam could feel the muscles in Julia's body tense. "I will. Are you alright?"

"I guess I just shocked myself when I opened my eyes this morning."

"What do you mean?"

"I never do this sort of thing. I'm not a loose woman, although right now, it looks like maybe I am."

"Oh, that makes two of us...I really never did this sort of thing, I mean never."

"Not even in college?"

"No, I was engaged."

"Oh my, I've corrupted you...." Julia faces Sam and caresses his cheek. "Seriously, this is so sudden. I don't know if I can do this."

Sam leans in and kisses her. "I'm sorry, listen...let's get up and talk. This is strange for me too...but I haven't felt this way in a long time...I mean so close to someone."

Julia burrows her head in his shoulder. "This frightens me."

"Hey, I'd never hurt you, never."

"No, I believe you...you wouldn't...I'm not so sure about the universe."

Julia gets out of bed, and Sam watches her put on her bathrobe, trying to hide her naked body from him. He waits for her to leave the room, puts on his clothes from the floor next to the bed, and then follows her into the kitchen.

Julia makes coffee and takes out a package of Stella D'oro cookies. He sits down at the table, still barefoot.

"I hope you weren't expecting me to make breakfast like some girl in a Neil Simon movie."

"No...this is fine. Just being here is well...wonderful."

"Please...don't get your hopes up...I don't think I can do this...it's oh my, too good to be true."

Sam is quiet for a moment debating if he should say anything. "Julia, I think I know what you're afraid of...I had a phone call from your friend Linda the other day."

"Linda? Why would she call you?"

"That's a good question...she was one of Angie's friends,...well, church friends."

"You didn't answer the question, Sam." Julia sets her cup down with a clunk.

Sam puts his head down. "She called to *warn* me about you...I hung up on her."

"Linda? She's been one of my best friends forever. What could she warn you about?"

"Some of the things that happened to you...that's why I'm telling you this...I mean..." Sam looks down and brushes imaginary crumbs back and forth on the table. "Things don't always have to end bad...this could work."

"But what did she say about me exactly?"

"That you were troubled...nothing like my wife...be careful...that kind of thing."

Julia picks up a cookie and bites down hard, crunching it angrily. "Jesus Christ...Miss Nothing Bad has ever happened to her in her life! Miss Fucking Perfect!"

"Julia, don't be upset...I want you to know that I understand why you're afraid."

She stands up. "Sam, I don't know how much Linda told you in her little phone call...but you can't even begin to understand."

Sam is surprised by her anger but not put off. He acknowledges her pain and stays planted in his chair.

Julia slams the cabinet door shut and leans over the counter, breathing heavily. Her face is red. "Sam, maybe you should leave."

He gets up, pushes his chair in, and starts to walk away until something in him snaps. He pivots and moves back toward Julia, arms outstretched to enfold her, reassure her, keep her safe. "No, I'm not leaving you like this."

Her eyes fill with tears. "No, go…go, Sam…Linda is right…I'll end up your worst nightmare."

Sam embraces her, and she shudders in his arms. Her breathing slows, and she quiets in the warmth of his body pressing against her. They stand melded together in the middle of the kitchen until Julia tries to push away.

Sam whispers in her ear, "Julia, didn't the universe bring us together?"

55

Meanwhile, Back in Florida

Lorraine guides Enzo through the halls back to the waiting room. A crowd of relatives surrounds them, and she waves them back. "Pete's fine! He had a little heart attack…he's going to be okay!"

"Thank God! Jesus, Mary, and Joseph, he had us scared, that son-of-a-bitch," one of Pete's cousins shouts.

"You can all go. They want him to rest."

Enzo spies several sandwiches neatly piled on an end table and grabs one, sitting down to take a bite. He nods as various relatives stop by and express their good wishes for Pete's recovery as they take their leave.

Pete Jr., who just arrived, makes a beeline toward his mother and hugs her. "Thank God, Mom. I think I drove ninety miles an hour to get here. Can I see him?"

"Yes, Petey, go ahead in. Take your Uncle Jim in with you. Then can you take Pop to your house? Chelsea took Bobbie there."

"Yeah, sure, Mom…what about everyone else here?"

Pete's cousin, Dom, overhears the conversation and winks at Lorraine. He shouts to the dispersing crowd, "Hey, everyone come over to my house. I'll order pizza. Bring your bathing suits!"

Lorraine is relieved that someone else will orchestrate the post-hospital gathering, "Thanks, Dom. Maybe I'll stop by later."

"Yeah, Lorraine. Don't worry about anything…I'll take care of this crowd."

One by one the relatives come up to Lorraine and kiss her before they leave. Her sister-in-law, Tina, sits by her side as the room empties.

"I'll stay with you, Lorraine. You can't be alone all night."

"What about your husband?"

"He can go over to Dom's. I'm sure Johnny would rather be there than here."

"Well, ya' know…I could use the company. It's been a long day."

"What on earth happened over at Pop's?"

"Your mother…we have to talk about that…well, she was shouting things, and everything got out of hand. You know your brother…he got himself all worked up, and it was so hot out…oh, I don't know."

"Poor Mom…I've been trying to ignore her little incidents, but we have to do something."

"Yeah, she's not herself anymore."

"I know...I'm having trouble accepting it. She was a fire-cracker in her day...now look at her. Can't even figure out what shoe goes on what foot."

"It's too much for Pop to handle anymore."

"Yeah...oh, look, here comes Petey and Jim."

"Petey, go ahead home with Pop now...maybe you could all go over to Dom's."

"Maybe, Mom...Pop looks pretty beat." Enzo is slumped over in his chair, sleeping with the wrapper from his sandwich in his lap.

"Well, you decide. I'll call you later, and we'll figure out what to do with Pop and Nonna. Maybe bring them to my house."

"Why can't they go home?"

"I'll explain later...Aunt Tina and I are going to go stay with your father now."

"Okay, call me if you need anything else."

* * *

Everyone starts to arrive at Dom's house by five-thirty. No one comes empty-handed. Gina and Paul bring their homemade soppressata, Anna holds a tray of pastries, Vinny has four loaves of bread tucked under his arm, a bag full of olive containers, and two family-size bags of potato chips. There's a pasta salad in a giant aluminum pan from the deli that delivered the pizza. Cousin Paul looks at it. "Mayonnaise on pasta. See Dom...this is what's wrong with the world."

Lorraine and Pete's son, Little Enzo, arrive with his family, takes fifteen folding chairs out of his minivan's back, and sets them up on the lawn. Dom yells at him, "Put them on the patio!

You see that Paul…what kind of landscaper is he? He's killing the grass!"

All the adults find a seat, fill their plates with food and watch as the children jump into the pool. Then the conversations and conjecture begin. Cousins, aunts, uncles spin the afternoon's events into a web of misinformation. Words fly down the line of relatives in a game of telephone.

"What were Pete and Lorraine doing over there on a Sunday afternoon? Don't they go to see the grandchildren every Sunday?"

"Where was Petey?"

"Why did Chelsea rush Bobbie out of the hospital like that? She must have been sick."

"Where's Big Enzo?… Hey Little Enzo! Where's your grandparents?"

"Did Lorraine tell anyone that Pete had a heart condition?"

"He has to eat healthy living with Lorraine. She's a cracker counter."

"What's a cracker counter?"

"You know she looks at the calories on the box and then takes five out and nibbles on them for an hour."

"No wonder she is so thin. How did she let Pete get so fat?"

"He sneaks food at the club. Have you gone with him? He calls it his hamburger paradise."

"Who was that guy at his house last week?"

"I think it was Lorraine's boyfriend from high school."

"C'mon, Pete wouldn't let him in the house."

"Hey, Little Enzo…who was that guy staying at your parent's house?"

"Some guy from New York, an old friend. I don't really remember him."

"Did you know your dad had heart trouble?"

"No, nobody tells me anything! Ask Petey."

"Look, here comes Chelsea and Petey with Bobbie and Enzo."

"Why's Enzo in a suit? Was he at a funeral?"

Chelsea helps her children get their shoes and tee shirts off so they can join their cousins in the pool. Pete Jr. walks his grandfather over to sit with Dom and Paul and his grandmother to sit with her younger sister, Carmella, who moved to Florida a few years before her.

"Bobbie, what happened?"

"I don't know, Carm. They said Pete is in the hospital."

Carmella tries rephrasing the question. "I know but, why did they take Pete to the hospital?"

"I can't remember Carm. You know me."

"Yeah, yeah…don't worry about Pete. He's going to be fine."

"Is Nino here?"

"No, Bobbie, he's gone."

"Where did he go?"

"Out somewhere." Carmella decides not to remind Bobbie that their brother died three years ago. "Remember our old neighborhood, Bobbie? Now, look at us, living like millionaires."

"I was just talking to my friend Gracie. She called me on the phone."

"Gracie? Yeah, I remember her. She was so beautiful…but she had that *cornuta* for a boyfriend."

"What did she say?"

"Something about that."

"About what?"

"That boyfriend...Where's Pete?"

Carmella keeps trying to have a coherent conversation with Bobbie but finally gives up. She is kind and patient with her older sister but still mourns the loss of her once vibrant confidante. Bobbie stares at the children playing in the pool. Carmella vaguely remembers Gracie visiting her family's house, but there is one memory from her sister's bridal shower that stands out. Gracie's husband refused to come in to get her when the party was over. He leaned on the car horn until she frantically ran out. After the screen door slammed, Bobbie advised Carmella, "Never marry a man who doesn't come to the door."

Carmella carefully stacks an assortment of food on paper plates, and they sit down next to Chelsea. Bobbie starts to eat and loses interest in what is going on around her.

"Chelsea, what happened this afternoon?"

"Oh, Aunt Carm, what a day! Petey took the kids to a game. I thought I'd have the whole afternoon to myself."

Carmella pulls her folding chair closer to Chelsea.

Chelsea is glad to be talking with someone she considers an ally in this big family. She checks on her children then continues, "Lorraine called me and said I had to come to the hospital right away to pick up Enzo and Bobbie. I don't know what happened over at their house, but something is just not right,"

"What do you mean?"

"Well, Enzo, you know Big Enzo, said at the hospital, it's all his fault...then he shut up like a clam."

"They must have had a fight. You know how Enzo picks on your father-in-law all the time."

"I don't know...maybe...well, then after I brought Bobbie home, she kept on asking for this woman, Gracie. I don't know any Gracie, do you?"

"Bobbie was just saying she talked to her on the phone this morning. She's an old friend from the neighborhood...but I know Bobbie hasn't seen her in a million years."

"I don't understand how her mind works anymore. It's so sad."

"I know...God forbid if that happens to me...no one will remember anything about the old days and the family."

"Well, Aunt Carm, funny you should say that. That's the other thing...we went out with Petey's parents for his birthday, and this thing came up with our family tree. Lorraine just shut me down when I asked about it." Chelsea crosses her arms and lets out a pouty sigh.

"Oh well...who knows what that was about.... I hope Pete is okay. He has to take care of my sister."

"Yeah, but Aunt Carm...do you think I should ask Lorraine about it again?"

"Maybe when things calm down...I could ask her for you...I have to talk to her about Bobbie."

"Yeah, we have to do something about her...she's too much for one person to handle...thanks...I just feel like something is going on that they're not telling us."

56

Bedside Manners

Pete has finally been transferred out of the Emergency Room. Lorraine and Tina take the elevator up to the cardiology floor and step out into a cacophony of beeping. Both women carry cups of coffee in their hands and a look of resignation on their faces.

Tina waits outside the door to Pete's room. "Do you want to go in alone first, Lorraine?"

Lorraine wants to say yes, but instead says, "No, come on in with me."

Pete is lying in bed attached to wires and an I.V. looking uncomfortable in his hospital gown. "Here come my two favorite girls."

Tina maneuvers through all the wires and tubes to hug and kiss her oldest brother. "You gave us all a good scare."

"Sorry, Sis, maybe next time I want to see you, I'll just call."

Tina is relieved to hear Pete sounding like himself. "Everyone is at Dom's house. I don't know how there can be a party without you."

"Well, at least it's not for my funeral."

"Honey…don't talk like that!" Lorraine cringes at the thought of life without Pete.

Tina sits down next to him. "What did Pop say to you to get you so upset?"

"It wasn't Pop."

"It's always, Pop…you two need to cut this out."

"Yeah, yeah…I need to go on a diet, that's all."

Lorraine sees the conversation is going in the wrong direction. She doesn't want Pete to relive the scene from earlier in the day. "Maybe we should go on a little vacation, maybe New York, when you're feeling better."

Before Pete can respond, Tina starts peppering him with questions again. "I heard your friend Sam was here…how was he?"

"Good…man, I should follow him around and eat what he eats. He still looks like he could play ball."

Lorraine sits down on the opposite side of the bed and takes her husband's hand. "We'll get you back in shape…don't worry…like the doctor said, this was a warning."

Tina stands up and picks up the little booklet on the nightstand. "Look, Pete…it says right here that you have to eliminate stress. See, I'm right about you and Pop."

"You're stressing me out talking about Pop. He's never going to change."

"But you can…Don't let him get under your skin."

"I'm telling you, Tina, it wasn't Pop!"

Tina backs away from the bed. "Okay, okay…don't let me upset you now."

Lorraine looks at her husband. "Hey, …you look tired…why don't you close your eyes for a little while…Tina and I can go down the hall. There's a nice new visitor's lounge."

Pete thinks he knows what Lorraine has in mind but is too tired to argue. He closes his eyes.

"Do you think we should leave him, Lorraine?"

"Yeah, he'll be fine…we'll just be down the hall. I have something I wanted to talk to you about."

"You mean Mom?"

"Yes, but something else, too."

Pete is snoring by the time Lorraine and Tina leave the room.

The two women find a quiet corner of the visitor's lounge, a brand new space with soft leather chairs, a cathedral ceiling, and long windows looking out at tall palm trees that border a manicured lawn. A small snack bar offers baskets of apples and bananas for sale.

Tina looks around at the posh surroundings. "When did they build this? It's like a hotel lobby in here."

"Last year…Pete and the boys donated some of the landscaping…who would ever think we would be staring at it from in here…my God, what a day."

"Are you okay, Lorraine? You need me to get you anything?"

"No, I'm fine…just worried about Pete. He was supposed to start taking something for his cholesterol last year, but he kept saying he didn't need it. I should've put my foot down."

"Don't blame yourself. He's stubborn… always taking care of everyone except himself."

"I know."

There is a pause in the conversation. Tina checks her cell phone for messages. "Johnny says there's quite a crowd at Dom's house."

"Ask him if Mom and Pop are there."

Tina gets a quick response. "Yes, they're eating."

"Okay, good. I guess Petey and Chelsea decided to go over. Your mother was probably too much for Chelsea to handle alone."

"So…what happened over there this afternoon?"

Lorraine looks down and wrings her hands, then slumps into the deep cushions of a nearby chair.

Tina is surprised to see her sister-in-law anxious. She is the stalwart of the family. Tina has never seen her so frazzled.

Lorraine looks up and away. "I don't know how to tell you this."

Tina's heart starts beating fast and she breaks out in a hot flash. "You're not sick, Lorraine, are you?"

"No, no…Tina. What you said about stress was right…we should've told everyone when we found out."

"Found out what? What…what are you talking about?" Tina's black curly hair flops over her eyes as she leans forward, and she pushes it off her face.

Lorraine blurts out, "Your father had an affair when your parents were practically newlyweds, and you have a sister!"

"Pop? No way! And a sister? C'mon, Lorraine…that's ridiculous." Tina feels sweat trickle down her back as Lorraine pulls her cell phone out of her purse.

Lorraine pushes the photo under Tina's nose. "No, it's not. It's for real."

Tina recognizes the hair that won't stay tamed, dark eyes, and the way her lip dips down in the corner, same as her own. There is no doubt that she is looking at someone who could be her older sister. "I think I'm going to have a heart attack!"

"I can't keep this secret anymore…it's going to destroy Pete and me if we try to keep this to ourselves any longer."

Tina holds Lorraine's phone and studies the photo. She runs images through her mind of her parents' seemingly happy marriage: the family picnics, laughing around the kitchen table at dinner time, the fiftieth wedding anniversary party. And the way her father never loses his patience with Mom now that she isn't well. He's devoted to her in every way.

"Lorraine, how do you know this is true? Maybe it's his brother's daughter. Uncle Tony was not such a nice guy…really awful."

"No, she's his daughter. She found him on the ancestry site. They matched…you all matched. Remember we did that family tree thing about two years ago?"

"Did Pop know? I mean, did he admit to this?"

"No…he never knew about his daughter, but he admitted to an affair."

"I still can't believe this whole thing. What the hell?"

"I know, but what makes it worse was that she was one of your mother's friends."

"Did he admit to that?"

"No, not until this afternoon when your mother...well, I don't know how it's even possible...she heard the call we were making in the kitchen. She was in the family room with the television turned up loud."

"Wait...you spoke to this woman today?"

"Yes. Her name is Julia."

Tina's mind is spinning, trying to process the information that Lorraine has burdened her with. The cell phone drops out of her hand, and she grips the arms of the chair to steady herself. She keeps repeating, "This can't be true."

"Tina...listen, your mother came running into the kitchen when she overheard Julia's voice yelling, 'Gracie, Gracie.' That's Julia's mother's name. Your father turned beet red and yelled to turn it off. One of us slammed the laptop shut...I don't even remember who."

"So, what happened?"

"Pop ran into his room and locked the door...wouldn't come out...Pete was sweating like crazy trying to get them calmed down, and he went out on the patio. Next thing I know, he is flat on his back moaning."

"So, it was stress...why didn't you tell us?"

"It was too much of a shock. Pete wanted to tell everyone, but I convinced him to wait."

"Wait for what?"

"Pop didn't want anyone to know. I thought if we could ease him into it, then he would be okay telling everyone. I had no idea it was your mother's friend...we really didn't see that coming."

"Damn Catholic guilt. He must be so embarrassed. For all we know, my mother knew and forgave him...but we will never know, will we?"

"That poor woman, Julia. I have to call her back."

"Does she know about Pete's heart attack?"

"No, all she knows is we hung up on her very abruptly."

"Do you think she heard Mom?"

"Yeah...I think so."

"What are you going to tell her?"

Lorraine shrugs her shoulders. The weight of today's events has been too much for her to bear. She can't make a decision.

Tina's inner voice pulls her out of this muddied conversation. Suddenly, with crystal clear clarity she sees what needs to be done.

"Lorraine...maybe you did do the right thing, not telling everyone. I mean, what's it going to help knowing something like that with Mom sick? Listen, this woman hasn't known any of this her whole life...maybe she can wait a while longer. We have to take care of Mom now...that's enough for one family to worry about."

Lorraine is relieved to hear Tina approves of her decision. "You mean call her and explain that it's not a good time?"

"Exactly. I don't think Pop needs to dredge up his past either. Let him keep his dignity...I mean, he's over ninety...I've read about these ancestry tests unearthing things better kept quiet, but I never thought it could happen to us. My God."

"I don't know...if you spoke to Julia, you could tell she was a good person. We sent Sam to meet her. He said she was lovely...I don't know."

"Let Sam have her then...we don't need any more relatives...we have enough troubles with our own."

"Maybe you're right."

"No, maybe about it...we have to protect ourselves. Who really knows what she wants."

"You sound like your brother now."

57

Crossed Signals

Lorraine and Tina take turns sleeping on the reclining chair in Pete's hospital room. Nurses filter in and out every hour in the twilight glow of the monitors. At daybreak, Lorraine finally convinces her sister-in-law to go home and get some rest. She waits until one of her sons arrives to run home to take a shower. Meanwhile, she tries to sleep a little more.

Weary from the constant disturbances, Pete drifts in and out of sleep. He is half awake when his sister leaves and a little confused. Now Pete watches Lorraine sleeping on the chair opposite him. Her mouth is slightly open, making tiny whispers. Suddenly, yesterday comes back to him in a blunt thud. A wave of guilt washes over him, and he vows to shape up.

A nurse enters the room, accidentally bumping into Lorraine's chair. "Sorry, sorry...how are you this morning Mr. Russo?"

"Hungry!"

"That's good. On a scale from one to ten, what is your pain level?"

"Two for physical, ten for mental."

"We do have counseling services if you're interested," the nurse quickly adds as she leaves the room after recording his vitals.

"She doesn't get your sense of humor, Pete."

"I'm not joking...I'm wiped out."

"I know, honey...Tina and I talked last night."

"You told her, didn't you?"

"Yes...I couldn't lie to your sister."

"I know, I know."

"Well, for everyone's peace of mind, we kind of decided to put this whole thing on hold for now. Tina promised to keep it to herself until we figure out what to do."

"Yeah...you know, I think that's the right thing to do after seeing how upset Pop was and Mom getting so riled up. He's going to be lying in the bed next to me if this keeps up."

"I think I'll go home and take a shower...then call Sam. I won't be gone long. Petey is coming to stay with you. I'll leave when he gets here."

"I can be alone for a little while. I'm not some damn baby...why don't you go ahead?"

"No...I'll wait."

"Okay, boss...but I'm fine. I promise to eat egg whites for breakfast if that's what you're worried about."

"Turkey bacon?" Lorraine fixes the blankets on Pete's bed and combs back his hair, checking to see if he is feverish.

"Come on...that's torture now...next, you'll make me eat avocado toast," Pete laughs.

"Look...Petey just texted me...he's on the way. I'm going to fill out this menu for you and drop it off at the nurse's station and then go."

"Yeah, yeah, okay. I don't have my reading glasses anyway."

Lorraine checks off the boxes on the heart-healthy menu and then kisses Pete goodbye. "I'll be back in a few hours...listen to the nurses."

Petey arrives as his father is looking down at his breakfast tray of berries and a cup of plain non-fat yogurt. "I might as well be dead if I have to eat this shit."

"Dad, come on...man up...it's just yogurt."

"Yeah, you're right...it's just fuckin' yogurt...I got more to worry about than this."

"What do you mean?"

* * *

Lorraine drives home in a daze. She drops her purse on the floor in the kitchen and looks at the pool. How good it would feel to swim in the warm water. Instead, she heads to the shower and stands under the hot water for a long time, lost in thought. As she steps out, she realizes it's Monday morning and she was supposed to substitute teach today. Dripping wet, she grabs a towel and picks up her phone to call the school and apologize, but it starts ringing. It's Sam calling.

Lorraine hesitates. She hasn't rehearsed what she is going to say but then answers anyway. "Hello, Sam."

"Hey, Lorraine…is everything okay there? Pete didn't pick up…I didn't call back right away…figured you needed some time."

Lorraine holds her towel close to her body. She feels guilty about what she hasn't said yet. "Well, Sam…it's a…things didn't turn out quite as we planned yesterday."

"I guess that's an understatement, huh?"

"Is Julia with you?"

"She is, actually…right in the next room."

"Where are you?"

"Her house." Sam evades telling the whole truth. "Thought it would be best to call you from here since I'm sure you want to speak to her."

"Oh, Sam…I'm sorry I dragged you into this."

"Hey, it's okay…where's Pete, anyway?"

"First…did Julia hear Bobbie shouting Gracie?" Lorraine sits down and crosses her legs.

Sam lowers his voice to a whisper. "Yeah, she did…put two and two together. It still doesn't make any sense to her."

"I promise you, we had no idea! Bobbie's memory is so erratic…and we didn't mean for her to overhear the conversation…really, what a mess."

"No one's blaming you guys."

"It was so upsetting for everyone…especially Pete."

"I bet…so, can I talk to Pete?"

"Well, I was getting to that…he's fine, now…but like I said, he got really upset with his father yesterday, and well…he had a heart attack…not a bad one…."

"What?" Sam is shocked into silence.

"Not ten minutes after we hung up, he collapsed on the patio, the ambulance came, they whisked him into the Cath Lab, put in one stent, and he was back in the ER sitting up in bed…it all happened so fast."

"Oh, geez…that's…wow, unbelievable…is he okay?"

"He's worn out, but the doctor said he should make a complete recovery…he'll be in the hospital for a day or so for observation. But, you know…well, Julia seems wonderful and all," Lorraine pauses. Sam can hear the bad news telegraph in the empty space. "But, I think we have to put this whole thing on hold."

Sam cringes at Lorraine's decision. "She's right here…do you want to tell her yourself?"

"No…no…you tell her Sam…I'm really overwhelmed about now."

"But, she'll understand…I'm sure she will."

"No, no…we'll call… well, I don't know when…but not for a while. We have to get things straightened out here. You know Bobbie needs some extra care…I don't know…we just have a lot to figure out."

"I get it…you have a lot on your plate right now…but I think it would be the right thing to do if you spoke to Julia directly."

"No, I can't," and with those final words, Lorraine ends the call.

* * *

Sam knows Julia is expectantly waiting on the other side of the door. He knows she did not anticipate good news, but this denial adds one more disappointment to a cascade of trouble. His head swells with an instant headache. The last time he had one like this was the night after Angie died. He stands up and quietly turns the doorknob, trying not to appear shaken.

Julia studies his face. "Sam, you're so pale."

He is still barefoot and suddenly feels an urgent need to put on his shoes and socks and leave. Even Sam, who has handled everything for everyone throughout his life, feels like running for the door. But he knows he can't do that to Julia. He doesn't want to hold a truth that will hurt her.

"I'm okay." Sam sits down at the kitchen table and gets his bearings. "Is there any more coffee?"

"Yes...you look like you saw a ghost. What did Pete say?"

"Well, there's no easy way to say this...but after they hung up, Pete had a heart attack...he's in the hospital."

"Oh my God! No!" Julia leans her head down and massages her temples. "Is he going to be all right?"

"Yes, Lorraine said it was a mild one."

"This whole thing is turning into a nightmare...it's my fault."

Sam can see Julia begin to spiral down like she did earlier this morning. "Julia, no...no...how can this be your fault? You're an innocent bystander in all this."

"Am I? Someone gave me the *malocchio* the day I was born...trouble follows me."

"The evil eye? You don't believe that do you?"

"How else can I explain everything? Or is it just me...I'm the trouble."

"Sometimes there isn't a good explanation."

"You sound like my therapist now."

Julia watches Sam drink his coffee and looks down at his bare feet. There is something so innocent about him sitting there, trying to find the good in everything. A part of her wants to believe him. She closes her eyes and breathes deeply, re-centering herself. "Sam, why didn't they want to talk to me?"

Sam doesn't answer right away but pretends to look for something in his pocket. "Look, Julia...I don't know. Lorraine is having a hard time. She said they will call when things settle down."

"I feel so terrible...maybe I should send flowers or call later in the week."

"No...maybe you should give them some space for now."

"They're shutting me out, abandoning me, aren't they, Sam?"

"Maybe temporarily...."

"No, I know...it's the story of my life."

Sam doesn't know what to say. He feels the defeat in Julia's voice. Some unknown part of him knows what she was saying is true. He can't save her from the harsh reality. They sit there silently drinking coffee until she speaks. "Maybe I really should drive you to get your car. You probably have a ticket."

"That's okay. Do you want me to come back here?"

Julia has an appointment with Dr. Blanding this afternoon. She doesn't want to share that information with Sam, so she tells a white lie. "I have a meeting this afternoon about a commission...some little project."

"Oh...well, hey, I can Uber there if you don't have time."

"No, no...it's actually on my way."

Sam rises to finish getting dressed and turns to Julia. "Maybe I can call you later?"

"Yes, Sam...we'll talk later."

Rush hour is over, and the drive to Andrea's house goes quickly. The easy banter of their first meeting is replaced by uncertainty. There are no unpleasantries, just awkward silences. Julia pulls up next to Sam's car, and he squeezes her hand. She lifts his hand to her cheek and holds it close for a moment. He reluctantly opens the car door and walks over to his car. Andrea is at the kitchen window watching.

58

The Doctor is In

Julia's phone rings as soon as she is two blocks from Andrea's house. She doesn't pick up and, at the next red light, listens to her voicemail. "Mom, I know you can hear the phone. I just saw you drive past my house and drop off Mr. Testa. What was that about? Remember, I'm home resting…call me."

Julia doesn't call back but continues to Dr. Blanding's office. There is too much to explain, and she needs to work through the past twenty-four hours before talking to anyone about anything. The weekend events have swung from high to low. On the elevator, up to the office, she wonders why she feels so calm. Her usual anxiety level is dialed way down. She thinks, "How can anything be wrong if I don't feel bad? Something's not right."

Dr. Blanding is in her usual chair, and Julia sits down and smiles at her. "Beautiful day, isn't it?"

Martina is taken aback by Julia's demeanor. "Yes, I think spring has actually arrived. Well, it's been two weeks since

303

I've seen you…how has it been, going a little longer between sessions?"

"Maybe we need to switch to on-demand." Julia smiles again.

"That would work in a perfect world, but we both know that doesn't exist."

Julia crosses her legs and twists her scarf between her fingers. "Well, my world's been turned upside down…but I think I like this side better."

"What do you mean by that?"

Julia rambles, dramatically articulating each phrase. "Okay, well, I found out that Andrea is having twins, the man who is my biological father was married to my mother's best friend, my biological half-brother, Pete, had a heart attack yesterday, and remember I told you about that little boy I loved in elementary school?"

"Yes, of course."

"I slept with him last night, oh and he's Pete's best friend, and my best friend Linda tried to sabotage me ….besides that, I ate a lot of pizza."

"First of all, is your brother going to be alright?"

"Yes… he's supposed to make a full recovery. But…it seems like they don't want to have anything to do with me anyway."

"This is all a lot to take in…where do you want to start?"

"I don't know. I'm so serene right now…something is wrong. I was so upset this weekend with the *other* family thing not working out as I imagined, but right now, I feel indifferent…un-bothered about it."

"Why…what happened that made you feel that way?"

"I don't know…Is pizza an anti-depressant?"

Stunned by Julia's giddy disposition, Martina stands up and walks around to her desk to look at Julia from another angle. She fears she is missing something in Julia's visual clues.

"Julia, are you sure you're feeling okay, stable?"

Julia giggles. "Yes…I mean half of what happened was really terrible, but the other things were kind of remarkable. It's like I put the fun back in tragedy."

"What do you feel were the remarkable things?"

"I'm going to be a grandmother to twins this summer. Andrea tried so hard to have another child for so long. Now out of nowhere, without all those shots and specialists…well, it's a minor miracle."

"Yes, it gives you something to look forward to, and that's so important to your well-being."

"The other thing…well, Sam…I haven't been with a man since the divorce. God, I'm surprised everything still worked…oh, you're too young to worry about that…but, I don't regret it at all. I hope I didn't scare him away."

"Scare him away? How?"

"I panicked a little this morning about starting a relationship…and I told him I wasn't sure I could handle it."

"Do you want to continue seeing him?"

"Yes…do you know Sam went out and backed my car out the driveway this morning while I was getting dressed? I mentioned in passing how much I hate to do it because the driveway is so narrow. I scratched my car the other day… he listens. I can't tell you how comforting that is…those little things when someone cares about you."

Julia cusps her hands around her face and rubs it. "But, Sam being best friends with my half-brother... complicates things, doesn't it?"

"Did he ask for a commitment? Or mention anything about Pete okaying the relationship?"

"No, of course not."

"Is there anything else holding you back?"

Julia wrings her hands. "Guilt...guilt about having strong feelings for this man. Feelings like I had for my first husband, Mike."

"Didn't you have strong feelings for your second husband?"

"Not in the same way, I was taken in by his flattery...made a fool of by him because I wasn't honest with myself. I was lonely. I turned out to be his golden ticket... I ignored the credit card bills, his excuses for everything."

"Are you afraid that will happen to you with Sam?"

"No...I know...you're going to ask me then what am I afraid of."

"Do you have an answer?"

"Losing him."

"What do you mean, Julia?"

"That's the trajectory of my life, isn't it? Losing the people I'm close to...my mother, my real brother, my cousin Tony...Mike... All of them tragic...even my half-brother, Pete, had a heart attack after meeting me. ... It's like I've turned loss into an art form."

"But not your daughter or granddaughter, even your son-in-law."

"No, no...don't even say that."

"But, it's the truth, Julia…you're a survivor. Guilt about that can hold you back. If you recognize it, sometimes you can move forward more easily. Not without a struggle, but maybe with acceptance."

"But why don't I feel more anxious right now?"

"Maybe because you're finding yourself focusing on the good things in your life…you said it when we first started the session…you like the flip side of the world."

"Yes…and I'm floating in a sea of mixed emotions…but not enough to drag me all the way down."

"Don't be afraid to feel those emotions, Julia…but give yourself the chance to accept the love people are offering to you…don't run away from it, don't feel guilty about it."

"Easier said than done…but what should I do about my other family in Florida that doesn't want anything to do with me now?"

"Let it play out…be disappointed, but it's out of your control right now. We all want a definitive solution to our problems. But life isn't like mathematics…it's fuzzy logic."

Julia gets up and stares out the window. "Bella said something to me this weekend that keeps playing over and over in my mind…aren't we enough?"

"She's perceptive for a teenager."

"She is." Julia's gaze returns to the room and, for the first time, she realizes what the little embroidered sign on Dr. Blanding's wall really means. She reads it aloud. "Survival is a beautiful thing."

"It is Julia…I understand it's a struggle to get there. It means different things to different people…and in your case, not only the physical implications but the emotional ones."

"I don't know if I can face Sam again…he's seen every side of me this weekend…I'm sure I don't measure up to his wife…that's what my so-called friend, Linda, implied to him."

"So she passed away?"

"Yes, almost two years ago."

"I'm sure he has some guilt, too…maybe you two need to have an honest conversation."

"You mean instead of sitting here talking to you about it?"

"Yes, listen, Julia…look at yourself. You've had an incredibly rough week. It's only natural to be feeling stunned, a bit disconnected emotionally. But, I see someone who has changed…someone who is…I think the best word would be well-balanced."

"Oh, I'm an acrobat, now?"

Martina smiles broadly. "Yes…you seem to be able to juggle all this at once."

"I don't know…I lost it a couple of times this weekend…in front of Sam."

"Feeling strong emotions is not abnormal…look, you rebounded. You are going to work it out. Focus on the positives."

"You're right…a few months ago, I would still be in bed in my sweat pants drinking chocolate syrup from a shot glass."

"That's quite an image…I can't even picture you like that."

"Believe it…it wasn't a pretty sight…so do I have a plan then?"

"Yes, call this Sam…talk to him. Enjoy your family right here in New York…be ready for your Florida relations to call you someday but don't sit around waiting…and call me if you need me."

"Shouldn't I come in two weeks?"

"No, I believe we actually are on an as-needed plan now if you're comfortable with that."

"You know, I think I am."

Julia strides out of the office with new confidence as Martina watches. She isn't the angry resistant woman who first walked through the door. Martina would have liked to take credit for Julia's turnaround, but she knows that it was mostly Julia's own doing. A determination to be there for her daughter and granddaughter. It is as if Julia looked in the mirror, saw a portrait painting, and critiqued it. She saw her flaws and imperfections and set out to correct them.

Julia sits in her car a long time before driving away. Martina has helped her see her life from a new perspective. She never shared with Martina the pulsing sounds and visions of her mother that she heard over the past months. The only one she can really talk to about that is waiting for her to call.

59

Loose Ends

Julia stays in her car and makes three phone calls. The first one is to her friend Linda. Linda is in her garden, starting to weed her flower bed. She brushes the dirt off her hands and answers her cell phone.

"Hello, Julia…are you calling to go for lunch? It's kind of late…coffee?"

"No, Linda…I'm calling to say I forgive you."

"Forgive me? Forgive me for what?" Linda stands up as guilt gathers into a knot in her throat.

"I think you know."

It doesn't take more than a moment for Linda to cave. "Oh, Julia…I did it to protect you as much as to protect Sam. He needs a different type of woman…his wife, Angie, was practically a saint."

"And who am I? Cruella de Vil?"

"No, no...I didn't mean it like that...you're too...you know...you."

"He's a grown man, Linda. He can decide who is right for him.... it's not your concern."

"Oh, Julia...I'm sorry, I'm so sorry...I just didn't want to see you hurt again."

Julia can almost see Linda's tears staining her face. She softens. "Please, Linda, just give us a chance...I really wished you talked to me first. You don't know the whole story."

"You're right...I've been kicking myself all week about it. I didn't have the guts to call you and tell you what I did."

"Look, maybe next week we can get together...just trust me on this, please."

"Yes. Yes...let's do that."

"Honestly, Linda...you put up with a lot of bullshit from me this year, so I owe you one...let's call it even now. I don't want to lose you...we've been friends for so long."

"Thank you, Julia...yes, we have been through it all, haven't we?"

Julia smiles and hangs up, then dials her daughter. Andrea is watching her favorite cook on the television and wonders how she seems so happy all the time. She hopes some of that positive energy will rub off on her while she sits and worries about her mother.

"Mom...where have you been? I called over an hour ago."

"Andrea, I do have things to do...I'm not on call 24/7, as you like to say."

"Oh, Mom...why did you drive Mr. Testa home this morning?"

"Are you spying on me now?"

"Stop! I thought we were going to be honest with each other."

"I said that before I knew you were planning to keep tabs on me."

"For real, Mom…you know I was worried about you after yesterday."

"Honestly, there's nothing to worry about…It got late last night, and he stayed over."

"What do you mean stayed over?"

"On the couch."

"Bella said he had a thing for you."

"Well, Bella is right…he's a wonderful man."

"Mom, really?"

"Why not? Maybe I can work out a grandfather for those babies."

"Oh, Mom!"

"Andrea…stop worrying…I'm fine. I really am. What are you doing anyway?"

"Watching a cooking show."

"Well, go back to your show and relax. The world isn't ending…do you need me to do anything?"

"No…but what happened with the Russos? Did anyone call back?"

"They put it on hold. A lot is going on down there. I guess we will have to wait for them to be ready to talk."

"And you're okay with that?

"I am, honestly I am. Let's concentrate on those babies, Andrea. Look, I have to call Sam. I promised I would this afternoon."

"Wait until Bella hears this…my goodness…. Did you talk to your therapist about this?"

"Yes…she's fine with it…and she released me on my own recognizance. Hey…if you don't need me…I really have to make that call."

Andrea watches the rest of the show but can't remember anything that the chef said but the sound of her laughter. She finds herself smiling when she gets up to check out what is in the refrigerator and decides to make something fun for dinner.

The last call is the hardest one. Julia starts the engine, rolls up the windows, and turns on the air conditioner. Sam is walking Yogi when his cell phone rings. He turns around immediately and quickly starts to walk home as he answers the phone.

"Julia…Julia, how are you? Did you get that commission?"

Julia forgot that she had told that little white lie earlier and hesitates. "Oh, no…she was looking for something else, I guess."

"That's too bad. I don't know how anyone would turn one of your paintings down."

"You'd be surprised, Sam…listen, do you want to meet somewhere this afternoon?"

Sam can tell there is a change in Julia's voice from earlier today. "Sure…as long as you feel up to it."

"Yes, it's such a beautiful day, so warm out…do you want to walk somewhere?"

"Where are you…are you far from Meadowbrook Parkway?"

"No, just a few minutes away."

"Do you want to meet at Jones Beach? It's empty this time of year."

"Oh, that's a lovely idea…it will be cooler there too. It's so unusually hot today. It's not even Easter yet."

"Great, meet me at Parking Lot One…I'll wait for you by the entrance to the tunnel to the beach…do you know where that is?"

"Doesn't everyone?"

***

Sam is standing by his trunk holding two beach chairs when she arrives. Julia wraps her scarf around her hair, puts on a pair of large sunglasses rimmed in bright blue, and then steps out of her car. Sam runs over to meet her.

"You look like a movie star, Julia."

She realizes she is giggling like a teenage girl. They walk through the tunnel to the beach and call out ridiculous curse words just to hear them echo like two adolescents. By the time they emerge, they are doubled over in laughter.

"Oh, Sam…what's wrong with us?"

"Nothing…I am just so relieved you called me. I was sure you were calling to end it."

"No…I'm sorry about this morning. Everything is all so new, confusing. And I have been so selfish…not thinking that you have your own issues to deal with."

Sam is touched by the concern Julia has for him. He had been afraid to admit to her that he too was struggling with his new feelings for her.

"Well, yeah…I guess I'm on a bit of a guilt trip."

"We wouldn't be Catholic without guilt," Julia pushes into Sam, and they both laugh, understanding exactly what she is talking about.

They walk the curvy concrete path to the boardwalk with smiles on their faces and stop at the railing to look out at the ocean.

"Can you smell that, Julia? The salt air?"

"Yes, we used to drive to Sunken Meadow Park on Sundays when I was young. And just before you reached the crest of the hill where you could see the water, there was that wonderful wall of air, the smell of the ocean. It was my favorite part of driving to the beach."

"You know, in Florida, the ocean doesn't have a scent. It's so strange…at first you don't know what's missing." Sam hopes that Julia will say something about the Russos, but she remains quiet and starts to walk down towards the water.

They reach the sand, roll up their pant legs, and pop off their shoes. Hand-in-hand they walk down the beach to an isolated spot and set up their chairs in the warm white sand.

Sam pulls his baseball cap out of his back pocket and puts it on. "Do you want to sit for a while?"

"Yes…let's talk…you know the truth of it is we hardly know each other."

"I know…we have over half a century to catch up on."

"My God, when you say it like that, Sam, it sounds like we are a couple of dinosaurs."

"Or Fred and Wilma?"

They both laugh and stay quiet for a moment. She reaches for his hand, and they sit there staring at the ocean, listening to seagulls, the small waves brushing against the shoreline. She closes her eyes and feels as though she is in a sanctuary, removed from all the noise in her life.

What Sam said just a few minutes ago returns to Julia, and she starts to wind her way back to finishing her thought about the Russos and Florida.

"I don't think I could ever live in a place where it's always summer."

"Yeah, it's a different mindset...I don't think I could ever leave New York."

"No, me neither...well, Andrea needs me now too."

"You're lucky to have her close to you. I wish my kids stayed here, but well, they have their jobs, lives to live...."

"Maybe they'll move back someday."

"I doubt it...but you never know...."

"Speaking about Florida...I'm so sorry you got stuck in the middle of all this thing with Pete and his family."

"I'm not...I never would have found you again if it wasn't for Pete."

"I decided to sit and wait for them to contact me...if they ever do...I don't see what other option I have."

"Don't give up, Julia...Pete really wanted to meet you. His father, I mean your father too...is a salt of the earth kind of guy.... but like you said, Catholic guilt gets a death grip on you sometimes. Maybe it will work out."

"Maybe...but it's like what you said about the ocean; something is missing...I know they are there, but I don't feel an urgency anymore to know them. It's hard to explain."

"You seem so calm, Julia...are you sure you're alright?"

"Andrea asked me the same thing…really, how could I not be? Do you want to go for that walk now?"

Sam and Julia head to the shoreline, where the sand is wet and flat. The water is still frigid, and they run when a larger wave bubbles up close to them. There are a handful of other beach walkers heading towards them. Sam keeps his eye out for Gloria or any of that group of women even though he knows they walk in the early morning hours. Finally, he relaxes when they pass by the last person on the beach.

"Julia, I have to tell you something," Sam stares down at his feet as he speaks. "I know it sounds crazy, but I have been dreaming about you for over a year, and…well, I felt terrible about it…not about you, but about my wife, Angie. I mean, I really loved her…and I miss her every day."

"Sam, I know…after Mike, my first husband died, I stayed single for over twenty years. I couldn't bring myself to love anyone else…to be open to it anyway. I think I waited so long I forgot what love really was."

"But you married again."

"Yes, to a fool. I was so lonely, Andrea was married…busy, all my cousins moved to the west coast. I let myself be taken in…I was tired of being alone… it was a time in my life when I wasn't making very good decisions."

"Hindsight is perfect…isn't it?"

"Yes, if only we had a crystal ball."

"Maybe we do now…There's something so odd in how we met again…it's like it was always meant to be."

"Our second chance, Sam?"

"Yeah, it almost felt like Angie was telling me it's okay last week…just a strange feeling."

"My mother visited me…Andrea said it was the sleeping pills, but oh, it felt so real."

"We really are a couple of ghostbusters or something."

"Whatever it is…maybe this is our second chance, Sam."

"I hope so."

60

True Confessions

Lorraine spends Monday morning packing enough clothes for her mother-in-law to stay temporarily with her and Pete. Bobbie is in her lounge chair watching television, and Enzo is busy making scrambled eggs and toast in the kitchen. The smell of melting butter wafts through the condo. He has become more and more self-sufficient as Bobbie's memory falters, and Enzo actually enjoys his new domestic tasks.

Although Enzo is over ninety years old, he has a quick mind and stays active. He still owns a car to drive short distances. It is hard for him to accept that he can't drive a golf ball over one hundred yards anymore and has to take a cart instead of walking, but he persists and plays twice a week in the senior league. Despite being fit for his age, he knows Lorraine and his daughter Tina are right. As hard as he tries, he can't take care of Bobbie alone anymore. The past few weeks have been difficult, and it finally culminated on Sunday afternoon in full view of

Lorraine and Pete. Her outburst about Gracie was evidence of how disoriented she has become.

Lorraine comes out of the room with Bobbie's suitcase. "Pop, so you understand the plan, don't you?"

"Yeah...I stay with you during the day, and at night I come back here to sleep."

"You could stay with us too, you know."

"No, I don't want to leave this place empty. Besides, I can't sleep good away from my own bed."

"Okay, Pop, it's your choice. It's just until we figure out a better plan. We have that meeting with the social worker at the hospital next week. She's going to go over our options."

"We're not locking her up in a nursing home." Enzo is adamant. "I get the final say, not someone who doesn't know us."

"Of course, Enzo...don't get upset now...we'll do the right thing for Mom."

Enzo puts Bobbie's breakfast on a plate, opens the kitchen door, and places it on the snack table next to Bobbie.

"Bobbie, look...I made the eggs the way you like them. C'mon, eat."

"Okay, Enzo...what time is it?"

"Nine o'clock."

Lorraine watches as Enzo patiently hands Bobbie her silverware and unfolds the napkin on her lap. "C'mon Bobbie, eat a little."

"Okay, what time is it?"

Enzo walks back into the kitchen. "I'm only agreeing to this because I think your house is the only other place where she feels at home."

"I know, Pop, I know…maybe we can get her back here with an aide…let's just listen to what the social worker says…Are you ready to go soon?"

"Yeah…do you want any eggs?" Enzo stands with the frying pan in his hand, mindlessly scraping at the crust of the eggs with a spatula.

"No thanks. You know this is for the best, don't you?"

Enzo throws the frying pan into the sink with a little bit too much force. "Yeah…but I made a vow to take care of Bobbie in sickness and health."

"Oh, Pop…this is taking care of her, really it is."

* * *

Lorraine leads Bobbie into the guest room near the front of the house and away from the pool. They spend a long time unpacking the suitcase. Lorraine has Bobbie help her sort her clothes and then uses masking tape to write down what is in each drawer.

"See, Bobbie, here are your socks."

Bobbie sits down on the edge of the bed and looks around. "Why am I here?"

"Just a little vacation, that's all. You know it's Easter this Sunday. I thought you'd like to be here with the kids and all."

"Easter, already?"

"Yes, Bobbie…see, look at this nice outfit you have to wear."

"Yes, it's nice…is it mine?"

Enzo waits out in the kitchen. He sits on a high-top chair at the marble island and runs his hand along the smooth, silky top. The phone, a pile of magazines and mail, is next to him, and he casually starts to look through the papers. He finds a scrap of paper with Julia's telephone number crinkled up under the electric bill. He takes it and shoves it into his pocket, then goes to look in the refrigerator for something to eat. A small bowl of strawberries is at eye level, and he takes them out and brings them by the pool, where he quietly eats.

* * *

Pete is coming home from the hospital Wednesday morning. His discharge papers have a long list of dietary restrictions and a physical therapy schedule. His sister, Tina, drives to the house to stay with her mother while Lorraine picks up Pete at the hospital. Enzo plans to come over after his senior league golf game. Instead of going to Pete's house after the game, Enzo heads to our Lady of Perpetual Sorrow for twelve o'clock mass. It is a small church only a mile away from their condo development on the main road through town. Pete and Lorraine always take him and Bobbie to the cathedral on the other side of town. Enzo had promised everyone that he wouldn't drive outside of his neighborhood anymore, but he wants to pray alone, in peace, that he makes the right decision for Bobbie. The prospect of living apart for the rest of their lives frightens him.

The mass is short without music. There are less than twenty people there. After the closing prayer, the priest announces, "Since this is Holy Week, I am holding confession right after mass," he laughs, "You can beat the crowds later in the week."

Enzo studies the priest. He is young and so different from the harsh ones he remembers from his earlier days. The ones who had belittled him and pounded their fists when he confessed to saying a bad word or lying to his mother. He has done his best to avoid confession over the years except for the times Bobbie forced him to go with her. It is almost as if a voice is whispering to him, "Enzo, go…this is your chance."

The priest enters the confessional, and no one lines up. Enzo hesitates but feels maybe he can step inside since this parish still had confession like he remembered from the olden days, no face-to-face conversations in a conference room. Enzo walks over and pushes the dark curtain of the confessional aside. He notices a bench against the wall instead of a kneeler and thinks to himself, *This is a church for old guys like me.*

"Bless me father for I have sinned; it's been, well, a long time since my last confession."

"That's fine. I'm glad you chose to be here today."

Enzo is shocked by the priest not admonishing him and relaxes a little.

"Well, uh, well, I have lied in confession…many times."

"That's okay…it must be something that has troubled you for a long time."

Enzo is caught off-guard by the priest's reaction and starts to stumble on his words. "I only came to, uh…pray for my wife today…she can't remember things anymore."

"I'm sorry to hear that. I'll pray for her too…but what else is troubling you?"

"I never confessed my worst sin…I should go straight to hell for it."

"No one goes straight to hell…and an evil man wouldn't be here in the confessional."

Enzo holds his breath for a moment and then lets the words flow. "I cheated on my wife. It was when we were first married. I stopped it…but now, I just found out I have a daughter. She called. I can't let my whole family know; my wife is sick. I don't know what to do."

"What does your heart tell you to do?"

"I want to talk to this daughter and explain…."

"Explain what?"

"It wasn't what it seems like…but, I never knew about her… I'm not that kind of guy."

"What kind of guy is that?"

"One that runs around with other women."

"First, you have to forgive yourself. We are imperfect beings…all of us."

"I can't. I caused so much trouble for my family. My son had a heart attack because of it."

"People have heart attacks for a lot of reasons…but not usually from someone else's sins. I can't tell you what to do about your family, but, nothing should stop you from a private conversation with your daughter."

"Isn't that a sin…to not tell everyone?"

"No…the sin is not being true to yourself."

"You say you never knew about this daughter?"

"Yes."

"Well, maybe she will be a blessing in your life."

"I never thought of it that way."

"Do you have any other sins to confess?"

"Yes, I yell at my oldest son too much for no damn…I mean good reason."

"You are forgiven…Go…and sin no more."

"Don't I have to say some Hail Marys or something?"

"No…I'm leaving the penance part up to you."

Enzo blesses himself, stands up by the altar, and says *The Act of Contrition.* He is still shocked at how casually the priest reacted to his sin of adultery and how easily he was forgiven. He feels a cloud lift from him and carefully drives home to put his golf clubs in his garage.

61

The Unexpected

Tina helps her mother dress and makes her breakfast. Bobbie has basked in the attention everyone has been paying to her in the last few days and is more responsive than usual. She remembers the names of Tina's children and is aware that Pete is in the hospital. Tina relaxes a little seeing her mother's improvement, and wonders if all she needs is to be around more people. After Bobbie finishes her breakfast, Tina settles her in front of the television.

"Mom, I went to the gym this morning, and I didn't have time to take a shower. So, I'm just going to go take a quick one in your bathroom."

"Okay, go ahead. Do you have clean clothes?"

"Yeah, they're in my gym bag…You'll be okay?"

"Sure…why wouldn't I be?"

Tina quickly takes her shower and peeks out at her mother. She is still in the chair watching television. Tina decides to try out the new hairdryer she just bought that straightens curly hair.

While Tina is still in the bathroom drying her hair, Pete and Lorraine arrive home from the hospital, but the house appears empty. Worried and confused, they call out, "Mom? Tina? Mommmm?"

"Where do you think they went, Pete?" Lorraine goes into the kitchen to look.

Tina pops out of her mother's room. "Hi, you're back. How are you feeling, Pete?"

"Good, where's Mom?"

"Isn't she with Lorraine?"

"No."

Tina frowns. "She was just sitting here watching TV five minutes ago."

They hear Lorraine shouting from the back of the house by the pool, "Pete! Tina! Come quick!"

Outside, they find their mother's clothes in a pile on one of the deck chairs. Bobbie is floating naked on her back in the pool, singing an old Italian folksong.

Lorraine calls to her gently, "Mom, come on out...you're going to catch a cold."

Bobbie doesn't cooperate and starts to splash. "No, I'm playing now."

Tina looks at her brother and sister-in-law, touches her newly dried straight hair, and says, "Oh shit." She jumps in the pool and tries to keep her head above water.

Pete shields his eyes from seeing a little too much of his mother. "I'm going to let you girls handle this."

Lorraine waves him away. "Yeah, you go rest, Pete."

He walks away slowly, shaking his head back and forth.

Tina curls her arm around her mother and guides her to the steps that lead out of the pool. "C'mon, Mom…it's time for lunch."

"Okay, that sounds good."

Lorraine and Tina dry Bobbie off and help her get dressed again. They bring her into the family room, and Lorraine locks the door to the pool and turns on the alarm.

"Oh my God, Lorraine…I only left her for a minute."

"It's like having a baby again, isn't it?"

Tina picks up a towel and wraps up her now wet hair. "Let's not tell Pop when he gets here."

"I don't know…maybe we should. I don't want to lie."

"We're not lying…just omitting."

"Well, maybe it will help him understand the situation better."

"No, he knows the situation. Let's not stress him out, at least for today."

* * *

Sam and Julia spend the night together. The next morning, they are in the guest bedroom at Sam's house. Sam stares at the ceiling waiting for Julia to wake up. He feels as though he is in a movie. This moment feels like young love. He asks himself, "How is this happening to me?"

Julia rolls over and nestles her head against his chest. Sam wraps his arm around her. Neither one wants to let the warmth of the bed go.

Sam whispers, "Julia, are you awake?"

"I am, but I don't want to wake up from this dream."

"Listen, I've been thinking about something."

Julia doesn't open her eyes but moves her arm over Sam's. "Is it something I want to hear?"

"I hope so…I promised my daughters that I would visit next week. The kids are on vacation after Easter…I thought maybe you would want to drive down with me."

"And meet your family…or do you plan on hiding me in a hotel?"

Sam laughs. "No, of course not …but yes, meet my family, why not? I don't want to leave you for a whole week."

"What about Easter? I'm going to be at Andrea's house."

"We can leave Monday morning…my daughters aren't expecting me until Tuesday. They are seeing their in-laws on Easter."

"I don't know, Sam…I'd have to ask Andrea."

"Why?"

"Because that's a good way to stall answering you." Julia giggles. "Well, a road trip would be exciting…we would find out if we can really stand each other."

"Oh, Julia….My daughter told me to bring one of my friends with me. She didn't want me driving alone."

"Well, I'm sure I'm not the friend she's expecting."

"No, but…I think they'll love you."

"Don't let me be a surprise. You have to warn them."

"I will…we can stay in a hotel *together* to ease the shock for them, okay?"

"Okay, let's do this…but then you have to come to Andrea's house for Easter."

"Do you have to ask Andrea about that?"

"No…I'm telling her, especially because I'm cooking with my sous chef Bella."

Later that day, Julia calls Andrea to tell her about what she has planned.

"Mom, aren't you rushing this? I mean, you hardly know this man."

"You know him…you're the one who told me how wonderful he was."

"Oh, Mom…that's different…I mean, you weren't dating him. You're acting impetuous, like a teenager, a bad one at that."

"Look, Andi…I'm getting old. I don't have time to contemplate every decision I make. This feels right."

"But, I was counting on you spending time with Bella. She's off from school, and I'm going back to work next week."

Bella hears her name mentioned from the other room. "Mom, why are you talking about me?"

"Your grandmother wants to go away to North Carolina next week with Mr. Testa."

Bella lights up. "Put the phone on speaker!"

Andrea does so without thinking and regrets it immediately.

"Grams! Grams…I have a great idea…bring me with you!"

"I don't know, Bella."

"Where's Mr. Testa?"

"He's in the other room."

"Go ask him. I can babysit his grandchildren, and he can take his daughters out to dinner. I can walk Yogi. It would be so much fun. Does his daughter have a pool?"

"Well, hold on…let me go talk to him."

Julia leaves the phone on the table and goes to ask Sam about Bella's idea.

"Sam, I know this is coming out of the blue, but Bella wants to come with us. She's off from school too. What do you think?"

He is taken a little off guard, "Well, what do you want to do? I'll do whatever you want."

"She offered to babysit and help take care of Yogi while we are there. And honestly, I think it would be good to give Andrea and Phil some alone time before the twins arrive."

"Well, okay then…besides, my daughters will love Bella."

"It won't be the romantic getaway you were planning."

"That's okay; honestly, it probably is a bad idea to stay at a hotel while we are there…I just want to be near you. Oh, and tell Bella to pack a bathing suit. My daughters have pools."

Julia kisses Sam and runs back to the phone. "If it's okay with your parents, Bella, then pack a bathing suit."

Andrea is ready to say no but concedes that maybe her daughter has a good idea. She gets back on the phone as Bella runs upstairs to start packing.

"Listen, Mom, you can't be sleeping with Mr. Testa with Bella there, separate rooms."

"Yes, of course. We will be staying with one of Sam's daughters. Bella and I can share a room."

"Well, I still think you are taking this way too fast, but I know I can't stop you. At least Bella will slow you down."

"You're right …maybe I am. But, it will be fun to take a little vacation after this dreary winter."

"Okay, Mom…we'll talk more on Sunday. I suppose Mr. Testa is coming."

"Yes, and his dog. It's a package deal."

62

Easter Weekend

Lorraine spends Saturday afternoon preparing trays of lasagna. Her sons and their families are coming for dinner after eleven o'clock mass tomorrow. The rest of the extended family is dropping by for dessert in the afternoon. Everyone plans to bring something this year instead of depending on Lorraine to cook the entire meal. Pete's heart attack is a wake-up call for the whole family. Everyone has relied on them for so long, and now, suddenly, they seem vulnerable.

After all the commotion earlier in the week, Lorraine finds assembling layers of ricotta, pasta, and sausage a relaxing diversion. She makes Pete a low-fat version, so he won't feel left out of the celebration. After some initial resistance, Pete is working hard at changing his diet. He even plans to start doing laps in the pool as soon as his cardiologist gives the okay.

Enzo busies himself doing the little chores around the house that Pete usually takes care of. Both men settle into maintaining the peace with each other. But Enzo is anxious to get Bobbie back home with him. He walks into the kitchen to talk to Lorraine after taking out the trash.

"Lorraine, why don't I bring Bobbie home tomorrow night?"

"Pop, I thought we agreed to wait until we talk to the social worker on Tuesday?"

"Yeah, but what is she going to say? How does she know what Bobbie wants?"

"I don't think that's the issue anymore."

"Isn't it? I want to do right by her."

"Oh Pop, I know this is hard…please, let's not get ahead of ourselves. C'mon, help me put the lasagna in the refrigerator. It's going to work out."

* * *

On Sunday afternoon, the rest of the family arrives in waves. They have all changed out of their church clothes and wear shorts, bright floral blouses, and flip flops. Their arms overflow with boxes of pastries, chocolates, and homemade cannoli. Pete splits one cannoli with Lorraine and then leaves the table to avoid temptation. Bobbie enjoys seeing the relatives, but by the end of the afternoon she walks around in circles repeating, "I have to go home." She turns all the doorknobs in the house in an attempt to leave.

Chelsea watches Enzo follow Bobbie around the house trying to reason with her, then saddles up next to Aunt Carm.

"Aunt Carm, did you say anything to Lorraine about what I told you?"

Carm turns around to see if anyone is listening. "Yes, I spoke to her. It's nothing. Lorraine just wants to be in charge of everything. You should know that by now."

"Yes, but what did Enzo mean at the hospital when he said it was his fault?"

"Just like Lorraine told everyone…Pete and Enzo were arguing over nothing as usual. You know how they are."

"Yes, unfortunately, I do. They seem to be acting nicer to each other today."

"Yeah, they learned their lesson the hard way. Really, Chelsea, nothing's up."

"Okay, Aunt Carm, if you say so."

Chelsea leaves to check on her children, and Carmella takes a handful of jellybeans and sits by herself for a long time, eating them one by one.

* * *

Julia and Bella are up early to start preparing their traditional Easter meal before leaving for church. Bella has eaten two chocolate Cadbury eggs before eight o'clock and thrown the wrappers out in the bathroom, so her mother won't know.

"Bella, you're not going to fool your mother. She probably counted those eggs before putting them in that basket."

"Grams, she's not that OCD. What do you want me to do?"

"Peel some garlic for the leg of lamb…Are you packed?"

"Yes, two bathing suits. So I always have a dry one."

Phil walks into the kitchen already dressed for church and grabs one of the chocolate eggs. "Bella, when your mother notices the missing eggs, blame your grandmother."

"Very funny, Phil. Do you want a slice of chocolate bacon to go with that?"

"That would be spot on. Wouldn't it?"

"That's really gross, Dad."

"To you maybe...look, I'm off to the bakery in Garden City to pick up our order before the crowd. It's the only place where they have decent hot cross buns."

"I hope you ordered some Italian pastries too, Dad."

"Of course, especially with, you know, Mr. Wonderful, coming for dinner."

Phil heads out to the garage, and Bella turns to Julia. "Grams, don't listen to him...he is wonderful."

"Thanks....I think we have time to make the pesto for the lasagna...get the basil over there on the counter."

Bella buries her nose in the handful of leaves. "This is the best smell in the world."

"Are you sure you're alright with me seeing Mr. Testa?"

"Grams, I know this sounds crazy...but every time he came over to our house, I thought I heard this music...not out loud like on a radio, but a melody playing in my head. Don't tell Mom. She'll make me see the school psychologist."

Julia is taken aback by Bella's admission. "I won't tell her...because I really saw a ghost."

"Maybe it's just because we have good imaginations. Do you think so, Grams?"

"That has to be it. So...you like him then?"

"Oh yeah, definitely."

They hear Andrea walking down the stairs and go back to cooking talk. She has on a muumuu and is beginning to look very pregnant. She holds the railing to keep herself balanced.

"Who ate the chocolate eggs for breakfast?"

"Dad!" Julia and Bella secretly smile at each other.

They leisurely finish up all the prep work in the kitchen, put the lamb in the oven, and then go upstairs to get dressed for church. In front of the house by the purple hydrangea bushes, the four of them gather for a family picture. Andrea and Julia beam in their swing-style linen dresses and matching flats. Bella wiggles on her high heels on the soft grass while Phil towers next to her in his light blue button-down shirt and tie.

Sam arrives by ten-thirty, and they all drive to Easter mass together. Bella's classmates recognize Mr. Testa. A few popular girls rush up to her and ask in their friendliest voices, "Why's he with your family?"

Bella beams with pride. "He's my grandmother's boyfriend….and I'm going on vacation with them."

The day sails by seamlessly. It's as if they have been a family unit for years. Artie comes by later in the day to say goodbye to Bella. They leave to go for a walk.

Sam stays a little longer and has one more cup of coffee. "I have to finish packing, so I'll pick you and Bella up around seven?" He leaves the itinerary on the table for Andrea and Phil. "In case you need us for anything."

As Sam leaves, Phil, Andrea, and Julia stand by the door to wave goodbye. Andrea puts her arm around her mother. "You know, Mom, he's such a thoughtful man…it does feel right."

Phil chimes in, "Yes, a true prince."

63

Ambushed

Tuesday morning arrives in Florida with thunderstorms on the horizon. Enzo did not sleep well last night worrying about this meeting with the social worker. He is groggy, so he drinks an extra cup of coffee and then hurries to get ready. Lorraine, Tina, and Bobbie's sister Carmella plan to pick him up at ten o'clock. Everyone agrees that it would be best for Pete to stay home.

Lorraine, dressed sharply, arrives right on time and rings the bell. Enzo opens the door wide and is surprised to see Bobbie in the back seat of the car.

"Bobbie is coming? You didn't tell me that."

"Yes, the social worker spoke with her yesterday and thought she should be part of the discussion."

"How come no one told me the social worker was going to talk to her?"

"You had your golf league. We didn't want you to miss it. And, you know Bobbie is more with it in the morning."

Enzo tries to hide his agitation. He doesn't want to upset Bobbie, so he doesn't press the point and gets into the car.

They arrive at the doctor's office building adjacent to the hospital and head towards a conference room. A middle-aged woman in a sundress, rubbery sandals, and a long necklace made out of shells greets them at the door.

"Welcome, everyone, just take a seat...anywhere. Hello, Bobbie, how are you?"

"Good, do I know you?"

"I'm Estelle, your social worker."

"Oh, yeah, yeah...Enzo told me."

Enzo knows Bobbie is faking it since he has never met this woman. He feels a profound sadness that he can't begin to explain. Estelle starts the meeting with several brochures of assisted living facilities with steps up to memory care.

"This one is only a mile away from your condo. It's beautiful. See this lovely dining room, you'll never have to cook. A beauty salon and all sorts of communal activities."

Enzo is puzzled. "What about me?"

"Oh, Mr. Russo, you would move in there with Bobbie. And then if you or Bobbie needs to *step up*, everything is right there to care for you."

Lorraine and Tina look down and remain quiet. Carmella looks grim.

"I thought we could get help at our condo?"

Estelle leans in sympathetically. "Mr. Russo…that just isn't practical at this stage. You want the best for your wife, don't you?"

Enzo turns to Bobbie. "Honey, do you like these places? Is it what you want?"

"I want to go home." Bobbie has the frightened look of not understanding. "The green house."

Enzo realizes she means their home on Long Island, where they lived for fifty years. He starts to break down and excuses himself saying, "I need some air."

Carmella follows him into the hall. "Enzo, you owe her this."

He is holding in tears. "Owe her what? Don't you think I am going to take care of my wife?"

"Taken care of like she deserves. Especially for what she's been through all these years."

"What are you talking about?"

Carmella stands in front of him and looks straight into his eyes. "She knew…she knew about you and Grace all these years. She kept it a secret to protect you. To protect the family."

Enzo looks through Carmella as what she just told him settles into his mind. Then, suddenly, he asks, "She knew about the girl?"

"Yes, she knew everything."

He is overwhelmed with feelings of confusion and betrayal. His whole life is swirling around in his head. He feels dizzy and leans against the wall.

Carmella presses him. She is fiercely protective of her only remaining sibling. "If you really love my sister, you will do what she did…keep it to yourself."

"But Lorraine and Pete know."

"Lorraine will take care of Pete. We talked about it yesterday."

"How could Bobbie know I had a daughter and not tell me?"

Seeing Enzo's obvious distress Carmella speaks more compassionately. "She didn't want you to leave her and the children."

"I never would have…I broke it off."

"We all agree the best thing for the family is to keep this quiet. Look what happened to Pete because of it. Tina doesn't want her children to know."

Enzo contemplates what Carmella just said but then is struck with a new fear. "I know…but what if Bobbie remembers now?"

"That part of her memory is long gone…and no one would believe her anymore if she did say something."

"Does the social worker know?"

"Of course not…. Look, Enzo, Bobbie forgave you a long time ago and put it behind her."

Enzo speaks in a whisper. "I guess everyone wants me to take this to my grave, huh?"

Carmella nods and touches his elbow. "C'mon, let's go back in."

"Just give me a few minutes."

Carmella walks back into the conference room and closes the door. "He'll be back in a few minutes. Just needed some fresh air."

Enzo walks outside. The tops of the clouds are growing higher and grayer. Thunder is in the distance. For a fraction of a moment, he wishes he would be struck by lightning and put an end to it all. This was not how he thought his final years on Earth would be…. dragged down by the unintended consequences of one unfortunate decision. He takes a deep breath and forces himself back inside to face his reality.

Enzo sees the reflection of the storm clouds in the glass doors. He opens them slowly, walks back to the conference room, sits down next to Bobbie, and takes her hand. "Okay, we can move there, but I get to keep my car."

64

Southern Pines

Sam arrives precisely at seven o'clock and leaves the car running in the driveway with Yogi in the back seat sleeping in his crate.

"Everyone ready? We might have a little rush hour traffic on the Belt Parkway, but after we get over the Verrazano, it'll be clear sailing."

"Mr. Testa, how long is it going to take to get there?"

"Nine or ten hours, it all depends…if we stop a lot."

Julia has her suitcase by the door and a small cooler. She hands Sam a cup of coffee in a disposable paper cup. "I packed us some sandwiches and drinks. This will save us from those greasy fries and burgers at the rest stops."

"Grams…that's part of the fun."

Sam smiles, remembering that Angie always packed their lunch. It was part of their tradition when they took road trips.

Oddly, it is comforting for Sam to put another red Igloo cooler into the trunk.

Andrea and Phil left for work earlier this morning, so Julia locks the door, and they all settle into the car. Yogi wakes up and wags his tail at Bella. She reaches in and pets him. "He looks like a stuffed animal, so cute…can I take him out?"

"For a little while, sure…but he can get wild in the car."

Bella puts Yogi on her lap, and he snuggles up to her and falls right back to sleep.

"Yogi's a good judge of character, Bella…I guess we'll keep you." Sam laughs as he looks at Julia.

They crawl through traffic until they finally reach the Verrazano Bridge. Bella sits up to peek over the railings and spots the Statue of Liberty in the distance. By the time they are in New Jersey, she and Yogi are quietly sleeping.

"Sam, it's really so nice of you to take Bella with us…did you talk to your daughters?"

"Yes…they're a little surprised but are happy about it. They're probably googling you right now, though."

"Oh…well, I think I only have a paper trail. But, I promise to be on my best behavior."

"Just be yourself…I hope you like a lot of commotion. My grandsons are, well, the nice way to put it is active."

"It will be a new experience for me, but Bella was a handful when she was younger…climbing on everything."

"Good, then you won't be in shock when they start jumping out of trees. It drove Angie crazy…oh, I didn't mean to mention her."

"Sam, it's fine…really. We shouldn't be afraid to talk about our past. It is what it is…there's no denying it. Don't you think this week proved that when people hide things from one another, it's a recipe for disaster?"

He nods, "You're right, you're absolutely right."

"Then is there anything you want to tell me? Does Yogi have a puppy somewhere?" she teases him.

"Oh, Julia…Since I met you, I haven't laughed so much in my life."

"It makes up for all my drama, I hope."

Sam reaches over and takes Julia's hand. "It does, it does."

* * *

The trip seems to fly by. Sam and Julia talk away the morning while Bella sleeps or listens to music on her headphones. They sing along to the seventies channel and play Twenty Questions with Bella. Lunch is under the shade of a maple tree at a rest stop in Virginia. They sit at a rickety wooden picnic table and open the cooler while Yogi runs around. It feels like a scene they have all been in before. When they arrive at Caroline's house in the northern suburbs of Raleigh, the air is soft with the scent of pine trees. The sky is lit a vibrant blue.

The house is set on an expansive lawn and has a wraparound porch. Intricate millwork fills the space in the three steep gables. It is the antithesis of the miles of Cape Cods that line the shores of Long Island where Caroline grew up. Bella peers out the car window. "Wow, look at that…it's so beautiful."

The front door opens, and Sam's family rushes out to the car to greet them. The boys jump up and down and try to reach

Yogi, who is in Bella's arms. She puts the dog down, and they run off chasing him, the leash dragging around the yard.

Caroline warmly greets Julia while Vi cautiously approaches. The smell of barbecue drifts in from the backyard. Caroline brings Julia and Bella into the house and shows them to the guest room, beautifully decorated with shiplap walls and matching white and blue striped curtains and comforters. A floral chair in the corner faces the screened-in porch that is adjacent to their room.

Caroline leaves them to freshen up, and Julia turns to Bella. "Dorothy, we're not in Kansas anymore. Look at this. I feel like I stepped onto the set of HGTV."

"I know. Mr. Testa didn't mention we were going to a mansion. Wow." Bella opens the door to the bathroom. "The shower floor is made of black pebbles...Grams, come look at this!"

Julia can see Sam walking Yogi outside her window. His daughter Vi looks agitated as she walks alongside her father. She feels anxious and decides to change into her nicer sundress before heading back outside. Everyone sits around the fire pit, and Sam introduces Julia and Bella to his sons-in-law. In the center of the patio table, there is a plastic container full of strawberries and melon with Piggly Wiggly stamped on the label.

Vi is the first one to speak, "So, Julia, I hear you moved back to your family home in Astoria."

"Yes, it's been very nostalgic being back in my old neighborhood."

"But, don't you miss living close to your daughter?"

"It's not very far, really."

"So, why did you move?"

Sam interjects, "Vi, tell Julia about that painting class you're taking."

"It's really amateurish. I'm sure Julia is not interested."

Sam takes out his cell phone and shows Julia one of Vi's paintings. "Oh, that's lovely. I can see you have talent."

Vi picks up where she left off. "Dad, stop…so, Julia, your daughter, and her husband are doctors?"

"My Dad is only a radiologist, not like a real doctor," Bella shouts out.

"Oh, Bella…he's a real doctor," Julia laughs.

"Well, he doesn't have patients like my Mom…that's what I meant. I guess he's a *real doctor…* but he doesn't talk to real people."

Vi's interest now switches to Bella. "Do you want to be a doctor too, Bella?"

"No, I want to be famous, an influencer. You know… I don't want to be one of the other people on the plane when it crashes. I want it to be *my* plane crash."

"Oh, my goodness, Bella…you obviously didn't get the memo to be on your best behavior." Julia pretends to laugh, and Bella looks puzzled.

"Not a real plane crash…Grams. I'm just saying it metaphorically."

"Metaphorically?" Vi looks astonished.

"Oh yes, I learned that word in English class last year…did I use it right?"

Sam lets out a belly laugh. "Bella, you're doing fine…Okay, Vi…enough with the third degree. What happened to that Southern hospitality?"

Caroline answers, "Well, bless her heart, Vi's acting like an obnoxious New Yorker. I'm sorry, Julia…can I get you a drink? Iced tea?"

"Yes, please."

Caroline has her husband turn up the heat on the grill so they can eat sooner, and she brings out cans of hard seltzer, beer, and red wine for Sam. Finally, the mood mellows, and the conversation turns to everything they miss about living on Long Island.

Caroline picks up the strawberries and places them on the patio table. "I long for our fruit markets and bakeries in New York."

After dinner, the children and Bella go swimming under a moonlit sky. Smoke from the fire pit curls toward the stars and glows from the lights around the patio. Julia and Sam are tired from the trip, and they decide to turn in early.

Bella comes into the guest room wrapped in a towel. "Gram, did I say something wrong before?"

"Oh, no, Bella…what can I say…we say what's on our mind."

"They are going to have to get used to us, that's all," Bella laughs.

"It might be a big adjustment. I'm going to hop into the shower first, okay? I won't be long."

"Yeah, my bathing suit is practically dry already. It's so warm here."

"Did you text your mother that we are here?"

"Oh, Grams…she was texting me every hour."

Julia heads into the shower, and Bella puts a dry towel on the chair and sits down to see if she has any messages from Artie.

There is buzzing coming from under Julia's pile of clothes on the bed. Bella answers it. "Hello?"

A voice that sounds like a cross between congestion and a croak answers, "Julia? Is this Julia?"

Bella looks down at the number. "Unknown Caller."

"No, this is Bella, her granddaughter. She's in the shower."

Enzo hears something familiar in Bella's voice. It shakes him for a moment, but then he continues, "Hello Bella, this is Enzo, Enzo Russo. I don't think you know me."

"Oh, Mr. Russo…wow, no…I know who you are."

"I…I wanted to talk to your grandmother. But, I don't want to bother her if she's busy."

"Oh, no…she would really like to talk to you."

"Maybe I can call back in a little while?"

"No, wait, wait, talk to me…she won't be long."

Enzo hears a sweetness in Bella's voice and can't hang up. "All right, how old are you?"

"Fourteen, how old are you?"

"Ninety-two."

"Wow, you're the oldest person I ever spoke to."

"Well, I don't feel that old.…"

"How old do you feel? I mean, you sound old, oops, I didn't mean it like that."

"Sometimes I feel like I'm still your age."

"Look, Mr. Russo, I'm so glad you called. My grandmother is probably the best person you will ever meet, except maybe Mr. Testa."

"You know, Sam?"

"Yes, we're at his daughter's house in North Carolina."

"With Sam?"

"Yeah…here comes my grandmother…hold on."

Julia enters the bedroom in her robe with her wet hair settling into curls on her shoulders. "Is that your mother on the phone?"

Bella stretches her arm out and hands Julia the phone. "No, it's your father."

65

Borrowed Time

Julia swooshes Bella away towards the shower, then she takes the phone off speaker. "Hello? This is Julia."

"Julia, Julia…I don't mean to bother you."

"You're not bothering me." She sits down on the edge of the bed. There is a long silence, and Julia finally asks, "How is your son, Pete?"

"He's good. He's going to be all right…I wanted to apologize for hanging up on you last time…my wife, well…she gets confused."

"I understand, really. How is she doing?"

Enzo looks around at the boxes that line the walls of his condo and sighs, "They're making us move."

"Move? Who's making you move?"

"My kids…they're sending us to a place called assisted living…I don't need any help living."

"I'm sorry to hear that, Enzo."

Julia is the first person who has shown any empathy towards him about the move. He softens. "Listen, that's not why I called…I, well, I just wanted to get something off my chest. It's not just the move…they want to take you away from me again."

"What do you mean?"

"They want me to forget about you."

"Who wants you to do that?"

"Everyone…well, the girls do. They keep saying it's better for the family that no one knows about you…. but I can't stop thinking about you and what happened."

"I haven't been able to stop thinking about you either…and my mother."

"I'm an old guy. I can't go to my grave like this. I have to make it right." Enzo's voice is cracking.

"Are you alone?"

"Yeah, Bobbie is staying with Lorraine and Pete until we move next week."

"Are you okay? You sound very upset. Maybe you shouldn't be alone."

"No, I like being alone. No one listens to me anyway. They treat me like I don't understand anything…like I'm some old fool."

"Enzo, I'm listening to you. I know families sometimes have a hard time understanding each other."

There is another long pause, then he starts again. "I just wanted you to know that I really didn't know about you. I hope your father didn't treat you like he treated Grace."

"No, he never hit me…but he wasn't very kind. He drank…a lot."

"I know."

"Enzo, what happened between you and my mother?"

"It's not an excuse; I was in the service… Korea. I came home and married my girlfriend, Bobbie…but I wasn't right. I saw too many bad things. I wasn't thinking straight."

"But, what did that have to do with my mother?"

"She was beautiful, really beautiful and well, one night she came over looking for Bobbie. She had a bruise on her face, and she was crying, really crying. And I just wanted to comfort her. But, you know, one thing led to another…It only lasted a few weeks. Then, we both agreed it had to stop. She said she wanted to give your father another chance." Julia can hear Enzo pounding his fist on his chair. "I loved my wife…I don't know. I was broken by the war…all that death and everything. I thought maybe I could fix this one thing, like I was helping Grace…but it was wrong, really wrong."

"Oh, Enzo…so you never saw her again?"

"No, we both decided it was for the best."

"Didn't your wife notice her friend wasn't around anymore?"

"Yes, but…she told Bobbie that her husband wouldn't let her see her anymore…you know, women obeyed their husbands back then…no one questioned it."

"And Bobbie believed that?"

"Well, that's what she told me."

"What do you mean by that?"

Julia can hear Enzo taking deep heaving breaths on the other end of the line. "Please…I'm so grateful you told me all this. I don't blame you for anything. Please…don't cry."

Enzo takes a few minutes to gain control of himself. "You don't understand, Julia…there's more."

"More?"

"My sister-in-law told me this morning that Bobbie knew all along."

"That you were having an affair?"

"Yeah…and about you."

"And she never told you?"

"No, never. Carm, her sister, said she was afraid I'd leave her."

"Her sister knew?"

"Yeah…just the two of them…kept it secret all these years."

Julia is stunned by this revelation and falls back flat on the bed and stares at the ceiling. Bella walks out of the shower and into the room as Enzo continues, "I never would've left Bobbie…but I would have never left you either. I'm not that kind of guy."

"No, I know it now…you're not that kind of guy. But, Bella, my granddaughter is here, I have to go…listen, call me anytime you want to…maybe we can make a fresh start…just the two of us."

"Yeah, yeah…that would be good. Could I talk to Bella too?"

"I'm sure she would love it."

Julia ends the call and just lays there. Bella's curiosity gets the best of her, and she cuddles up next to Julia. "What did he say, Grams?"

"He didn't say it, but I think he loves us."

66

Six Months Later: Summer's End

"Dad, can you help me with this box?" Caroline walks down the ramp of the U-Haul with a box marked *LAMPS*.

"Yeah, coming…do you think you're going to fit everything in this house? I mean, your real moving van isn't even here yet." Sam grabs the other end of the box.

"I don't know. Did you and Julia take everything you wanted?"

"Yeah, I left what you wanted of your mother's things in her closet for you."

"Thanks…Where is Julia, anyway?"

"Today is her morning to babysit the twins. Andrea went back to work part-time last week. So she'll be here later."

"That must be hard. I can't imagine having twins."

"Everyone is helping, even me."

"That's great, Dad...the boys are going to enjoy being near you again. You sure you're all right helping out when they have school breaks?"

"Sure, no problem."

"This is some kind of karma, isn't it?

"What do you mean?"

"Me getting offered the professorship at Hofstra, Ed's job offering a remote option, you and Julia renting a condo near her daughter. Who would believe in a million years that I would be moving into the house I grew up in?"

"That was a beautiful house in Carolina...are you sure you want to stay in this little place?"

"For now, it's perfect. We could never afford a house like that here."

"I guess so. How was Vi when you left?"

"Well, her head is spinning...she's still a little worried about you, Dad. Making such a quick decision, well, getting engaged, moving out of the house."

"I know...it seems rushed, but I'm getting older...I don't have time to waste."

"Oh, Dad! Please, don't say that... Listen, Julia is the best thing that's happened to you since Mom died... I can't believe Andrea asked me to be Gracie's godmother."

"Yeah, you two really hit it off. I hope Vi wasn't upset that she isn't Charlie's godmother."

"Oh, no, Dad, she's fine with it. Listen, Vi and I talked, and I think she is going to try to move back too. She has to convince Steve; he misses his family here too...and the fishing."

"Now, if only we could get Matt a job with the Mets…even the Yankees."

"I know this sounds crazy, but when I was driving in all that traffic this morning, people cutting me off on the expressway, I felt calm…like ahhh, I'm home again."

"I've missed you."

"I know, Dad…believe me, Vi isn't going to last through the rest of another summer down there in that heat. She'll be moving back before your wedding. You can bet on that."

"I hope so. But don't pressure her. The last thing I want to do is make her feel guilty. I mean, you all had a good life down there. Are you sure about this, Caroline?"

"Dad, yes. I've been trying for so long to get a full-time college position…at Hofstra no less, just perfect. And, I guess I'm like you. I missed the ocean. Ed is excited about getting a boat. The boys always loved visiting you and Mom here…they'll adjust."

"Okay, I'm not complaining. I just want to make sure this is what you wanted."

* * *

Julia steps out of her Mini Cooper and meets Caroline, who is carrying a box into the house. "I stopped at the deli on Broadway in Massapequa. I hope you're hungry."

"Oh, thanks, Julia. Dad and I haven't stopped to eat all morning. God, I missed real salami." Caroline puts the bag on top of the box and walks into the kitchen, and Julia follows.

"There's a wedge of provolone in there for your father, oh…and bread from the bakery."

"I think Dad's in the basement."

"Don't call him. I wanted to talk to you for a minute."

"Julia, is something wrong?"

"No, no…I just wanted to thank you."

"Thank me?"

"Yes, for well, being so welcoming to me, my family. I know how hard this must be for you…I've been told your mother was everything to everyone."

"Thank you for saying that, and yes, it is hard…but not because of you. You really brought my father back to life…and well, I mean…who couldn't love Bella?"

"Bella, I think she saved us all. Do you know she talks to my father almost every day? She checks in on him when she gets home from her counselor job at the day camp."

"Really? What on earth do they have to talk about?"

"He tells her stories about growing up in Astoria back in the day, about my brothers and sister, Korea…she says she is going to write a book about him."

"Does he know that?"

"I'm sure Bella told him…you know she can't keep a secret."

"She's so open…caring…you must be so proud of her."

The cellar door creaks, and Sam appears. "Julia, you're here."

She walks over to Sam and hugs him. "I brought provisions."

"Did I miss anything?" he asks.

Caroline opens the bag and begins to make a sandwich. "No, just talking about Bella….Are you hungry, Dad? Julia brought us some goodies."

"Yeah, let's take a break."

They sit around the kitchen table in the now half-furnished house. The sun pours in through the bay window in the dining room, making the room seem full of life.

"I hope you don't mind, Dad, if I donate some of this furniture. It's pretty old."

"No, no…maybe someone else will get some use out of it."

"No sentimental attachment?"

"They're things…I have all my good memories tucked away."

Julia winds her hair into a bun and ties it. "When is the van coming?"

"In a few days…Ed and the boys will be here. I start teaching next week, and then the boys start after Labor Day."

"This is cutting it close, isn't it?" Julia asks.

"Yes, but we'll be okay. I taught this freshman class before, so I'm almost ready, but I do have to run up to campus. Why don't you two take off? The truck's empty…I can finish putting things away later."

"Are you sure, Caroline?" Sam looks around at the piles of books and folders on the floor.

"Positive."

"Sam, let's take those folding lounge chairs to the beach. I'm exhausted from this morning with Gracie and Charlie…I could use a break."

"Me too…yeah, it's a perfect day; let's go."

67

The Perfect Day

Sam finishes packing the car trunk and turns to Julia. "How about going out to Fire Island today? It will be quieter there."

"Good idea…Let's park at the far end near the lighthouse."

They arrive at the easternmost part of the beach and find a secluded spot to set up their sparse encampment. The ocean breaks in white foamy waves on the shore. Towering behind the dunes is the lighthouse and an American flag flapping in the wind. The air is warm enough to languish in the sun but not hot enough to need the shade of the umbrella, which remains stashed under their chairs with the small cooler.

"It feels good to put my feet up. I must've carried a hundred boxes up and down the stairs this morning."

"I was lucky. The twins took turns napping, so I only had to watch one at a time, but it still was exhausting. We're getting old, Sam."

Sam closes his eyes and can feel sleep is about to come over him.

Julia clears her throat. "We never really talked about a honeymoon…is there anywhere you want to go?

"Right here is fine with me."

"In April?"

"I guess not…where do you want to go?"

"I was thinking of Italy. You know our families are from Abruzzi… it's not far from Rome."

"You're not planning on digging up any more lost relatives, are you?"

"God, no…I just thought it would be nice to see where we came from, that's all. Neither one of us has ever been there."

"Well, it will be warm and on an ocean…so yes, why not?"

"That's one thing settled…Did you call Pete?"

Sam mockingly pulls his cap down over his eyes. "I thought we were going to relax?"

She lightly slaps the side of his arm. "This is my last question, really…so, did you?"

"Yes, I invited him. He said Lorraine feels terrible about everything that happened."

"You mean exiling me?"

"Well, yeah…give them time… they're trying to figure it out."

"You're right." Julia bristles thinking about it. "I should know that nothing is ever simple."

Sam reaches out and takes her hand, and she immediately calms down. "Even if they don't come, we'll be fine. The day will be fine."

"It would be a perfect ending of our little love story if they came, but perfection is overrated, isn't it?"

Julia pulls her towel over her shoulders and hugs herself. "You know, I started doing this little mental trick every time I start thinking about what they did."

"What's that?"

"It's like counting sheep…I start naming all the people in my life since I met you and since Grace and Charlie were born. I know it's silly, but sometimes I have to remind myself how lucky I really am."

Sam lifts his hat. His eyes crease into a smile. "I only have to look at you, Julia."

"Stop…we sound like a lovesick couple in a sappy movie now, don't we?"

He sits up and laughs. "We do, but I don't care."

She stands up and takes Sam's hand. "Let's walk."

They head towards the lighthouse gliding their feet through the warm water of late summer. A steady breeze blows salty air. The sky is a pure cerulean blue. Clouds crawl across the sky spilling shadows along the beach. They stop on a crescent of sand that bends around the lighthouse. The ocean murmurs, sending a vibrating melody into the air as each wave breaks on the sand.

Julia wraps her arms around Sam's waist. "This is all I need."

About the Author

Ava Zacardi was born in Queens, New York, and raised on Long Island. She studied writing at the State University of New York at Binghamton. In addition to writing, she is an artist and educator. She currently lives in Upstate New York, surrounded by the beauty of nature and the warmth of her friends and family.

Acknowledgments

Thank you to my remarkable art students at the OASIS Senior Program in Upstate New York. Over the years, they have told me they not only come to my classes to learn to paint but also for the stories I tell. Their willingness to not see age as a barrier and follow their passions and dreams inspired me to rekindle my desire to write. My writing journey began again when I enrolled in a "100 Word Story" class at OASIS.

A special thank you to my editor, Linda Lowen, for convincing me to temporarily put down my paintbrush and take up the pen. Her support along the way was immeasurable.

Sincere appreciation goes to the members of my writing group who provided invaluable insights and advice: Susan Diane Hynds, Leslie Archer, and Elle Anderson. Also, thank you to my beta readers: Terry Guido, Caryn Atlas, Marlene Roeder, Katie Vecchiarelli, Maureen Santiago, and Wendy Tetro.

This novel would have never come to life without the support of my children and their spouses, grandchildren, and large, warm, and gregarious extended Italian-American family. Special thanks to my husband for always understanding my need for a creative space.

Visit **avazacardi.com** for updates. The second book in this series, **Honestly Julia** is coming soon!